A
YEAR
SINCE
YESTERDAY

BY
GEORGE EDWARD ZINTEL

PublishAmerica
Baltimore

First printing

ISBN: 1-4137-2667-4
PUBLISHED BY PUBLISHAMERICA, LLLP
www.publishamerica.com
Baltimore

Printed in the United States of America

To my wife and daughter

Acknowledgments

Thanks to my wife and daughter, for putting up with me during the writing of this book; to my aunt, Gertrude Potash, for her honest evaluation of the first draft; to my good friends Jeff Mayer and Joyce Mayer, for their hard work on the cover design; and to my sister, Linda Maguire, for being an inspiration to me throughout my life.

A very special thanks to my mother, Lucille Zintel, for more than words could ever say.

CHAPTER ONE

Charlie Marshal's knocking didn't immediately pull Evan Hayden out of his deep, drunken sleep. It was only five-fifteen in the morning and Evan hadn't swallowed his last shot of whiskey until nearly midnight, and, had things gone as they should have, he could have slept in until eight or nine o'clock.

When knocking failed to get results Charlie added some muscle and banged. He rammed his dirty, calloused hand into the door over and over as if he was a heavyweight boxer who had his opponent against the ropes. His thrusts were delivered with such force that the entire building seemed to shake.

"Evan!" Charlie yelled as his fist slammed into the door. "Evan, wake up. Shit-for-Brains is late again and I got a line of boats waiting for gas!" His voice was intentionally loud for the benefit of several agitated fisherman who were standing downstairs holding empty bait buckets. He looked down at them and grinned, exposing a few of his blackened, tobacco-stained teeth.

Shit-for-Brains as Charlie called him, but not to his face, was Derek Anderson, a twenty-two year old high school dropout Evan hired to run the marina's bait house. Derek never held a job for more than a few months at a time and had spent a summer in the county jail for breaking into a Laundromat, but Evan didn't know about the jail time when he hired him. Not that it would have made a difference, considering the other characters who applied for the position. There wasn't one in the bunch without a criminal record, and most committed crimes that were quite a bit more serious than stealing quarters out of washing machines.

Charlie's hammering persisted until the door slowly opened. Evan Hayden, the marina's dock master, stood with a mop of uncombed hair and bloodshot eyes and rubbed his face with the palms of his hands. "I'll be right down," he said, fighting back the urge to puke all over Charlie. His lips were covered in that white, glue-like substance that develops almost magically in the mouth of a person sleeping off a hangover, and as he spoke it stretched across his teeth like thin strands of cheese from a very hot pizza.

"This is the third time this month that he's pulled this crap. You should—"

Evan lifted a hand and shook his head in agreement. His temples were pounding, and his vision was muddled, and all he wanted was for Charlie to shut up before he found himself wearing a chest full of vomit. "I know. I'll take care of it. Just get them boys gassed up," Evan said before he shut the door and rushed to the bathroom. His stomach twisted and rolled as he fell to his knees in front of the bowl and launched the half digested remnants of the previous night's supper into the water.

After a glass of stale-tasting ice tea, Evan ascended the staircase from the back of his apartment which was attached to, and above, the bait and tackle shop. He opened the back door of the shop and flipped on the light switch. The intensity of the fluorescent lamps jabbed into his brain, and another urge to vomit was suppressed as he made his way to the front door. Six irritated fishermen, all regular customers, entered and began bitching about missing the incoming tide. Evan apologized but offered no explanation, and, after seeing the condition he was in, they didn't expect one. They knew Evan on a first-name basis and liked him too much to add additional pain to his obviously battered condition, but they weren't above a little friendly teasing.

"What happened to you? Some old girl get a hold of you last night?" one of them asked, which brought a wave of laughter from the others. Evan didn't reply. His mind was preoccupied with the thought of a hot cup of black coffee and his body was instinctively in motion towards the coffee maker. He filled it with grains, giving two extra scoops to insure its strength, then hit the brew button. It came to life quick and within seconds was discharging a thick, dark, robust liquid.

While the coffee brewed he made his way to the bait counter and began filling buckets with live shrimp and pinfish. The lively creatures fought to avoid capture as Evan struggled to scoop them up with a small net. He didn't bother counting them, not that he could in his state; he just put them in by the handful until he was close and then added a few more for good measure. The fishermen paid no attention to his disregard for accuracy. They knew Evan well and were confident they'd be treated fairly regardless of his condition.

"Where's the kid this morning?" one of them finally asked as his bucket was being stocked. It wasn't the first time the guy missed an incoming tide on account of Derek's tardiness so the question was more conversation than inquiry.

"Don't know. Haven't heard from him," Evan said. But that wasn't the whole truth. He had a pretty damn good idea where Derek was. In the same place he was the last time he didn't show, and the time before that as well. Probably in jail, and most likely drunk and full of cuts and bruises from picking fights with guys who looked a whole lot smaller through intoxicated eyes. Derek had a bad habit of becoming Superman after a few drinks.

"When Candy opened I never missed a tide," another one said, taking a friendly jab at Evan, who was still holding back an esophagus full of chunky matter that wanted out.

Candy had been around for as long as most locals cared to remember, which amounted to about ten years. She was originally hired as a deck hand on the charters, but transferred to the bait shop when she got married. Her husband, the jealous type, didn't care very much for his wife being out to sea every day with a boat full of men, so transferring to the bait shop was an improvement over quitting the marina altogether. For years after leaving the charters she worked mornings, until Evan hired Derek and gave him the pseudo-title of bait shop manager, putting him on days and switching her to afternoons. Although she wasn't thrilled about the change she liked it more than her early morning customers did; it gave her more quality time with her husband who worked afternoons at a nearby phosphate mine.

With full buckets and arms stocked with beer and chips the men made their way to the cash register. "It's on me this morning," Evan said and waved them to the door. He was in no shape to count bait, not to mention money, and it wasn't coming out of his pocket anyway. He was in charge of the books and could write off almost anything within reason, and at that moment nothing seemed more reasonable than getting them out of the shop so he could die in peace. They yelled back an entanglement of appreciations and then headed to their boats as Evan headed to the coffee maker.

The first hot cup he drank at the counter, with one hand firmly attached to a shelf for added support. The second he sipped as he stood out front and watched Charlie maneuver a forklift into the dry storage warehouse. He worked the controls as if they were extensions of his own arms. The forks lifted, spread apart, and tilted at precise angles as he pulled a vessel from the towering rack and gently lowered it to the ground. His short, stocky frame and overall mechanical posture, as well as his greasy complexion, made him appear at one with the machine.

Charlie was a good worker, an excellent worker as a matter of fact, and had been around long before Evan arrived. He knew a great deal about boating and fishing, as well as how to run a marina, but he wasn't the type of man to be put in charge of others. He was rude, short-tempered, and generally disagreeable. So when the previous dock master passed away Charlie wasn't even considered for the position. The owners fed him some line about needing someone with management experience, which justified their reason for hiring Evan. In an attempt to pacify him they increased his pay by fifty cents per hour. To Charlie the entire ordeal was a slap in his face, and more proof the world was full of assholes.

The air outside was still and warm and held a very faint fog that was only evident under the lights of the dock. The roar of the forklift broke the silence in a most unnatural way as Charlie went to and from the warehouse carrying Donzis, Chris Crafts, and Sea Rays. On the north end of the marina Sheila Stone was unlocking the door of The Blind Minnow Diner, which meant it was six o'clock sharp. Within the hour the marina would be crawling with people and the bait shop would be as packed as Grand Central Station on Christmas Eve. It was Saturday, Evan reminded himself, the busiest day of the week. The day bankers and lawyers and real estate agents become fishermen and water skiers and scuba divers.

Evan stepped back inside and hit the button on the weather radio, hoping there was a storm brewing somewhere in the Gulf that would keep the weekend water rats, at least the smart ones, away from their boats. But the forecast called for partly cloudy skies with a ten percent chance of afternoon showers, a light wind two to four knots out of the west, and calm seas. It was a perfect forecast for those wanting to be on the water, and the worst for a hung-over dock master wanting to be in bed.

When the radio went silent he picked up a cordless phone and dialed Derek's number, which he knew by heart, then leaned against the counter top and rubbed his throbbing temples with his free hand. "Come on, kid, pick up the phone," he said to himself. Four rings, five rings, six rings, nothing. He hung it up. "Shit!" he said out loud before he reached under the counter and retrieved a bottle of Tylenol. He popped the top and put the container to his lips. Three, maybe four gelcaps rolled onto his tongue and were washed down with the remaining coffee in his cup.

Although his stomach had settled down a bit the pounding in his head had gotten worse. It had migrated from the base of his skull to directly between his temples and was hammering on the backs of his eyes, which gave the sensation that his brain was being torn in two pieces. He sat down on a chair between a rack full of candy bars and a freezer full of squid and closed his eyes. The room moved in a slow wobble and his stomach churned as if it was full of spoiled butter; he'd gotten more than he bargained for when he swallowed that first shot almost nine hours before. The hangover was expected of course, but it was worse this time, worse than yesterday and the day before.

Early on, after the accident and before he left Syracuse, he tried other things to help him get through the night. The pills prescribed by his doctor made him sleep, just as intended, but did nothing to stop the dreams. In fact they made matters worse by paralyzing the part of the brain responsible for waking the body, which in turn made it more difficult for Evan to break free of the nightly torture. The counseling sessions did even less because he refused to talk to the doctor, or anyone else, about what happened. Angela, his wife, managed to find solace in the empathy of the parish priest, and all but begged him to give the reverend a chance to help. But Evan didn't share her convictions when it came to matters of religion. So, as she looked to the spiritual world he looked to the bottle.

The bell attached to the bait shop door rang and Charlie came in searching for a cup of java.

"Did you get hold of Shit-for-Brains?" he asked, passing the counter.

"He didn't answer his phone. Might be on the way here," Evan replied, relieved to see Charlie instead of another customer in need of bait.

"Yea, right," Charlie said with a sarcastic chuckle. "He's not on his way. He's face down on the floor of a cell lying in his own puke just like the last time."

Evan didn't bother arguing. Charlie was probably right and he didn't want to provoke an "I told you so," even though he HAD told him so several times over. On Derek's very first day Charlie said the kid was too stupid to pour piss out of a boot with the instructions written on the heel and about as reliable as a weather forecast, and he'd been proven right about the reliable part on more than one occasion. But Evan saw something in Derek, something in his eyes, something he could relate to. It was the look a person gets from experiencing grief and turmoil and disappointment, and Evan, better than anyone, understood that. So he listened to his heart and not his head and hired the kid, which had proven so far to be a mistake. A mistake Charlie reminded Evan about every chance he got.

Charlie filled his cup, the large insulated type, with coffee, milk and about a dozen sugars. On the outside of the grungy container was a picture of a guy giving the middle finger. Underneath it were the words, "Who says I never lift a finger around here." He grabbed a double pack of Twinkies and settled at a spot on the counter across from Evan where he tore open the package and swallowed the cream filled bombs without chewing.

"You look like hell," Charlie said before taking a large gulp of piping hot coffee. "If you want to grab a shower and a bite to eat I'll watch things here for a while."

The offer caught Evan off guard; it was so obscenely out of character for the man who hated everyone and everything. But Evan didn't care from whom the offer came. He was on his feet before the word "thanks" could escape his lips.

Evan didn't like Charlie much when he first met him. He was rude and obnoxious and carried a chip on his shoulder, but he worked his ass off and kept things running smoothly around the marina, which made Evan's life a lot easier, and Charlie'd been damn near a permanent fixture since the complex was built some decades before. Plus, there were those rare occasions when he was actually quite civil, which led Evan to believe Charlie wasn't quite as much of a jerk as he led people to believe.

Evan climbed the stairs to his apartment, sixteen total, as if he was carrying two sacks of concrete on his shoulders. His shaky legs fought to lift his heavy feet, and they came down with a thud that could be felt inside the bait shop. When the apartment door closed behind him he undressed and made his way to the bathroom, where stood naked in front of the shower as the water heated up. The last eighteen months had been like a roller coaster ride with the daytime being a slow anxious climb to the top and the night time being a treacherous ride down, and his posture and appearance said as much.

As he stood on the cold tile he thought about his wife and their baby girl, Emily, who was named after her great-grandmother. Without warning, from somewhere deep in his head, the past came forward. He was home in Syracuse, standing in the shower holding his young daughter. She was small, only ten pounds, and she wiggled around as the water sprayed on her and tickled her belly. He held her tightly and lifted her to the spout so she could stick out her tongue and lick the spray. Evan laughed as the water sprayed on her face and made her little legs kick and her tiny butt shake. He turned her around and kissed her small wet nose, the way he had the very first time he held her and a million times since. Her fine hair was pressed to her head and her large blue eyes were wide with excitement as she smiled at him.

Outside the tub stood Angela, Evan's wife, pointing a video camera and laughing. She was beautiful, like the little soapy girl he held in his arms. Their features were almost identical, separated only by time, and Emily's gestures, her laughs and frowns and smiles, were echoes of Angela.

It was like a childhood recollection, where the images seem so real but are so far away they feel like they're from a different person's life. But he watched them anyway, and smiled at the memories that felt stolen from someone much more alive than he was. He watched them for a long time until they faded and left him staring at a moldy plastic shower curtain. He stepped in and let the water run over his head and down his back, carrying with it the tears that had bled from his eyes.

CHAPTER TWO

Sullivan's Secret was a forty-five foot sailboat owned by Arthur and Mary Sullivan, a friendly retired couple in their seventies dedicated to reliving their thirties. The bright white vessel was back in her slip at seven-fifteen when Evan returned from bailing Derek out of the Sarasota County jail. Evan hadn't seen the Sullivans in quite some time and decided to stop by to hear about their latest adventures. They had set sail two weeks earlier on a trip to Ambergris Caye, a small island off the coast of Belize, to visit several excavated Mayan sites. It was the latest in a series of trips that took them all over the eastern and western Caribbean.

The Secret, as the Sullivans referred to the boat, always docked on the far south end of the marina, well within view from Evan's apartment above the bait shop. He kept an eye out for her and maintained a mental log of his friends' travel plans and he knew when to expect them back, give or take a day or so, and wouldn't hesitate to send the Coast Guard out after them if he felt they were in trouble. They were seasoned sailors with common sense and a sturdy vessel, but he'd heard many stories of experienced sailors underestimating the seas, overestimating their abilities, and ending up capsized.

He had been dock master only two months when a twenty-five-foot day sailor was lost with four people aboard. They ran into a storm they couldn't outrun and their boat went down a mere twelve miles from shore. The next day the Coast Guard recovered the bodies, and Evan was there as they were loaded onto the coroner's wagon and hauled away. The memory of that event was always present when his friends were out to sea, and he worried about them as if they were family and waited impatiently for their return each time they left.

Evan met the Sullivans, Art and Mary, a few weeks after taking the job as dock master. They sailed in one afternoon looking for a temporary home for *The Secret*. Coincidentally a slip had come available only hours before and Evan let them have it on the spot, without even asking for identification. At the time he didn't know about the waiting list, or he conveniently forgot, and didn't bother with the customary forms. They paid cash for a year's rent in advance, and were friendly—iced tea on the front porch type of friendly. Evan immediately felt a connection to them, as if they were friends he hadn't seen in a very long time. They were intelligent people who had seen many sides of life and learned to take the good and the bad in stride, and their years together forged a shackle of mutual respect and love that bound them in a way Evan came to admire.

He walked the dock towards *The Secret* in a lazy way, hands deep in his pockets and shoulders slightly forward. He was still feeling the aftershocks of the night before and was tired from a busy day of scooping bait and selling beer. "Thank God for Candy," he thought as he reflected on the chaos of the day and how much worse it would have been without her. She came in early when he called her and she didn't complain about Derek not showing, even though she, more than anyone, had a right to. He had screwed up when he bumped her to afternoons and put Derek in charge and he knew it, and he added that decision to the list of many he wished he could annul.

When he approached slip two sixty-one he heard a soft sound rolling smoothly from below deck. It was Bach's "Concerto for Two," and it filled the air with a sweetness that could almost be tasted like fine powdered sugar. The harmony, along with the fact that Arthur wasn't on deck, acted as an invisible force field to Evan, who knew from experience what activities might be accompanying the orchestra. Without hesitation he turned to leave, and had walked only two steps when he heard Art's inviting voice.

"Evan," Art yelled. "Long time no see. Come aboard, my friend, Mary's making her famous seafood gumbo." Art had emerged from below carrying a snifter of brandy in one hand and an unlit cigar in the other. His large round face sported an equally large smile as he gestured for his friend to join him. He put the cigar in his mouth to shake Evan's hand, and his strong grip felt comforting and reassuring. Mary heard Evan's voice from the galley and yelled topside, "I'm making gumbo and corn bread. I hope you brought your appetite."

"Grab yourself a beer," Art said as he affectionately rubbed his hand across Evan's shoulder. The cigar was lodged tightly in one side of his mouth and he spoke out of the other, sort of like Popeye did in those old Saturday morning cartoons.

Evan hadn't planned on eating because his appetite, normally quite healthy, was still out to lunch. Earlier in the day Sheila sent food from The Blind Minnow for the crew at the marina, something she did on weekends, and he hardly touched it. He ate a few French fries but didn't even try the grouper sandwich, the house specialty, and when it became apparent it would go to waste Charlie snatched it up and inhaled it. Watching that guy eat would lead a person to believe he had teeth in his throat.

Once below deck Evan was greeted with a big warm hug and a kiss on the cheek. A heavenly aroma emanated from the stove and caused an unexpected pang of hunger in his stomach. Mary lifted the spoon from the pot and held it out for him to taste and his appetite came awake the instant the gumbo hit his dormant taste buds. After that he spent several minutes updating her on the happenings around the marina. There wasn't much to tell outside of a few minor thefts and one small boat fire, and he intentionally ignored the problem with Derek since he was still too pissed off to talk about it. He took another taste of gumbo before he grabbed a beer and went back on deck.

Art offered a cigar that Evan accepted and they sat together drawing on the stogies and sipping their drinks as Art told of the trip to Belize. His face lit up as he described their adventures on the high seas as if he was a child on a pirates' ship, and Evan listened with sincere enthusiasm. He hoped someday to be able to see first hand the many places Art and Mary have visited.

They departed the marina on a Tuesday heading southwest towards Mexico. The first day the weather was great, but on the second they hit a storm that was forecast to be relatively mild and ended up being anything but. They were about ninety miles north of the Yucatan Channel when they sailed into forty mile-an-hour winds and rough seas, and, although they managed the storm, they were pushed off course and wound up in Cuban waters where the Cuban navy, on a very intimidating Soviet Pauk II fast patrol boat, greeted them.

The Navy captain, a young man with a chip on his shoulder towards Americans, was at first rather hostile toward Art and Mary. He softened when Mary demonstrated her abilities to fluently communicate in his native tongue, and when Art made an offering of a case of twelve-year-old scotch. He, in turn, threw Art a box of Cuban cigars, two of which he and Evan were enjoying. After that encounter they hit one more storm, much smaller than the first, just east of Isla Cozumel, but managed to stay on course until their arrival in Ambergris Caye.

Their adventures always captivated Evan. He wasn't taken so much by where they went and what they did, but by the fact that such things were being done by a married couple in their seventies. While other people their age were playing shuffleboard or bingo, they were sailing across the worlds' oceans and exploring its lands. It was the type of retirement he used to envision for himself and his wife. But that seemed like a long time ago.

The resonant pitch of a bell sounded from below deck and put an immediate halt to Art's narrative. It was Mary's way of saying dinner was served, and although she could have just as easily yelled, she preferred to use the bell. It reminded her of the big cast iron one her mother used to ring to summon the troops to dinner. Her tiny replica was purchased in the Bahamas, at Nassau's original straw market, before some crazed local burned it to the ground.

During dinner the stories continued with a comedic turn. Mary took the stage and described how Art had gone skinny-dipping one morning after breakfast. They were several miles off the shore of Cozumel and well out of sight of beach goers, not that there were many out that time of the morning, when Art undressed and dove off the bow of the boat. He must have been splashing about for nearly ten minutes when two scuba divers surfaced no more than fifty yards away and started whistling. In typical fashion Art finished his swim and unabashedly climbed back on deck and waved. The story brought tears of laughter to Evan's eyes as he pictured his friend floating unsuspectingly over the divers wearing nothing but his birthday suit, and his own private thought of a grouper or tuna mistaking Art's genitals for a dangling piece of bait made matters even worse.

When they were finished eating they all went topside to catch the sunset. They sat together in silence and breathed deeply the fragrant air that floated in from the Gulf as they watched a flock of gulls dive for their evening meal. A few minutes later the sun approached the horizon and colored the sky in such brilliant purple and yellow streaks it was as if God wrung them out of a giant towel soaked with paint. When the ocean's waters extinguished the last little bit of glow Mary went below to make coffee, leaving the men on deck.

Art brought out the chess set, a game he and Evan found they had in common early on in their friendship, and the two men set to playing. Art sat comfortably in his aluminum-and-canvas chair and re-lit the Cuban cigar he'd held earlier. He leaned back and blew two perfect smoke rings that seemed to float forever before vanishing in the evening air. Evan looked at his friend, with such peace in his life, and wondered how such bliss was possible in a world full of so much hurt.

Evan came to know Art as a person who was easy to talk to, a person who listened and sincerely cared about his feelings. He found himself opening up to him on several occasions and he always felt better afterward, as if an evil poison had been sucked from a bite. When he had first met Art he had been careful about what he said, steering away from why he left Syracuse for fear of losing his regard. But, in time, he made the decision to tell him everything, and from that day on the friendship grew and became the strongest Evan ever had with anyone outside of his immediate family.

After a few bad chess moves Evan fired up the remains of his stogy and took to copying Art's smoky halos. He puckered his lips and shot out a patch of smoke that could have just as well been blown out the tailpipe of a backfiring sixty-five Dodge Dart.

Art laughed and blew a few more floating sculptures before offering some advice. He told Evan to pop his jaw and to exhale fast but not to blow. So Evan put the cigar to his lips and drew in deeply, then opened his mouth and let it rip. The smoke poured from his lips and rolled up his face and into his eyes. His jaw popped, but not before he inhaled and nearly caused himself to hemorrhage. He coughed and wheezed for five minutes as if a live bug was caught in his throat.

"You better stick to chess," Art said, taking pride in the fact that his smoke rings were still unchallenged.

Evan, eyes watering and throat scratchy, made a very decent move with his queen that Art hadn't seen coming.

"And you'd better stick with cigar tricks," Evan shot back with a teary-eyed wink.

Just then Mary came topside with two large mugs and placed one in front of each of them, then returned below to finish cleaning up from dinner. Art picked his up and studied his chess pieces carefully before reaching out and castling, putting Evan in check. He nonchalantly sipped the brew and grinned as he set the mug back down.

The game continued through two cups of coffee during which the tide turned from Evan's side to Art's several times, but ultimately Art pulled a brilliant knight/rook combination that had Evan mated before he knew what hit him. The old guy was smug about beating his younger challenger in such a tricky manner and he let his pleasure show by throwing up his hands as if he just knocked out Joe Frazier in the final round of a championship fight. Evan leaned back and allowed Art to gloat, and, despite the fact he lost, he found pleasure in the spectacle before him. His friend was an admirable opponent, and could lose with the same enthusiasm in which he could win, a noble trait Evan admired.

After a replay of the final move and a refill of their cups, Art inquired about Angela, and asked if Evan had spoken with her recently. Evan thought seriously about the question before answering.

"No. I don't know what I'd say if I called her," he replied honestly.

"Have you given any more thought to going home?"

"Are you trying to get rid of me? I have to win a few before I can leave, you know," Evan said lightly as he thought about an honest answer. "I think about it every day, but something tells me it's not time. I don't know, maybe I'm stalling for some screwed-up reason that I don't understand."

"It's never gonna be the right time if you two don't talk," Art added.

"But every time we do it just ends up a mess. All she wants to talk about is when I'm coming back."

"Well, of course she wants to know when you'll be back, she's your wife. You shouldn't blame her for asking you that."

"But I can't give her an answer. I'm just still..." Evan stopped and turned his head towards the moon that was growing brighter by the minute.

"Afraid?" Art asked.

"I guess," Evan said, before sipping his coffee.

"You know, when I was younger—hell, even now for that matter—if I over-think something, reluctance takes over and I end up not doing it. Take this boat, for example. Mary and me had the idea one day, while we were sitting around watching television and wasting our golden years, to sell our house and buy a sailboat and travel the world. Well, at first I was filled with excitement and gung-ho to get on the ocean and live like a free spirit. But then my darn brain took over and I started reasoning. I had all but convinced myself that I was too damn old to sail and that I didn't know anything about handling a sailboat." He paused and took a sip of coffee.

"Well, let me tell you. When I told Mary I was having second thoughts she said she was going with me or without me. She gave me the entire "life's too short" talk and before I knew what happened our house was sold and we were enrolled in a two-week sailing school. It's been the greatest adventure of my life, and I almost reasoned myself right out of it," Art said.

"Sometimes you gotta just jump in with both feet and say to hell with reason," Art finished after a brief pause.

Evan nodded his head to acknowledge Art's way of thinking, but it seemed to fit every situation in the world except his. The water was just too deep and dark to take the plunge, and he was afraid he'd end up washed up on shore.

The conversation ended naturally and comfortably with both men knowing instinctively that enough had been said. Evan knew Art was right, and Art empathized with Evan's feelings. They left it at that and reset the chess game for another battle. After a second game Evan thanked his hosts and headed back to his apartment. A lonesome feeling came over him when he left *The Secret*. He walked the dock and periodically glanced over his shoulder at her silhouette, which faded a little more into the darkness with each step he took. By the time he reached his apartment door all he could see was the outline of her tall sturdy mast gleaming in the light of the full moon and seemingly reaching to the clouds above.

CHAPTER THREE

Evan awoke at eight-twenty-six according to the clock radio next to his bed. Charlie hadn't banged on the door, which meant Derek had been on time to open the shop as he had promised when Evan bailed him out of jail the day before. He lay still for several moments and surveyed his vital signs before sitting up. He had a headache, a small one, and a dry mouth, but he wasn't at all nauseous. A late start drinking due to dinner with the Sullivans, coupled with a full stomach, made the effects of the six or seven shots and four or five beers comparatively mild. By the time he passed out it was from exhaustion rather than over-indulgence. But the dream still came, waking him four or five times through the night. The same dream that had been haunting his nights for the past year and a half.

When he was sure his legs would support him he pushed himself off the mattress and went to the window, which overlooked the marina to the west. The sky was clear and blue, which meant another busy day was ahead. But with Derek downstairs and Candy due in at eleven, Evan knew Sunday would be better than Saturday had been. He could stop at The Blind Minnow for breakfast and a helping of Sheila's southern hospitality before dealing with the day's issues, which, with some luck, would be minor ones. As he looked out across the yard he noticed Charlie and one of the marina's two mechanics busy at work on a customer's boat. They were bent over the engine of a large Donzi under the watchful eye of a young fashionable couple anxious to get on the water. Charlie was talking with his hands in an apparent attempt to convince the mechanic of where the problem lay. The mechanic, younger and more capable, was shaking his head and pointing to an electrical schematic to make his point.

Evan's eyes turned south and, in the distance, he noticed *The Secret* tied securely in her slip. She sat, quiet and still, her only movement a gentle sway driven by the remnants of a subtle wake. Seeing her there gave him an easy comfort, the type of comfort a child feels when riding his bike while his father has hold of the seat. He managed a small smile before heading towards the bathroom.

Standing over the toilet he looked in the mirror as he relieved his bladder. Two days worth of tiny salt-and-pepper hair formed the beginnings of a beard, and he thought for a second before deciding that he wasn't in the mood to shave and maybe wouldn't be again for some time. He had worn a beard when he was younger, in his twenties, and liked it, and wondered why he'd ever shaved it off. For an instant he considered growing a goatee before dismissing the idea of facial hair altogether and deciding to shave when he got to it.

After rooting around for a clean pair of shorts and a shirt that didn't stink like a high school locker room, he headed down to the shop. When he entered, Derek was giving a lesson on the do's and don'ts of baiting a hook with a shrimp to a skinny pimple-faced teenager. He held a large one in his left hand and pointed with his right to the round pellet-like mass in the head.

"That there's its brain. You can hook 'em in the head but make sure ya don't run ya hook through his nugget or you'll kill 'em, and they'll just lie there on the bottom and the fish won't eat 'em. I hook 'em in the tail but no way's better than the other," he said.

Evan poured himself a coffee and waited for the shop to empty out. Derek took notice when Evan entered, but avoided eye contact in the hope he would fill his cup and be on his way. Only Evan had no intention of leaving without spewing out his practiced lecture about responsibility, the one he'd gone over in his head the night before on his way to see the Sullivans. When the pimple-faced kid was gone he spoke in an uncharacteristically formal tone, "Derek, we have to have a talk." He felt hypocritical but continued all the same. Derek lifted his head from the cash register and turned. He was a few inches over six feet tall, not muscular, but big-boned and barrel-chested like a lumberjack, and his expression was in sharp contrast to his size. He was clearly ashamed and embarrassed about getting arrested and having Evan post his bail. He looked like a child who had accidentally hit a baseball through the stained glass window of a church.

"What happened yesterday can't happen again. I have to be able to count on you opening this place on time. If you can't handle that, I'm gonna put

Candy in charge and switch you to the afternoons. You told me last time that it would never happen again, but this time I'm telling you that if it does I'm gonna have to replace you with someone I can count on."

Evan felt silly sounding so serious about a bait shop. Eighteen months earlier he was in charge of fifteen technicians in a nuclear power plant and rarely spoke with the intensity he now heard in his own voice.

"Look, all I ask is that you show up on time and keep the place organized and stocked. I don't care what you do when things are slow. Throw a line in the water and relax for all I care. But you have to be on time." He felt better about his second sermon.

Derek apologized and reinforced his desire to run the shop, and he promised it wouldn't happen again and thanked Evan for posting bail. "I'll pay you back as soon as I can. I swear," Derek said. Evan believed his sincerity but wondered if the kid would be around long enough to come up with the hundred bucks it cost to get him out.

After a handshake Evan left the bait shop and headed for The Blind Minnow. He was barely ten steps out the door when Derek yelled, and when Evan turned he was handed a piece of paper. "Some lady called for you this morning and left her number. Said her name was Angela. Angela Hayden," Derek said curiously, having never heard mention of her before.

"Did she say anything else?" Evan asked, attempting not to appear startled but failing terribly.

"Just to have you call when you get a chance."

Evan glanced at the writing, and then back at Derek who was waiting to learn the connection the woman had to his boss. Evan never talked about any relations, not even of Angela, who he'd promised to honor in sickness and in health until death do them part. It was a conscious choice he made when he took the job, to not mention family or friends or anything about his life before coming to Florida, and, with the exception of the Sullivans, he never told anyone at the marina that he had a wife and son twelve hundred miles away.

Having been caught off guard it took him a minute to realize the number was his, rather Angela's, home number. His calls, since forgetting to pay the phone bill for his apartment for two months, were now taken in the back of the bait shop on an ancient rotary phone that smelled like fish.

After thanking Derek he walked to the dock and looked at the number again, as if it might have magically changed in the previous ten seconds. His initial thought was that his six-year-old son was hurt or sick or even worse, and he had the urge to run to the bait shop and dial the number as fast as his fingers could turn the sticky disk on the fish phone. After a minute or so reason took over and he convinced himself nothing was wrong. Nothing except the fact that he and Angela lived in separate states and hadn't talked to each other in well over a month. He remembered their last conversation, the one where they talked about marriage counseling. He recalled how Angela got mad when he said he wasn't ready to come home, that he needed more time to work things out. She said it wasn't fair to her to be put on hold and forced to wait for him to decide if he was coming back or not. He countered by reminding her she threw him out saying she never wanted to see him again. Angela mentioned Emily and what she would have wanted for them; he got mad and hung up the phone. When he called back only minutes later Jeremy answered and said his mommy didn't want to talk anymore. That was the last time they spoke.

After replaying their last conversation it became very clear to him why she called. It had been a year since he left and he was no closer to going home now than he was a month ago or a month before that, and he knew her well enough to know she wasn't the type of woman who would sit idly by and wait forever. He knew she still loved him, but he also knew she had a limit and would only wait so long before asking for a divorce. That was why she called. To tell him she went to a lawyer and to give him a heads-up that papers were on the way so he wouldn't be caught by surprise. She was a good person and wouldn't want to hurt him. She would certainly start crying when she told him she wanted the divorce, and he would probably cry, too.

It was a lot to think about. It had been a year and yet it seemed like yesterday when he had pulled out of his driveway heading for God knows where. By the time he entered Florida, New York was frozen in his mind. Left in a state of infinite preservation like a time capsule shot into space. The first days went by and turned into weeks and before he knew it a month had passed. Then another and another until he found himself with a job and an apartment and another life far away from Angela and Jeremy and the house he once called home.

He stuffed the note deep into his pocket and continued towards the diner. The marina was alive with activity as people rushed to get on the water. Chugging sounds came from every direction as outboards and inboards idled in the no-wake zones headed for the Gulf. Young couples unloaded jet skis alongside beer-bellied fishermen, and weekend sailors raised their masts and hoped for wind as over-tanned skiers donned their vests and checked their gear. Seagulls flew nearby with sharp eyes for anything from chewing gum to fish guts, while pelicans sat lazily on dock poles waiting for handouts.

A unique odor found only at marinas filled the air. It's best described as a mixture of two-stroke motor oil, seaweed, suntan lotion, a dabble of beer and potato chips, and a smidgen of dead fish, blended together and dried in the sun.

Evan walked along the dock taking it all in, trying to forget about the piece of paper wadded up in his pocket. He realized, looking around, how familiar everything had become, which only emphasized the fact that yes, indeed, a year had gone by. A full year. A Christmas, a New Year's, birthdays and anniversaries had all passed in the time he'd been gone. He stopped walking and stood, staring out at the water. What he saw wasn't boats and jet skis, but rather a house at the end of a cul-de-sac with a big front porch and an evergreen tree next to the driveway. He focused on the front door with its stained glass windows, the one Angela fell in love with when she first laid eyes on it, and the terra cotta flowerpots on both sides filled with daisies or mums or roses, depending upon the season. He saw the back yard and the above ground pool he put in when Jeremy was a baby, and he saw the garden Angela planted. He saw her, bent down pulling weeds, with her hair pulled back in a ponytail and covered with the large floppy hat she wore to keep the sun out of her eyes.

He stood and looked, stared, as she worked. He wanted to walk up to her and reach out and touch her shoulder and tell her he was there, then the screen door slammed, the way it always had, and Emily emerged from the house carrying her butterfly net. She ran around the yard swatting at anything that moved and she laughed and smiled the way she had from the moment she was born. She ran to the garden and stopped long enough to kiss Angela before running away again in pursuit of a blue or orange or green little creature that flew too fast to be caught. He watched her carefully and took notice of everything. Her small white sandals with flowers on them and her beach pants, called that because she had outgrown the length and would wear them to the lake so she could walk in the water up to her knees. She wore her soft blue shirt, her favorite because her grandmother bought it for her at a yard sale, and he noticed her smile, big and happy and real. She was everything he remembered, clear in his vision as if she was there in front of him. His ears heard the crunch of the grass under her feet and his nose caught the smell of the garden.

She ran around for some time before suddenly stopping. Then she turned towards Evan and yelled, "Daddy's home," and ran at him with her arms stretched out in front of her. The butterfly net hit the ground and she jumped into his arms. He kissed her on the nose, then lifted her high into the air; her soft brown hair shot out in all directions like fireworks filling the sky. Her smile was large and true and her love apparent and deep. Just as his emotions exploded he was pulled back into real time.

An engine backfired. A jet ski sped by with total disregard for the posted "No Wake Zone" signs, sparking a wave of yells and horns from other boaters. An instant later a kid on a skateboard passed behind him and pulled one of those numbers where the board rotates three hundred sixty degrees while the rider is airborne. He executed it perfectly and was gone before Evan had a chance to tell him to stay off the dock, not that he would have. He was still preoccupied with the fading memory of his precious little girl.

When the memory was completely gone he continued on to The Blind Minnow. Sheila saw him coming and met him at the door, something she liked to do with people she considered friends. She grabbed him by the forearm, and, in a drawl reminiscent of times long gone in Florida, asked him what you call a woman without a brain. She loved jokes and would repeat the last "good un" she heard to every friend she had. Evan smiled and shrugged his shoulders, giving her the chance to yell, "A widow," before laughing so loud it was as if it was the first time she heard it herself. Then she walked him to the counter, sat him down, and yelled, "Dana honey, we got a hungry man here."

Dana, a tall pretty woman who displayed subtle signs of a hard life, emerged from the kitchen carrying a box of frozen butter pats. She smiled at Evan and wiggled her fingers in an attempt at a wave, which Evan returned in the same manner.

"Coffee, tea or me?" she asked as she passed by. She was outgoing and friendly, and her relationship with Evan had evolved into one of playful flirtations. She hoped it would eventually turn more serious, but Evan discounted her attention as mere friendliness.

"Well now, that's a hard decision. I'll take the hottest one," Evan replied, playing his expected part even though he wasn't really up to it. The trip down memory lane had taken the playfulness right out of him and had all but erased the appetite he'd had earlier.

"I'm not sure that would go over too well in the diner," Dana whispered as she passed close by him.

Sheila managed to scrounge up most of the pieces of the daily newspaper, which she placed on the counter at about the same time Dana brought a coffee. She bent over and put her arm around Evan and said jokingly, "If I was twenty years younger..." to which Evan replied, "You'd be hugging a little boy."

"And I'd show that boy a few things he'd never forget," she said before slapping Evan softly on the head and walking towards the door to greet another friend. She was the type of woman blessed with eternal adolescence, and judging strictly by her actions one would most certainly swear she was thirteen years old.

The Minnow gave the Delcast Marina an edge over other newer and larger marinas built after it. It served as a central meeting hub for most everyone that docked their boats there, and it was a convenient place to grab breakfast in the morning or a sandwich in the afternoon. Technically, it was under Evan's control, like everything else on the property. But he followed the previous dock master's way of doing things by allowing Sheila full autonomy in managing it. The same way he allowed Charlie full rein in the warehouse, which in his mind was a good thing considering he didn't know the first thing about food service or what it took to run a dry storage facility. That left him free to run the charters, bait house, and docks, the meat and potatoes of the operation. At the end of each month he would meet with Sheila and Charlie to review the books and discuss any issues, and, if there were any, they would already have the answers, making their get-togethers more academic than anything else. But Evan didn't mind. It was a chance to eat a nice dinner, usually home cooked by Sheila, and fill his thoughts with something other than the past.

"You want your usual, hon?" Dana asked as she stroked her hand up and down Evan's back. Her long nails felt nice along his spine; something that reminded him of quiet evenings at home with Angela after the kids went to bed. They'd get under the covers and pop a movie in the VCR and lie together tangled up like pretzels in each other's arms. She would rub his back the same way and many times, after the movie or during it, they'd make love and her nails would sink into his skin as she pulled him close.

When his breakfast arrived he picked at it, managing only to eat the toast and two strips of bacon before pushing the plate away. The call from Angela and the memories of Emily were still on his mind, which made his stomach too upset to digest anything more. Sheila stopped by and told him another joke and said something about a delivery of spoiled milk, to which he nodded his head although he wasn't really paying attention. Before long Dana's section filled up and she was busy taking orders and filling coffee cups, and Evan slipped out unnoticed.

Outside he ran into Bill Baxter, a crabber who thought that anything that went wrong in his life was the marina's fault. He bitched and moaned about some stolen crab traps and asshole jet skiers and taxes and his arthritis and every other damn thing he could think about. Evan just agreed with him, something he had learned to do after his first encounter with Bill.

"Stop by the shop and I'll see what we can do about replacing those traps," Evan said when Bill took a break to breathe. "I'll have Derek fix ya up," he added before taking the opportunity to escape.

When he was in the clear he reached in his pocket and took out Derek's note. If there was magic in the world it wasn't at work that day, because the writing still held the same message it had an hour earlier. After a brief look he rolled his hand over it and wadded it into a ball. With a gentle throw he tossed it off the dock into the salty water below.

CHAPTER FOUR

After calling and leaving a message at the marina, Angela and Jeremy went to church and then to her parent's house for Sunday brunch. Her mother, a bit quirky and on a constant quest to be trendy, changed their traditional Sunday lunches together to Sunday brunches. She served a mixture of breakfast and lunch items that had no appetizing qualities when seen on the same table—like rare roast beef alongside omelets, and cold cuts alongside fancy pastries—and she served it on the veranda, formerly know as the screened-in porch. Had she not been such a sweet, loving woman her husband would have complained a long time ago.

Their house was a colonial built in the thirties, and was on a prime piece of real estate on the shore of Oneida Lake. Most of the houses in the area were newer, larger, more modern homes built by people who had the resources to purchase the old homes, tear them down, and build new ones. But Angela's father had refused to sell during the building explosion of the late eighties and early nineties, when the first of the baby boomers were setting themselves up for their retirement years.

When Angela arrived her mother answered the door and led her in to the family room where her father was looking at cars on the Internet. He was talking to himself, like people sometimes do when they're frustrated, about the outrageous prices being asked for high-mileage luxury sedans. He had no intention of buying, although he would tell you he did, he just liked to look and dream and convince himself his vehicle was just fine considering the asking price of new, as well as abused ones.

Jeremy ran and jumped onto his grandfather's lap and got a hug and a kiss, which was happily accepted and returned. He was the old man's favorite grandson. Not because of what he'd been going through, but because the kid truly loved him and wasn't the least bit ashamed to show it, like his other grandchildren were when they visited. He would stay by his grandfather's side almost the entire visit and cry when it was time to leave, and although nobody knew it, not even Angela's mother, his grandfather sometimes cried too.

"How you doin', Pop?" Angela asked before bending over and kissing him on the cheek.

"Hi, sweetheart. Your mother and me are fine. How are you and my favorite grandson doing?" he replied, not at all shy about voicing his true feelings about Jeremy.

"We're doing O.K."

"Any word?" he asked, referring to Evan, who he knew hadn't called in over a month.

"Nothing yet. But we'll talk more later," Angela said, gesturing towards Jeremy who was rooting through his poppy's shirt pocket for a stick of gum, or a piece of candy, or some other goody he had become accustomed to finding in there.

"Getting a new car?" Angela asked, noticing a Lincoln Town Car on the screen.

"No. The LeSabre is running fine. I'm just looking," he said and she knew that, but she liked to humor him now and then, as he used to do to her when she was a little girl.

"You'd look good in that one, Pop."

"Not at these prices, I wouldn't," he said. Then he whispered, "Go see your mother and see if we can have lunch today like normal people instead of eating like the rich and famous."

She laughed as she left the boys alone and walked to the kitchen. Her mother was mixing a hollandaise sauce on the stove, which smelled very appetizing to Angela, who hadn't had a bite to eat all morning.

"Can I help?" Angela asked, hoping to speed things up for the sake of her growling stomach.

"You can set the table."

"Where are we eating today?" she asked, having felt a slight chill in the air when they arrived.

"Outside. It's a nice day and I hate to waste them when they're here," her mother said. "And you can get the wine out of the fridge."

"When the table was set and the food was ready, Angela's mother served the first course: Eggs benedict with sliced roast beef and fried potatoes. The food was delicious, but not to the liking of a six-year old boy accustomed to cereal or scrambled eggs for breakfast. The second course was a basket of French pastries with fancy names, and a cheese and vegetable tray. The old man rolled his eyes when his wife started explaining the difference between French and American baked goods. Everything she said was correct, but to him a donut was a donut, regardless of which side of the ocean it came from. Jeremy managed to find a sugar-coated job among them and ate half of it before asking to be excused so he could watch television.

"He looks a little thin, Angie. Has he been eating?" Angela's mother asked.

"He's a boy. They all lose some weight at his age. It's from all the running around they do," Pop said in defense of his little buddy.

"I don't think it's that, Pop. He's been upset lately, and he's been having some trouble sleeping," Angela said, pausing to sip some wine. "And the school called. He's been having some problems there, too."

Her father's brow tightened and his eyes squinted. Obviously bothered, his wife worried he'd get upset, and his heart would race, and he'd end up in the hospital again.

"What's wrong with him?" Pop asked.

Angela's mother looked at her with concern and gave her leg a cautionary tap under the table. It told Angela to sugar-coat the truth and hold on to what she wanted to say until the boys went outside to fish.

"Nothing really. He just falls asleep at his desk now and then, and the teacher was concerned. It's my fault for letting him stay up so late," she said and her mother smiled.

"Well, like I said, he's a growing boy. Hell, I fell asleep in class when I was his age, too. The only difference is they didn't call your parents, they bent you over right there in front of everyone and pulled out the switch," Pop said, his face relaxing.

Angela ate a helping of eggs benedict and two French pastries. She made Jeremy a peanut butter and jelly on white bread, crust removed like he liked it, and took it to him with a glass of milk. His poppy sat with him in the family room and convinced him to eat it by telling him it was his favorite when he was a kid. When the sandwich and milk were in the little boy's tummy, his poppy took him to the dock to try his luck fishing.

Three years before, Angela's father had suffered a heart attack. He was at work when it hit, without warning, and he went down hard. He arrived at the hospital with no pulse, and was clinically dead for almost five minutes before the doctors managed to jump start his ticker. Years of over indulgence in fatty foods and cigarettes finally took its toll, and gave him the wakeup call he needed. That's when he retired and stopped smoking, and took to walking around the neighborhood every morning.

Since the heart attack Angela's mother had done everything in her power to shield him from things that could upset him. Things like the large increase in property taxes she miraculously worked into the budget without his knowledge, and the problems her daughter Eve was having in her marriage. For that reason she waited until his line was in the water before asking Angie about Jeremy.

What Angela said earlier was true. Jeremy was falling asleep in class, but he had also been wetting his bed at night and losing control of his bladder at school, and he had lost weight, almost ten pounds in six weeks. She thought it was a phase he was going through, sort of a delayed effect from losing his older sister, and she thought it would pass, but it didn't. Then the school called and suggested she take him to a counselor, someone who could help him before things got worse.

Angela's mother listened, and felt the pain only a mother or grandmother can feel when something is wrong with a child in the family. Her life was so different when she was young compared to her three daughters' lives. She never experienced the sorrow that comes with the loss of a child as Angela had, and she never faced a problem in her marriage so severe that it ended in divorce, as her youngest daughter Kimberly had. So when those things happened to her children it was almost as if they happened to her, and now her grandson was having problems, problems that could affect him for the rest of his life.

"Has he asked about his father?" her mother asked.

"Not in the last few weeks," Angela replied. She turned from her spot at the table and looked out the bay window at a scene that could have been a Norman Rockwell painting. Her father and her son were sitting next to each other holding their poles as the noon sun lit the weather beaten wood dock below them. Off to the side was a large weeping willow with long branches that hung over part of the dock, but not over the boys. They were facing away so that only their backs, and the very tips of their poles above their heads, could be seen. The picture could have told a million stories of hope and love and family had it been viewed by anyone but Angela. To her it told a simple tale of a decent old man who truly cared for his confused and injured grandson.

"Have you heard from him lately?"

"No," Angela replied, still staring out the window.

"Maybe you should call him and tell him what's going on with Jeremy. Maybe he'll come home if you ask him again."

"I did call him, Ma, and his phone was disconnected. I thought at first that he moved somewhere else and I'd never hear from him again. Then I got the number to that marina where he's been working, and I called and left a message. The guy that answered said he'd tell him," she said, sounding sure he wouldn't call back. Her mother thought hard for a moment before asking what she'd avoided all along.

"Do you think maybe he, that he might have…" she struggled to ask the question but Angela got the gist of it before she could finish. Her mother suspected, but never before suggested, that Evan may have met someone in Florida.

"I don't know, Mom. I've thought about it. It's been a year, and for the last month or so he hasn't even called to talk to his own son."

"What are you going to say if he calls?"

"I'm gonna tell him about Jeremy, and about the doctor. I made an appointment with a children's psychiatrist, and I don't feel right about taking him there without telling Evan. He needs to know that his son is having problems, but I don't want him coming back just because of that. I mean, if he doesn't love me anymore," Angela said with a tear in her eye.

"I'm sure he loves you, honey, and I'm sure he loves Jeremy, too. But what happened after the accident, well, I'm not saying that what he did was right. Maybe he's just not a strong person," her mother said as she wiped away tears from under Angela's eyes.

"But he was strong when I married him, and I know how much he loved Emily. God, I loved her too, Mom. She was my little girl," Angela said crying some more and wiping the tears away so that her father wouldn't see through the window if he turned around. "But I couldn't let everything come apart when she died. I had to take care of my son."

"I know that, honey. I'm just saying that maybe it did something to him that we don't understand. You have to remember that he was with her when it happened. So maybe he blames himself. I don't know, but you have to realize that you're doing the right thing by taking care of that little boy."

Angela's tears came faster as she thought about the fight they had before Evan left. "It's just that I'm the one that told him to leave, but I didn't mean for him to leave forever. I was just angry and confused."

"Honey, you've been through a lot. Don't blame yourself for what you said back then. You were grief stricken, and when people get that way they say and do things that they don't mean."

Angela shook her head and dried her eyes with a napkin. She squeezed her mother's hand and felt the love in her touch. It was the same love she'd felt growing up when her mother would comfort her and tuck her into bed and kiss her goodnight. She felt like a little girl again, in a way. Sitting in the same house she grew up in and talking to her mother and crying just like she did when her very best friend moved out of state brought back many feelings. Her mother held her back then and told her it was God's will, and that everything has a purpose. But now, she just couldn't see the purpose in anything that had happened to her family in the past eighteen months.

When they were done talking Angela went to the bathroom to freshen her makeup. Then she climbed the stairs to her childhood bedroom, and sat in the window bench and looked out across the yard. Most of the houses were gone from when she was a little girl, and the trees were bigger, too. She had a partial view of the lake and could see the place where her first boyfriend lived. The original house had been razed, and a new one replaced it, but she didn't see the new one, she saw the blue and white, wood-framed colonial with the big back porch where she'd gotten her first kiss.

Her eyes crossed to a field where she and her friends spent hours riding bikes in the summer and throwing snowballs in the winter. She saw little girls and little boys dressed in warm winter clothes running through the snow. One little girl had long blonde hair and a funny smile. It was her best friend, the one who moved out of state when she was twelve. She watched her run and fall and laugh, and she saw herself laughing, too. She saw them cross the road to her house and enter the back door into the kitchen, where her mother would have hot chocolate ready for them to drink.

She wondered where her friend was now and if she ever thought about those fabulously innocent days of childhood, when all they cared about was laughing and playing and acting shy around boys. Just then her mother came up and found her in the room with a far-away look in her eyes, and she knew her daughter was somewhere in the past.

"This will always be your room, and you'll always be our little girl," she said from the doorway.

Angela nodded her head and smiled and reached out for her mother to sit with her, and when she did Angela put her head on her mother's shoulder and closed her eyes.

CHAPTER FIVE

Six months before leaving Syracuse, on the morning of the very worst day of Evan's life, he woke up early to make pancakes, eggs, and crispy bacon. His alarm went off at six-thirty, an hour earlier than it would have had he not taken the day off to spend with Emily and Jeremy, who were off from school because of a teacher's conference.

After making coffee he quietly retrieved the griddle form the cabinet below the sink and plugged it in. Strip-by-strip he laid a pound of bacon across its non-stick surface. While it cooked he prepared the pancake batter: two cups of Aunt Jemima pancake mix, two eggs, some milk, and some oil. As he whipped the batter, Angela's alarm rang. A minute later she was in the kitchen, squinting as her eyes slowly adjusted to the light. "Good morning, babe," Evan said as he flipped the bacon. Angela just nodded, not yet awake enough to talk.

Evan cracked half a dozen eggs into a large mixing bowl, added some cream, and began stirring. His apron, the one he used when barbecuing, caught Angela's attention. It was dark blue with two big pockets and stitched lettering that read, "Kiss the chef, he deserves it." In a sleepy voice she said, "If he comes back to bed I'll kiss the chef anyplace he wants me to."

Evan smiled. The offer was tempting, but with bacon sizzling on the griddle and pancake batter and eggs ready to cook he had to pass. "How about a rain check on that offer?" he asked, still half-tempted to turn off the grill and follow her back to the bedroom.

"Maybe if the chef prepares dinner tonight I'll provide the dessert," she said with a half-tired, half-sexy smile.

"And what would the lady like?" he asked while attempting a French accent.

She walked to him and put her arms around his waist, snuggling close. Wiping a small smudge of batter off his face she said, "How about an order of you, over easy?"

They kissed and she rested her head on his chest. Her body felt good against his and again he considered accepting her offer. It had been a while since they had made love in the morning, and he had the sudden urge to abandon the breakfast and carry her to the bedroom and tear her clothes off. But she had to get ready for work, the kids would be up soon and the bacon was close to burning. He gently pulled himself away, gave her another kiss and started removing the food from the grill. "You're gonna make me burn this breakfast if you keep that up," he said, smiling.

Angela poured herself a coffee, and before leaving the kitchen, gave Evan's butt a squeeze. "You don't know what you're missing," she said. On her way out she added, "I'll wake up the kids."

The day was originally planned as a family day, but an important meeting at work put the kibosh on Angela's chance to get the day off. She was still relatively new at the firm, only returning to work when Jeremy turned four years old and started pre-school, which put her at the bottom of the food chain when it came to discretionary time off. But Schewster and Brown was one of the best investment firms in the area, so being denied an unscheduled day off didn't really bother her. They paid well and had a reputation for taking care of their people, and she was glad to be with them.

The kids came out to the kitchen with sleep still in their eyes and Evan greeted them in standard fashion by kissing them on their noses, something he'd started doing for no particular reason when they were born and had continued ever since. Jeremy, being more of a morning person than his sister, opted to help make breakfast. He stood on a stool and pushed the runny mixture of eggs and cream around the griddle's surface while Evan filled three glasses with orange juice and put them on the table. Meanwhile Jeremy's older sister, Emily, laid her head on the table and fell back to sleep.

When the mixture stiffened Jeremy attempted to scoop it off the griddle and onto a plate but managed to drop almost as much onto the floor. When he was done Evan kissed him on the head and said, "Good job, champ, now wake up your sister so she can eat." Jeremy hopped off the stool and walked to the table where Emily's hair was laid out across the tabletop like a Japanese sensu fan. He reached out, grabbed a handful, and gave a tug and said, "Wake up, Emmy. Daddy said to wake up."

Emily's head rose quickly, tearing the hair out of Jeremy's hand. "Stop it, that hurts. Dad, Jeremy pulled my hair," she said angrily. It was a display of her usual morning grouchiness, a trait she seemed to acquire at about two and a half years of age.

"Come on, guys, let's get along today. We've got a fun day planned, so let's eat up and get ready to go," Evan said as he poured small round circles of batter onto the griddle. If only he could have seen the future in the tiny bubbles forming in the pancakes, he would have cancelled the trip and gone back to bed with Angela.

Breakfast was mostly uneventful once Emily got over having her hair pulled. There was one small argument over who got the last piece of bacon, but it was settled quickly when Jeremy started crying and Emily withdrew and gave it to her baby brother. Her morning disposition had gone from grouchy to agreeable in only fifteen minutes, and in another hour she would be her usual bubbly, happy self. All things considered she was a very good "big sisser," as Jeremy would say.

Most of the time she was sympathetic to the needs of her little brother. There were the occasional arguments—after all they were siblings—but nothing that couldn't be settled by the threat of a spanking or a few minutes of time out, and there was no shortage of love between them. They were inseparable from the very moment Jeremy was brought home from the hospital. Almost every night Emily would sneak out of her room and into his where she would sleep on the floor next to the crib. When he was old enough to sleep in a bed she would bring him into her room, and, in the morning, they would be found under the covers snuggled up together.

Angela left for work a little after eight o'clock. The transition from Mom in a bathrobe to Ms. Hayden in a business suit took less than thirty minutes, thanks to her planning the night before. She would always set her clothing out, along with her jewelry, before going to bed. Then she'd pack the kids' lunches and set their clothes out. She'd put her briefcase, purse and keys on the counter in the laundry room, next to the door to the garage. In contrast, Evan's lack of organization made it almost a miracle that he ever made it to work on time. He'd spend half of the morning hunting for a shirt to match his pants or trying to find two identical socks, and the other half searching for his car keys. Their happy marriage gave credence to the saying that opposites attract.

After kissing them all goodbye and reminding the kids to obey their father, who had the reputation of being a pushover in her absence, Angela backed out of the driveway and drove away from the house. Within a minute her car turned a corner and disappeared behind the long drooping branches of an old oak tree at the end of the cul-de-sac.

Evan filled Emily's school backpack with three sandwiches, a bag of chips and three bottles of water. He put two additional bottles of water in a small Mickey Mouse backpack of Jeremy's and carried another with him for the ride. By eight-fifteen they were piled in the Jeep Grand Cherokee and on their way out of Syracuse, heading towards Watkins Glenn State Park. The first half of the two-hour trip was quiet thanks to the few hand-held video games Evan had the good sense to bring. But by the time they hit I-14 the kids had turned them off and were getting fidgety, so Evan reached back and gave them a few coloring books and a box of crayons. Serenity returned.

I-14 runs north/south along the western side of Seneca Lake, one of the largest Finger Lakes. The area is home to over forty wineries, which, if combined, would produce more wine than any other place in the United States outside of California. It is also well known to people in New York, Ohio and Pennsylvania as a romantic place to get away for the weekend with someone special. Historic bed and breakfasts decorate the region from one end of the lake to the other and are often nestled in between vineyards with spectacular views of the water.

As Evan drove south on I-14 he kept an eye out for the shiny tin roof of the Blackberry Inn. It had been roughly seven years since he and Angela spent a weekend at the beautifully restored bed and breakfast, and although his memory held clearly the details of the place, he wasn't too sure of its exact location on the road. He took his foot off the gas pedal and let the vehicle coast down when he thought he was close. A large black sign with gold lettering caught his attention. It read, "Barr Hunters Vineyard, Established 1896," and he knew he wasn't far away from his destination.

He remembered the hayride he and Angela took at Barr Hunters, as well as the tour of the winery and wine cellar. They had spent the afternoon on a wine-tasting trip with three other couples, and Barr Hunters was the last stop. A limousine took them to several of the major wineries along the lake and by the time they reached Barr Hunters they were sauced. The hayride was the highlight of the day. All the wine Evan drank gave him gas and the first major bump the wagon incurred caused an explosion in his pants so loud it startled the horse. Needless to say everyone started laughing and for the remainder of the day they had the giggles. That memory brought a slight chuckle to Evan even after seven years.

Just past the third winery on his left the grand home appeared. Evan hit the brakes, pulled into the drive and stopped. The kids looked up from their coloring, curious to see if they were at the park. Evan told them where they were and pointed to the room that belonged to him and Angela for a wonderful weekend seven years before. After a curious glance they returned to their drawings, leaving Evan to his memories.

He looked up at the second floor of the three-level house. Small, lace curtains hung across old etched glass windows. Below them, on the porch, sat a row of wicker rocking chairs and a swinging love seat. Delicate flowers surrounded the house and gently stirred in the soft morning breeze. Two grand oaks stretched high into the sky and came together above the roof. The morning sunlight filtered through the leaves and laid golden sparkles of light on the ground below. It was just as he remembered, and seeing it made him sad. He shouldn't have let so many years pass without returning, without taking a weekend away, just the two of them, to taste wine and sleep late and fart on a hayride. Before leaving he promised himself he'd do that. Maybe for her birthday, or their anniversary, or just a long weekend, but he'd do it. He took one last look then pulled back onto I-14.

An hour and fifteen minutes later the Jeep pulled into the parking lot of Watkins Glenn State Park. It was relatively empty, as he expected, since it was a workday for most people. For an instant before killing the engine he thought about Angela stuck in a conference room, mulling through a pile of papers, and he wondered if she was thinking of him and the kids. There was an awkward feeling without her there, sort of like swimming in long pants.

Emily and Jeremy got out and wrestled with their backpacks until they were comfortably in place. Evan grabbed a camera, his water bottle, and the two raincoats Angela insisted he bring to keep the kids dry. She suggested he bring one for himself too, but he declined, saying a little water never hurt anyone. The truth was, the only raincoat he had was a large green poncho that got stuffed into his tackle box after his last fishing trip and was sure to have a permanent stench. If his memory served him correctly there weren't but a handful of places in the park where a raincoat would be of use, and he could just avoid them.

Evan put the slim bottle in the back pocket of his pants and bent down to tie the laces on Jeremy's sneakers. He had tied them himself at home, but history had proven his bows too loose to last more than five minutes. From mere habit he glanced at Emily's shoes and noticed they were fine. She had learned to tie her own at two, and by five could handle the job as well as any adult. With the sneakers secure and the backpacks in place, they took off towards the park.

Watkins Glenn State Park consists of a two-mile long gorge with elevations of up to four hundred feet in some places. There are four man-made stone bridges that cross the stream at varying heights, numerous waterfalls, and over eight hundred stone steps. A centuries-old foot trail allows visitors to walk through the gorge and enjoy the beauty from within its massive stone walls, and a stream winds its way through the park and descends hundreds of feet as it rolls over rock cliffs and cuts through stone channels.

At the entrance to the park the kids put on their raincoats. Jeremy's went over his backpack and left him looking a bit like a camel, which caused Emily take extra time to adjust her pack to fit over her coat. There was no way, she said, that she was going to walk around looking like a polka-dotted desert animal.

After paying the admission Evan stopped an elderly couple and asked if they would mind taking a picture of him and the kids. The gentleman, who could have doubled for Winston Churchill, was more than willing to oblige. Evan bent down between Emily and Jeremy and put an arm around each of them, and, in a voice that held a faint hint of an Irish accent, Winston said, "Let's see some teeth now," and took the shot. It was picture number eleven of a twenty-four-exposure roll, and the last picture ever taken of Emily. In it she was smiling, crossing her eyes, and sticking out her tongue.

Inside the park a slight mist hung in the air, the result of the first waterfall located near the park entrance, which slowly vanished as they made their way along the stone path. The ground was moist, but not drenched, and caused the rubber soles on Jeremy's sneakers to squeak as he walked, which incidentally served to notify Evan immediately when the little guy took off ahead. His squeaky feet raced along the trail and the hump on his back waddled back and forth as he went. Behind him was Evan, keeping pace by merely increasing his stride, and behind Evan was Emily, walking slow to admire the grandeur of the place.

As she walked Emily thought about how the gorge was scoured by glaciers millions of years before, and how Native American Indians blazed the trails centuries ago. Her dad had explained it the day before, and although she had acted uninterested, she listened and took note. Now she wondered what it must have been like to live when the Indians did, without electricity, or television, or ice cream. She liked nature, and learned at a young age to appreciate the smell of spring flowers and the colors of fall leaves, and she liked animals of all kinds, even snakes and bugs, and enjoyed playing outside and getting dirty. Those things she learned from her dad, and it made the loving bond between them that much stronger.

But she was also Angela's daughter and liked bubble baths, making cookies, and watching scary movies in the dark. She loved shopping with her mom and trying on new clothes and testing samples of perfume at the J.C. Penney's in the mall. But, most of all, she liked being together as a family, with her mom and dad and baby brother. So many of her friends' parents were divorced that she made sure to thank God every night that hers weren't, and she prayed for the angels to watch over her mom and dad and brother, and to keep them all together forever.

Evan raced along with Jeremy and looked back periodically to make sure Emily didn't fall too far behind. When the distance between them became too great he would grab the hood of Jeremy's jacket and hold him back. Once or twice, around corners, he lost sight of her and turned back, pulling Jeremy with him, until the shiny red and yellow raincoat came into view. At twenty-five minutes into the hike they reached the first of four bridges that crossed the river. Jeremy was the first onto it and was excited to be standing so high above the stream. At only forty-two inches tall his eyes just cleared the side, and on his tippy-toes he got a bird's eye view of the exquisite canyon below. A few minutes later Emily caught up and they all stood together, awed by the large ancient slice in the earth.

After a long look Jeremy took off towards a cave-like depression at the end of the bridge. He stopped long enough to satisfy his curiosity, then headed down the path towards a set of stone stairs and started climbing. Evan was a few steps behind and caught up with him before he was so high he might fall and hurt himself.

Before leaving the bridge Emily reached deep down into a side pocket of her backpack and removed a small, shiny credit-card-sized object with wires wrapped around it. It was the gift she got for her ninth birthday, an MP3 player that held about an hour's worth of music on a microchip. She clipped the tiny box to her waistband and inserted two cushioned, dime-sized disks into her ears. She pushed a button, and, in an instant, heard the voice of her one true love, Aaron Carter.

She reached the end of the bridge just in time to see her dad and brother turn a corner at the top of the first set of steps. Evan was looking back as he pulled on Jeremy's raincoat, and, once he saw her following, he let up on the reins and allowed Jeremy to speed ahead. Emily picked up her speed to a slow jog. She didn't mind trailing behind, but she didn't want to get so far behind that her dad would worry. At the halfway point between the bridge and stairway the MP3 player popped free of her waist, bounced three times, then slid through a drainage hole at the base of the stone wall. It fell four feet and came to rest on a thin ledge, mere inches from dropping fifty feet onto the rocks below.

Her heart sank as she imagined it at the bottom in pieces. She ran to the wall and at first glance didn't see it. Tears began to swell in her eyes before she spotted its shiny metal surface intact, but out of reach.

Her thoughts immediately flashed to the fuss she put up when she begged her parents to buy it for her. Several of her friends had gotten them for Christmas and were downloading songs off the Internet, and she wanted one so bad that she swore she would never ask for anything again as long as she lived. When her birthday came and she unwrapped it, from a huge box designed to fool her, she jumped up and down and said she had the best parents in the world. Now it lay there, her birthday present, on a dirty ledge, mere inches from falling.

She looked ahead for her dad, but he'd already turned the corner at the top of the steps, following squeaky feet. She looked again at the small shiny box, which magically appeared a little closer. She considered getting her dad but was afraid to leave it there alone, because of the finders keepers, losers weepers thing every kid knows about and considers a law. With her luck some other kid would jump the wall and snatch it in the time it took her to bring her dad back. Plus, her dad would probably say it was too dangerous to retrieve, and would give her a long lecture about being responsible for her belongings, the same way he did when she lost her Mickey Mouse watch at the mall.

She looked ahead, then back, then ahead, and then back again. The trail was empty and the little box wasn't really as far it first appeared, and she figured if she just grabbed it and caught up with her father and brother no one would ever know what happened. She loosened the shoulder straps on her backpack and let it fall to the ground. She sat on the wall, swung her legs over the top, and took a deep breath.

Her hands gripped the wall and supported her weight as she stretched out one leg to see how far she could reach. The tip of her foot extended slightly past where the MP3 player sat. If she could reach it with her foot, she reasoned, she could reach it with one hand while holding the wall with the other. Another glance at the trail proved it to still be empty.

Her heartbeat was double the rate it had been only minutes before. In part because of what she was about to do, but mostly because of the anguish of losing, or almost losing, her beloved birthday present. She slowly freed one hand from the wall and the thin muscles in the other tightened to compensate for the added strain. Her fingers tightened over the inside corner of the wall and her nails dug into the thin layer of dirt attached to the rock. She was completely supporting her sixty-five pound body weight using only four fingers and the very tips of her feet. She stretched out the other arm, slowly, hesitantly, until her shaking fingers were as close to the little box as possible. There were still inches to go before she could rescue it and climb back to safety.

She pulled back and took a breath. She'd remembered hearing someplace, probably on television, not to look down when in a high place. But the rescue required her to keep an eye sharply on the tiny box, which was incidentally in the down direction. She was back against the wall with both hands again holding her in place. She looked up and down the trail again and saw no one. Inside she hoped her dad might come back and put a stop to what she was doing. He would know then how much she wanted to get her player back and would most likely find a way, without a long-winded sermon.

She separated one arm from the wall and stretched out towards the player, and again she was within inches. She held the pose for a moment then relaxed her shoulder muscles to try and gain the last little bit of reach her body could provide. The tips of her fingers touched it, and her excitement grew. It was within reach. All she had to do was get it between her index and middle fingers and pull it to safety. But that would require another half inch or so, and her thin body was already at its limit.

She froze for what seemed an eternity, but in actuality was only seconds, before loosening the grip she maintained on the wall. She decided to transfer her weight to the very last set of joints on her fingers, leaving less than an inch of flesh between her and the bottom of the gorge.

Winston Churchill and his wife reached the bridge just in time to witness the fall. Her delicate body bounced and turned and flipped down the steep edge of the gorge and slammed into the rocks below. Their screams echoed off the canyon walls and landed in Evan's ears with the ferocity of a roaring tiger.

CHAPTER SIX

The state police, as well as a number of local authorities such as the village police and the county sheriff's office, had people on the scene. A park groundskeeper called his wife, an employee of the local paper, which led to an equally large group of reporters buzzing around. In addition there were paramedics, firemen and park employees. The place was crawling with uniformed officers by the time Angela arrived.

Two plain-clothes officers, both with tears in their eyes, showed up at her office to tell her the news and transport her to the park. Under normal circumstances relatives are not brought to the scene of an accident, especially one resulting in the death of a loved one. But what occurred shortly after the fall left authorities with little choice.

Winston Churchill reported the fall via his cell phone to a 911 operator. With a shaky voice, and the beginnings of an asthma attack, he described what happened as best he could. His wife was hysterical, which only added to Winston's struggle to maintain his composure long enough to summon help. When he ended the call he fell to his knees and fought for breath until his trembling hands delivered a small plastic life-saving device to his lips.

As the call was being placed Evan was sliding down the wall of the gorge screaming, "Oh God! Oh God!" He jumped the wall, and on his way down the face of rock, scratched and clawed at anything and everything to control his descent. His hands and feet grasped hysterically at loose rocks and frail shrubs. Dried sticks and sharp stones pierced his clothing, ripped his body at random, and severed his flesh until he finally slammed into the bottom, breaking his left leg and shattering several bones in his foot. When he hit the rocky bottom his body folded like a rag doll that had been tossed from a bed.

Despite his battered condition, and unaware of his pain or damage he'd done to himself, he stumbled upriver to the peacefully still body of his precious little girl and scooped her into his arms, and, in the very loudest voice the canyon ever heard he screamed, "NO!"

When he reached her she was motionless, absolutely and completely. There was no movement of fingers or toes or legs or arms. No rising and falling of her chest. Nothing. She was still and quiet and gone from this world. She lay face down in a mix of pebbles, dirt and rocks and tiny scraps of leaves and flowers from above.

Evan rolled her over and spoke her name again and again as he pushed the bloody hair away from her face and caressed her sandy cheeks. He lifted her eyelids and spoke to her gentle blue eyes now, rolled back in her head, and he begged her not to go and demanded God not take her. Tears flowed from his eyes and fell to the ground, where they mixed with Emily's blood and were carried away by the flowing river.

Ten minutes later, a lifetime in the clockwork of a father holding his lifeless daughter, the first rescue team arrived. Two young paramedics and a middle-aged park ranger came upon a scene they'd never forget. Evan had Emily in his arms and was rocking back and forth, crying and speaking in strings of words that sounded not of this world. The paramedics tried to make him release his grip but he wouldn't let go. Tears and snot and spit ran down his face and an awful sound emanated from deep inside his chest.

The park ranger, large and quite strong despite being near sixty, pulled Evan's hands away from Emily. Her lifeless body fell from his arms, and, within seconds, the paramedics were systematically trying to create a miracle. They worked with quick determination for what seemed like forever. Once or twice her tiny frame leapt off the ground in response to shocks from a defibrillator, and her chest rose and fell in harmony with a ventilator. But they were mirages, facsimiles of life, which served only to give a moment of hope before the reality of death set in. She had no pulse, or blood pressure, and her pupils didn't respond to light. When the decision was made to stop trying, the park ranger released Evan so he could once again hold his little girl. Evan rushed to her, pulled her close and fell to the ground with Emily wrapped tightly in his arms. The ranger, big and strong and seasoned, turned away for fear of losing his composure, and the two young men who tried cheating the reaper hung their heads.

A crowd gathered on the ridge above and on the bridge spanning the gorge. Evan's song of sorrow was the only sound but for the cascading water of the falls. Everyone was motionless and all eyes were fixed solidly on Evan as he held his daughter and cried long, slow, deep, wails of pain. Twenty minutes passed before the first attempt was made at retrieving Emily's body from Evan's grip. Then another twenty minutes passed when a state police officer and a fireman joined the paramedics and park ranger. All five men stood awkwardly as Evan held the little girl's bruised, bloody body close to his and begged God to give her back.

The state cop and the ranger knelt next to Evan to console him and convince him to release his grip so she could be brought out, and after ten minutes, he relented and they managed to lift her onto a stretcher for transport. The ranger held Evan in his arms and hugged him and cried with him as the paramedics and fireman prepared to carry Emily out.

Then, as what was later described by the ranger as a completely unexpected turn of events, Evan looked at the covered body of his little girl and completely lost control. He cried her name and started towards her yelling, "Leave her alone, you're hurting her!" As he struggled to break free the ranger applied muscle and tightened his grip. Evan's anger grew and his adrenaline kicked into full gear. The state cop, seeing the ranger's struggle, went to join in, but it was too late. Evan, despite a broken leg and numerous other injuries, broke free, and, when he did he had possession of the ranger's 357-magnum and was waving it back and forth in a frantic attempt to get everyone away from Emily.

The state cop's natural reaction was to pull his own firearm, but when he went to reach for it the ranger grabbed his arm and stopped him. "Hold it!" he said strongly, squeezing the cop's wrist and pulling him along as he backed up into the river. The paramedics immediately stopped what they were doing and backed into the water as well, and the fireman just froze, too scared to move.

From the ledge above there was a series of shouts and demands for Evan to drop the gun and put his hands on his head, but they went entirely unheard by Evan, who was in a state of hysteria.

The ranger released the grip he had on the cop, threw his arms above his head and shouted, "Don't shoot! Hold your fire! Don't shoot!" to the crowd of officers above, who all had their firearms out and aimed at Evan's head. Then he lowered his voice and spoke to Evan, who was still waiving the gun back and forth. "Take it easy, buddy. We're on your side here. Just take it easy."

Evan's hands were wrapped tightly around the butt of the huge gun and his tense finger was on the trigger. The ranger knew his weapon didn't sport a hair trigger like most of the semi-automatic jobs that the younger guys carried, and that made him feel a little better, but he'd also been around long enough to know that crazed men were capable of anything, and Evan wasn't only crazed, he was grief stricken as well, which made a bad situation even worse.

The ranger assumed the lead role in what was taking place, and all other law enforcement at the scene, regardless of rank, followed his lead. He yelled for them to put their weapons away, and they did so without question. He knelt in the water and told the cop, the fireman and the paramedics to do the same.

"We're not here to hurt you, man. We're not going to jump you or shoot you, I promise. But you gotta stop waving that gun. You gotta stop that right now!" He spoke with a mix of authority and sympathy, the result of many years of dealing with people in varying situations.

Evan's oscillating arms slowed until he was holding the gun straight at the cop, who still had his hand on his holster.

"Take your hand off your gun!" the ranger told the cop, who ignored the request.

"Take your damn hand off that gun right now!" the big man said. The cop complied the second time, aware he may have more to worry about than Evan if he didn't.

"Now point that thing at me if you want to point it at somebody," he said to Evan.

Evan's arm swung in the direction of the ranger and ended up aiming at the water in front of him.

"All right, my friend, now what do you want us to do for you?" the ranger asked in a calmer tone.

"Leave! Get out of here!" Evan yelled, motioning with his head in the direction from where they had entered.

The ranger told the others to leave, and, for an instant, the cop thought about standing his ground. After all, he was a state police officer, and in the hierarchy of things, further up on the totem pole than a park ranger. But he knew the ranger meant business, and, with every other law enforcement officer following his lead, he figured he better not make waves, especially since the media was probably filming everything. So, within a minute or so, it was Evan and the ranger, and Emily, alone in the gorge.

"Leave. Please leave us alone," Evan said to the ranger as he looked solemnly at his baby lying covered on the stretcher.

"I can't do that. If I leave they're gonna come down here, and I don't want to see that happen," the ranger said, pointing upward to the smorgasbord of armed officers above.

"I promise you I won't move if you put that gun down. I know you just want to hold her. You have my word." The big man's sincere expression was convincing. Evan lowered the gun, slowly walked to the stretcher and fell to his knees. It was the perfect opportunity for the ranger to leap out of the water and subdue him, but he didn't. He just watched and thought about his own children, all grown with babies of their own, and he understood.

Evan dropped the gun on the ground next to him and the ranger breathed a sigh of relief. He was unarmed so his counterparts above had no reason at all to shoot, and he kept his word and didn't move.

Evan uncovered Emily and picked her up off the stretcher to hold her in his lap, and he cried. He kissed her forehead and her cheeks and straightened her hair, and never once looked up at the ranger, who had a tear in his eye and was saying a prayer for the man who minutes before had him at gunpoint.

Up above, some savvy police work along with the information from Jeremy allowed Angela to be located in short time. One of the state police officers burdened with the miserable job of delivering the news was a female resource officer, named Toni Schaefer, from the state's grief counseling division.

When she arrived at Angela's office she requested a private place where she and Angela could talk. In a conference room she held Angela's hand, and with as much consideration as she could muster, delivered the bad news. As expected Angela broke down, and when she did, Toni held her and cried with her.

The two women sat in the back of an unmarked cruiser as another officer transported them to Watkins Glenn State Park. Toni had met with grieving relatives many times during her nine years on the job, but never in the back of a cruiser on the way to an accident scene. She didn't know exactly how to prepare Angela, except to tell her what she knew about the accident and what Evan did afterward. So she did just that as they sped along Interstate 90, with a remarkable blend of compassion and honesty.

When they arrived at the gorge the parking lot was overflowing with vehicles, among which were two fire trucks, an ambulance, numerous police cruisers and a number of other automobiles belonging to local news media and curious onlookers. The car Angela rode in pulled past all of it to a side entrance where a tall thin man in uniform stood waving his arms. He was the assistant park director and the man who would guide the two women to the scene.

The car rolled to a stop in front of him where he opened the rear door and offered Angela help getting out. She took his hand and stood on wobbly legs, glancing around fearfully at all the flashing lights and uniformed people. Toni exited behind her, stood at her side and held her hand, as the assistant park director introduced himself and expressed his heart-felt condolences for her loss. He then motioned the women to an employee entrance in the opposite direction from the media circus.

They entered through a large steel door and followed a corridor to a wooden staircase that led down fifty feet to the river's edge. Once below, the park director established radio communications with the officer in charge, who in turn used a different frequency to notify the ranger Evan's wife was on her way there.

While Angela was on her way to the gorge the ranger spoke slowly and carefully to Evan in an attempt to keep him calm. He reassured him that nobody would try to take his little girl away, and that she was in peace and in no pain whatsoever, but the words could have been spoken in Greek and would have had the same effect. Evan wasn't hearing or seeing anything or anyone except what was in his arms, and if the ranger was so inclined, he could have rushed him and tackled him to the ground and put an end to the entire situation in a matter of seconds. But he had no intention of doing that, or anything else for that matter. He was a man of his word and was confident it would end on its own when Evan's wife arrived. He wanted to give Evan a chance to talk to her and grieve with her before being hauled away to jail.

Toni and Angela walked carefully along the edge of the river towards the scene. When they reached the final turn before coming upon Evan, Emily and the ranger, Toni took Angela's hands in hers and looked her in the eye.

"We're almost there, honey. This is going to be hard, but I'll be right here with you the whole time. Remember what I told you about the gun. Don't run up to him when you see him until the ranger has it back," she said softly, compassionately. What she didn't tell Angela was that on the ledge above was a sharp shooter with a bead on Evan's head. If Evan grabbed that gun and aimed it at someone he would be taken out. Toni freed one of Angela's hands and tightened her grip on the other, and together they stepped forward and rounded the corner.

Angela's eyes first met those of the ranger. He was still in the water in a crouched position, shaking from the cold. His eyes showed the definitive signs of sorrow, and when he saw her he gave a compassionate nod and sympathetic half-smile. The big man almost looked like a grizzly bear waiting for a run of salmon, patient and powerful.

The next thing she saw brought her to her knees. Evan was sitting on the side of the river with Emily in his lap. They were both covered with blood, a mixture of father's and daughter's, and mud. Evan was scraped and cut so badly she hardly recognized him as the same man who had left the house that morning, and Emily lay in his lap, her bloody, muddy hair draped over his legs. Evan was rocking slowly back and forth and humming what sounded like a lullaby of some sort, tears streaming steadily from his eyes. He didn't notice them standing there, he just rocked in concert with his humming and cried.

Toni lifted Angela with both arms and held her tightly until she could stand on her own. Once she was on her feet Angela yelled to Evan, but he was so far gone he didn't respond. At that point it became clear Evan was no longer a threat, so the ranger left the water and retrieved his gun. Toni let Angela go and she ran to her husband and daughter, fell to the ground next to them, and wept.

CHAPTER SEVEN

Thursday was Evan's day off and generally the slowest day of the seven, and, therefore, the day he felt most comfortable leaving Charlie in charge. Early on he didn't take days off. Not because he was too busy or too vital a part of the daily operations, but because his thoughts would torture him when his mind sat idle. The Thursday-off routine began when Art invited him fishing one week and had continued ever since.

Mary didn't like fishing, at least not catching them, but she didn't seem to mind cleaning the day's take, and deep-frying them in her secret coating that was little more than Shake-n-Bake. So she made Thursday her shopping day, which left Evan and Art on their own to sail the open seas.

At first they would take *The Secret* out in the Gulf to challenge their luck until Evan became comfortable enough maneuvering the waterways to trust himself with the owner's yacht, a beautiful Donzi named *The Shark Bite*. He had full permission to use the vessel, and was actually encouraged to do so to keep her from sitting for too long a period of time, but he hadn't grown up around water and never captained a boat before. Truth be told, he had only been on a boat twice in his life prior to coming to Florida. The first time was as a kid when his father took him deepwater fishing on a charter in Lake Ontario. The second was the *Maid of the Mist* at Niagara Falls with Angela shortly after their marriage. Before going to Florida, all of his fishing was done from the banks of rivers in central New York.

Art had taken Evan under his wing, so to speak, and taught him the majority of what he needed to know to safely captain the thirty-seven foot vessel, which was quite a bit more than Evan had imagined. He learned how to keep her in the channel until hitting deep water and how to put her up on a plane at cruising speeds. He became comfortable using the global positioning equipment to find his way from place to place, even without the benefit of being able to see land, and he learned to anchor her against a fast current and retrieve the anchor from a rocky reef. He also learned what to do if the boat broke down or started taking on water. Art was a good teacher and knew the ocean well. His lessons brought Evan to the point where he could take the boat out on his own without worry, which he did when the Sullivans were off on their adventures.

One such Thursday started with Evan at the controls of *The Shark Bite* under the watchful eye of his instructor. He handled the boat with the confidence of a man who'd been boating for years, and Art took notice and felt pride in having taught Evan well. Evan watched the channel markers and kept his wake to a minimum until they passed Frog Island, the point where most boaters opened the throttle. Just outside the inlet he punched their destination into the computer and opened her up. The engines came alive and exhaled a deep throaty sound as the boat rose from the water. A light salty mist sprayed across the bow and Evan licked his lips to get a taste of the ocean. The wind blew his hair back as the boat accelerated west-southwest towards a reef that Art had overheard some fisherman bragging about.

Evan made it a point not to drink very much on Wednesday nights so he could handle the day on the water without becoming seasick. He looked forward to Thursdays, especially when Art was there, but dreaded the long nights before. The dreams were relentless, and managed to ambush him every time the whiskey didn't saturate his brain. The last one was particularly bad, and had him on his feet at two a.m. in a cold sweat. He paced the bedroom for nearly an hour before swallowing two shots and lying back down. But the dream returned, like a bad re-run, each time he dozed off.

The sky held small bursts of cumulus clouds here and there but experience told Art to believe the forecast, a thirty-percent chance of rain with seas one to two feet and a high temperature of eighty-eight degrees. He expected the clouds to burn off by noon and yelled as much to Evan over the engines' melody. Then he sat on the starboard side of the craft in a high swivel chair and watched with admiration as his young friend handled the boat like a pro. Art had a comfortable way about him that made Evan feel at ease, and Evan certainly did as he watched the bow rise and fall slightly as it cut through the water.

"A dolphin!" Evan yelled, pointing aft port to a fin that ran alongside in an up and down motion.

"They like the company," Art said, smiling at the sight of the ocean's smartest creature.

"Man, they can move," Evan commented.

Art nodded in agreement. He'd seen more dolphins than he could remember, even hooked one or two by mistake, but they still managed to capture his imagination, and he enjoyed seeing the excitement in Evan's face at the sight of them.

The vessel was equipped with every imaginable toy of modern technology. It had radar, sonar, global satellite positioning, and a number of other electronic miracles. It could steer itself to any destination with the touch of a button, and Evan knew that, but he kept control of her and used the equipment merely for navigation. He liked the feel of having control of the boat, being able to cut the waves and raise or lower the speed. He stood in front of the captain's chair with one hand on the throttle and the other on the wheel. Bursts of spray would periodically hit his face and each time he would roll his bottom lip to taste the salt. He looked like a man born aboard a ship who would die there, too. His skin, white only months before, had assumed a rich golden color. His slightly graying hair, which used to be kept cut above his ears, had grown out and blew in the salty breeze. Behind the stainless steel wheel of *The Shark Bite* he looked like a seasoned sea captain, completely at peace with the ocean.

An hour later they were circling the reef and setting up to anchor above it. Evan watched the liquid crystal display, which gave a color-coded diagram of the ocean floor below. He turned the wheel and bumped the throttle until he was at the reef's leading edge, then hit a button that released the anchor. He pulled the throttle back to let the engines idle and waited for the boat to settle. The anchor bit in just as planned and she came to rest at the exact spot intended.

"Impressive," Art said with a grin.

"Had a good teacher," Evan replied before killing the engines. The boat settled quickly and within minutes Art had two lines in the water, one baited with a pinfish and the other with a squid. He lowered the lines until they hit bottom then reeled them in three or four feet, set the drags and secured them in the holders. A few minutes later Evan's lines were also down but baited with shrimp. A fishing book he read said there were two types of bait for catching Florida fish, shrimp and shrimp, and he intended to find out how true that was.

"Let's hope our luck's better than last week," Evan said as he sat back in a swiveled fishing chair and removed his shirt.

"Can't be any worse," Art replied. "If we don't bring something back this time Mary's gonna think we've been out chasing women instead of fishing."

"We'd probably catch even less if that were the case," Evan said, watching his poles.

Mere minutes passed before Art got the first hit, a strong strike that left him with nothing more than an empty hook. A second later Evan reeled in a grouper that was below the legal limit so he had to throw it back. Then Art lost a second one at about the same time Evan hooked a keeper, a good-sized Red that Art was sure was the fish that stole his bait. Their luck had indeed improved and within an hour their cooler held four healthy fish, three of which were caught on shrimp. The next hour brought a few more keepers, and by noon they'd caught enough for several meals.

Evan broke out two sandwiches that Sheila made that morning, along with a bag of chips and a few beers, and they ate while listening to a Jimmy Buffet disk that Art brought along. The water had become calm, almost like glass, and the sky had cleared just as expected. There was a slight breeze out of the east, so slight that it barely ruffled the vessel's flag. When they finished eating Art lit a cigar and offered one to Evan, who politely refused. He'd opted for a swim instead and was in the water within minutes of taking his last bite of food.

"Didn't your mother ever tell you you're supposed to wait a half hour after eating before going swimming?" Art yelled to Evan, who was unsuccessfully attempting to float on his back.

"She also told me not to talk to strangers, and I didn't pay attention to that, either," Evan replied before splashing Art with a handful of water. When Evan was back aboard they lowered their lines again, but the following hour brought little luck. Evan caught two catfish and Art lost his bait multiple times to what he thought was either crabs or grunts.

The hour after that brought even less activity, so much less even the thieving crabs stopped biting. And it was during that hour that Evan made the decision to tell Art what happened with Emily. They had pulled in their lines to take a break when, out of the blue, Evan asked a question that started the conversation rolling.

"Art, have you ever lost anybody close to you?" he asked.

Art didn't expect the question and yet managed to answer it as if he'd been waiting for it all day.

"As a matter of fact, I have. We have, Mary and I. We lost one of our children many years ago," Art replied with an answer that Evan hadn't expected. When the revelation sunk in he continued.

"We were devastated, completely torn to pieces. In this life you expect to see certain people pass away like grandparents, parents, even uncles and aunts. But when a child is taken it's different. It feels like the world stops and then starts spinning in the opposite direction. You can never be prepared for something like that. Never." Art's face was somber and his voice low.

"I'm sorry," Evan replied. He was unable to say anything else. He didn't expect Art to have lived through the grief that he had, and lived through was the point. Art was still alive in every sense of the word. His life was full and happy and his marriage intact, despite the fact that he suffered the same loss Evan had, a loss that stopped the clock in Evan's world a long time ago.

"How about you?" Art asked, giving Evan that open door he needed.

Evan fought to say the words because he knew once he began there would be no turning back. He wasn't sure he was prepared to talk about Emily's death and his separation from Angela. But somewhere inside him it screamed to get out, wanted to be told. His body tensed and his throat became instantly dry as he spoke.

"My daughter died ten months ago," he said, pausing as he looked past Art and tried to picture her face. "She was nine years old." His eyes filled with tears.

Over the next hour they talked and Evan told Art all about Emily and the accident in the gorge. He stopped at the part where they took her body away, and they both sat silent and looked out at the water. Then after a long silence Evan continued.

"They put me under arrest for the incident with the gun, and I spent that night in the hospital with an armed guard posted at my door. After they patched me up I was sent to the county jail, and, eventually, to Country Side, a maximum security nut house in East Syracuse, where they filled me with drugs and strapped me to a bed. I didn't talk to anyone for days, and when I finally got to see Angela all we did was cry and hold each other.

"I spent the next few weeks at Country Side being analyzed by head doctors. Angela came to visit every day, but without Jeremy. She said he wouldn't be able to understand my being locked up. It hurt me so bad to be away from her, and then not to be able to see my son. When I finally got out I had to appear before a judge who ordered me to continue counseling for another six months. The worst part was that I missed Emily's funeral. She died in my arms and I wasn't allowed to say my last goodbye. The doctors thought it would be too much for me to handle. I could have killed the bastards when I found out they buried my little girl without me there," Evan said. He dropped his head in reflection for a moment before continuing.

"After that, things became worse. I was reassigned at work to a department that the company deemed less crucial, which in the nuclear power world means a place where I can't do anything that will inadvertently kill a lot of people. Once a person is considered unstable, they're put off in a nice quiet cubicle someplace and forgotten about.

"Things weren't any better at home, either. Every night I dreamed about the gorge. It's the same dream I had last night and every night since the accident. In it I'm holding Emily's hand as she dangles over the edge. The harder I squeeze the more her little hand slips from mine. I would wake up screaming, which in turn would scare the crap out of Jeremy and cause him to wake up screaming. No one was getting any sleep, and Angela and I started arguing all the time. That's when I started drinking. I just needed something to help me sleep in peace, and to make the pain go away.

"When six months was over I stopped seeing the doctor. Hell, I could have stopped seeing him after the first visit as far as I was concerned. He was an arrogant bastard who wasn't doing me any good, just prescribing me a bunch of pills that knocked me out, which only served to keep me locked in the dreams for a longer time. I stopped taking them when I realized the liquor worked better. It was after that when Angela and I had our big fight, the one where she threw me out and told me not to come back.

"I had called in to work sick four days in a row. All I did was lay around the house with the curtains closed and sleep in fifteen-minute blocks, the dreams made sure of that. I was hardly eating anything and wasn't taking the damn pills any longer, and I hadn't had a shower in about a week. On the fourth day Angela came home from work and found me drunk. We started arguing again, and for the first time in our marriage, she hit me, smacked me right across the face." Evan stopped and took a swig of beer. Art sat, silently waiting. Two more gulps and the beer was gone. Evan continued.

"What I didn't tell you was that I never went to Emily's grave, I couldn't. I wanted to so badly, but I just couldn't. Angela went every day for the first month or two. She'd bring flowers, or one of Emily's favorite toys, and leave letters and stuff at the grave. She begged me to go, but I kept telling her I wasn't ready. I didn't know what else to do, but I knew I wouldn't be able to see my baby's name on a headstone." Evan stopped and looked directly at

Art. "That sounds pretty shitty, doesn't it?" he asked, a little afraid of the answer.

"I've been there, Evan, and it's not shitty. Everybody handles pain differently. We all have different defense mechanisms, and yours told you to stay away," Art said.

"But I wasn't there for Angela. She handled all of that alone. What type of man would let his wife go through all of that by herself?" Evan buried his face in his hands and rubbed his eyes. "I was so damn weak and she was so strong. She took care of Jeremy and managed to go back to work while I lay around like a bum. I feel like such a damn coward."

"What happened after she smacked you?" Art asked, trying to get Evan back to the story. He wanted him to keep going while he was in the talking mood.

"She put a bunch of my clothes in a plastic garbage bag and told me to leave. She said if I loved Emily I would visit her instead of lying around and wasting away. She told me not to come home until I got my head straight and stopped the drinking. I got in my car and left. I didn't know where to go, so I just drove. I hit the highway and headed south and drove all night and into the next day until I was in Florida. It's a miracle I didn't kill anybody considering the state I was in. I grabbed a hotel room for a few days and intended to go home once Angela cooled down, but the days turned into weeks, and, before I knew it, I was here a month. Needless to say I lost my job, and I ran out of money pretty quick so I took the job at the marina.

"At first, while I was living out of hotel rooms, I called Angela every day and we would talk for hours. She apologized for throwing me out and I said I understood, and then we both agreed that I should spend a week or so down here to get my head on straight. But something happened to me that I can't really explain. It was as if my life in New York was cryogenically frozen. You know, like those people who have some deadly disease and freeze themselves in the hope that a cure will be discovered in the future so they can come back and be healed. Well, for me, being in Florida was like waiting for the cure. That's the best way I can describe how I felt, or rather, how I feel.

"Well, a few weeks went by and Angela started pushing me to come home. I kept telling her I needed a little more time and then the weeks turned to months, or at least it seems like it happened that quickly. Shit, I don't know. One day led to the next and here I am, gone from home for three months. Our daughter died because I screwed up, and then I screwed up again and landed in jail and missed her funeral. To top it all off I abandoned Angela and Jeremy when they needed me the most."

A tear rolled from Evan's face and he didn't bother wiping it away. He just sat still and looked out at the water. Art sat next to him and said nothing for several minutes.

"Where is Emily now?" he asked.

The question startled Evan and he didn't know how to answer.

"What do you mean?" Evan asked, unsure what exactly Art meant.

"Where do you think she is right now, as we speak?"

There was a long pause as the question was considered.

"She's gone. She's gone forever," Evan said sadly.

Their eyes met and locked as Art spoke.

"She's not gone forever. She's still with you, whether you realize it or not. And you'll be with her again someday, only in a much better place than this earth."

Evan didn't reply. He'd heard the same thing from Angela and respected that belief, but his brain told him differently. His parents were religious, and when his father died, his mother used to take him to the grave and they would sit on the grass and talk to the stone. He always felt sorry for her, but he understood. People who can't deal with death find comfort in believing that their relatives are in heaven. And he didn't believe in heaven, or hell, other than to say earth could be either depending upon what cards fate dealt a person. And he was dealt a bad hand and that was that. No luck, no divine intervention, no rewards or punishments, just consequences and incidents.

Evan shook his head as if he understood. Knowing that Art had also lost a child, he didn't want to argue the point. If Art took solace in the belief that his child was in a better place, and that he would be with him again, that was just fine with Evan. And he appreciated the fact that his friend listened to him and said what he thought would help, but it didn't change his mind.

Each Thursday after that was a chance for Evan to open up and talk about what was on his mind. It became like a weekly therapy session, only with fishing poles and cold beers instead of notepads and tape recorders. And Art listened. He listened because he wanted to and because he cared. But most of all he listened because he truly believed it was what he was supposed to do.

Chapter Eight

It was still dark outside when Angela hit the snooze button on the clock radio next to her bed. The house was quiet with the exception of an ever-present hum that came from the fish tank pump in the family room. She felt through the darkness until her hand landed on Jeremy's soft head of hair. He was at the foot of the bed, lying perpendicular to Angela with his feet over hers. Bugsy, his favorite stuffed animal, was pulled close to him to keep him safe. She stroked him a few times before lying back down for an extra ten minutes of sleep.

After a cup of coffee and a shower she lifted Jeremy from the bed and carried him to the living room, where she placed him on the couch to catch fifteen minutes of his favorite show, Pappy Drewit. His tired little head fell back against the cushion as he struggled between dreamland and Pappyland, giving in to the television when the surprisingly agile elderly-looking guy in a green shirt and suspenders started dancing around with a giant pencil.

Angela poured apple juice into a spill-proof cup and retrieved a children's vitamin from the cupboard above the fridge. She brought them into the living room and sat with Jeremy for five minutes as the hard chalky cartoon character slowly dissolved in his mouth between sips of juice. She rubbed his head and kissed him several times before returning to the kitchen to make his breakfast.

He had started sleeping with Angela when Evan left. At first he would fall asleep in his room, under the safety of a blanket on the bottom bunk—or capsule of his spaceship, as he referred to his bed. Then he would wander into her room sometime in the middle of the night. But when his nightmares started, she allowed him to fall asleep with her so she'd be there to hold him when he woke up screaming and crying. She'd pull him close and tell him she loved him, and explain to him that God was there watching over him. But God was somewhat elusive to him after the death of his sister and the loss of his father. He didn't comprehend the complexities of heaven and hell and everything in between. The world was small, consisting of his house, neighborhood, school, and Wal-Mart. And in his world his friends had brothers and sisters and mommies and daddies. And God didn't take any of them to heaven like he took Emily.

When his breakfast was ready she led him by the hand to his spot at the table. His plastic place setting, with colorful pictures of sea animals, once belonged to his big sister. Shortly after her death he started using it, along with other items that were hers, like her bike helmet and her skates. Her things were special to him in a way his weren't. He never left them lying around and he wouldn't share them, not with anyone. Not even his best friend Tanner, who he practically grew up with, was allowed to touch Emily's things when he came over to play.

Jeremy sat down and picked at his cereal and toast, not really eating it, just moving it around enough to give the impression that he was. He dipped his spoon in the bowl and retrieved a spoonful of milk that he sipped, and he broke his toast into smaller pieces and nibbled on the crust. His eyes scanned the plastic sheet of whales and sharks and sea turtles and manatees. But his favorite, like Emily's, was the dolphin. It was airborne above a wave, with glistening drops of water covering it and trailing behind it. Emily named it Sparkles, and she used to say good morning to it before getting to the age where she felt silly doing so. But even then she would say it in her head, imagining she was there in the sea with him holding his dorsal fin and being pulled through the waves. When she was no longer there to greet Sparkles, Jeremy took over the job, telling the two-dimensional coloring that his sister still loved him.

Jeremy's tiny teeth crushed a small piece of Cap'n Crunch as his imagination had him in the ocean with Emily and Sparkles. They rode the waves and laughed and Emily held his hand, like she used to do in a parking lot, or a mall, or at home when they watched television together. They rode the blue dolphin, around and around, without a care in the world, together again.

As Jeremy played with his breakfast Angela made his lunch and put his books in his backpack. She quickly did her makeup and hair, and threw on the outfit she had laid out the night before. When she was ready she cleaned up the cereal and toast disaster, and got Jeremy dressed in his blue and white school uniform. She combed his hair and helped him brush his teeth. At fifteen minutes after eight they were in the car and on their way.

She pulled into the school drop-off line and waited for a convoy of minivans and SUVs to unload their troops. When it was her turn she leaned back, gave Jeremy a big kiss and told him to listen to the teacher and pay attention. She said she loved him and that God loved him too, and that she would see him tonight and they would have spaghetti, his favorite, for dinner. The little guy gave an honest smile before donning the oversized backpack and heading into class.

As she pulled away she turned left towards work. This year she would have made a right and headed to Caper Middle School to drop off Emily, and she thought about that each and every time she made the turn. Most mornings she could handle it just fine, knowing that her little girl was in a better place, a place without pain or suffering or fear or death. But that morning something overcame her, and one hundred feet down the road she hit the brakes and turned the car around.

She made the three-mile drive to Caper and pulled into the teachers' parking lot opposite the school bus unloading area. She got out of the car and stared across the street at the swarm of children exiting the buses. She noticed every girl and studied each one's features, comparing them to Emily's. Some had similar hair, while others had similar facial features or walks. She tried to imagine how her daughter would have changed in the eighteen months since she last saw her. How much taller would she have grown, what style hair would she have and how would she have dressed after making the transition from elementary school to middle school. Angela thought back to her first day in sixth grade. She remembered feeling so different, so much more grown up. It was a changing point in her life, like it is for most children. An experience Emily would never have.

She looked at them for fifteen minutes as they got off the buses or out of cars and greeted their friends and goofed around like kids their age do. They were so alive and happy and unafraid of the world around them, despite the fact that in an instant it could all change. But kids don't think about those things. Parents do. Parents live with the knowledge of just how fragile life really is, and how easily it can be taken away.

It would have been Emily's first year there, and she would have been friends with some of the girls Angela saw. They would have been calling the house and asking to speak with her, and she would have gone in her room and closed the door and talked about this cute boy or that hunk, or what clothes they were going to wear or what movies they went to see. They would have fantasized about being famous like Britney Spears, singing and dancing onstage as the whole world watched.

Then Emily would come out and talk to Angela about things she could never speak to her dad about, like the changes her body might have been going through or the things she learned in sex education, and Angela would have been there to help her navigate her way through adolescence. Their relationship would have changed from mother and child to mother and daughter, and they would have become more like true friends.

When she had seen enough she climbed back in the car and pulled away. She cried a little bit, and, for just a moment, cursed Evan for not being there for her when she needed him. She carefully patted her eyes with a tissue so as not to smear her makeup, and put him out of her mind. It was what she learned to do, months earlier, before heading into work. She had to stay focused on her job in order to provide for Jeremy, and she couldn't afford the luxury of driving far away from her life and forgetting about everything and everyone.

When she hit Highway 690 she turned on the radio and tuned into her favorite station. After a few commercials and a report on the accidents in the area, the disc jockey played a block of The Eagles, one of Angela's favorite groups. By the third song she had pulled herself together and was singing along with "Hotel California", and when she exited the highway and pulled onto Clinton Street, Emily was in heaven, Jeremy was in school, and Evan was a million miles away.

CHAPTER NINE

Angela left work at four-thirty and was at her older sister, Eve's, house before five to pick up Jeremy. It had been a particularly trying day at the office and Angela hoped she could get in and out without being subjected to one of Eve's condescending conversations about how she would handle Evan if he were her husband. Angela knew it would all depend on how stressed out Eve was from following around her two sons, Kyle, six, and Brent, eight, and cleaning up after her husband who was the slob of all slobs and unappreciative of her servitude.

She parked in the driveway behind a minivan full of bumper stickers advertising the children's latest achievements in school. Things like, "Proud Parent of an A Student," and "My Child is an Honor Roll Student," and such. Angela paid little attention as she crossed the perfectly manicured lawn to the front door and rang the bell.

Brent answered the door and yelled, "Aunty Angela's here," then ran off upstairs to where Kyle and Jeremy were running around and making loud house-shaking thuds by jumping off beds and landing on the hardwood floors. Angela walked past the formal living room into the kitchen where Eve was bent over an open oven basting two large chickens. She wore shorts and a tank top and had a sweatband around her forehead as if she'd just returned from a tennis match. She always dressed like she was training for Wimbledon, even though she had never swung a racquet in her life.

"Hey, Angie, how was work?" she asked without turning her head from the golden fowl in front of her.

"It was a rough day. I'm still writing reports and gathering information for the upcoming merger," she said talking to Eve's backside.

Eve shut the oven and brushed her hair back out of her face, with an exhausted expression like she had just finished running a marathon. "Grab a chair, I'll get you something to drink," she said before quickly snatching a glass from the cupboard and filling it with crushed ice from a dispenser on the refrigerator door. Before Angela hit the chair there was an iced tea complete with sliced lemon on the table in front of her and Eve was back to preparing dinner.

Eve did most things at an exhausting pace which few people would be able to keep up with. She cooked, and cleaned, and helped with homework, and folded laundry, and cut the grass, and made the meals in a controlled frenzy that fatigued those merely watching her. Her days were filled with one activity after another that kept her mind occupied and off of the elephant in the basement.

Her twelve-year marriage to a man that knocked her up and was forced to marry her by his mother to save the family any embarrassment was far less perfect than she made it appear. He did his fair amount of drinking when he was home, and even more when he was at a local pub with his buddies watching football and chasing women. And Angela knew there were fights, the kind that resulted in unexplained bruises to Eve's arms and legs and neck. She brought it up, once or twice, in an attempt to help her sister, but Eve just denied there was anything wrong and became defensive. So Angela never mentioned it again and stopped asking when she noticed the blackened spots on her sister's frail frame.

"Did you get the raise they promised you?" Eve asked as she pulled biscuits out of one of those tubular cardboard packages they sell in the refrigerated section of the grocery store.

"Yes, thank God. I was beginning to wonder if I would have to wait until the new company was formed, and you know how that goes. Those that don't get laid off are usually considered lucky just to have kept their jobs," Angela explained. (Actually Eve didn't know anything about business. She'd been a stay at home mom since she married, and before that she was a full time student at one college after another on her parents' dime.)

"Dad thinks you should quit and go somewhere else. He says with the experience you have now you could make more money. He thinks you're wasting your education with that company."

"I've only been there a few years and the money isn't bad, especially with the raise, and they were great to me when Emily passed away," Angela said.

"Yea, I guess," Eve said, stopping as if she were instantly frozen. Her brain experienced what Angela came to call a brain fart, when she was doing and thinking so many things at once that everything just shut down as she tried to remember what she meant to do or say next. She stood catatonic for a few seconds before starting up again and reaching in the pantry for croutons to sprinkle on the salad.

"Did Mom ask you about the picnic?" Eve asked, meaning the family reunion that took place every June at the family's property on the shores of Lake Huron in Port Albert, Ontario.

Their mother's side was Canadian with relatives from British Columbia to Nova Scotia and almost every province in between, and for the past thirty years or so they'd gotten together on the last Saturday in June to have a family picnic slash reunion. Most of them had cottages or trailers along the lake on fifty or so acres that had been in the family for hundreds of years. There was always a huge feast to which everyone brought a dish. Her grandmother always made a three-bean salad that everyone pretended to like, but that ended up scraped into the trash, and her aunt made tiny little meatballs that everyone loved and which never lasted to the end of the food line. Then there was Angela's father, who made a huge pot of baked beans that he once jokingly said came from an age-old family recipe. The family ranted and raved so much that he didn't have the heart to tell them the beans were actually out of a can with a shot of whiskey added to them.

For a family picnic it was a surprisingly large, well-run event. There were games for the children and the adults, such as the potato sack race, the egg toss, the wheelbarrow race, and the shoe kick contest, with awards given for first, second and third place. For the little ones there was a piñata and a pony ride, and for the men there was the rock toss, the grandest of all the games. The rock was dug up on the very first reunion by Angela's Great Uncle Henry, who had since died. It weighed about five pounds and it was thrown for distance with varying styles and the winner got his name carved on an old maple tree on the property next to the names of all previous winners. Evan's appeared twice, and was the only American name on the Canadian maple.

Angela thought for a moment before answering Eve's question.

"Yea, Mom asked if I was planning on going. I told her I hadn't even thought about it yet. Heck, it's over six months from now, why is she asking already?" Angela replied.

"Because it's a big deal to her, and she doesn't want you to miss three years in a row," Eve said.

"I don't know. I've got too much going on to even care right now."

"The family really wants to see you and Jeremy. He probably doesn't even remember the last picnic. What was he, two years old at the time?" Eve said as she wiped off a counter top.

"Three," Angela replied.

"Alright, three. But still I bet he doesn't even remember seeing Aunt Flo or Uncle Freddy, or all his cousins."

"They're second and third cousins, Eve, and they live eight hundred miles away. It's not like he'd grow up with them and become friends or anything like that," Angela replied sounding a bit snippy. She was tired and wanted to get home. But Eve was nice enough to pick Jeremy up every day after school, which made Angela feel obliged to sit and talk with her for fifteen minutes, which some days felt like several hours.

"Well, I know that. But still they'd like to see you guys," Eve said.

"I'll think about it," Angela said as she squeezed the lemon into the glass. But her mind was already made up.

Eve excused herself and ran to the basement to transfer some clothes from the washer to the dryer. Angela sat alone at the table and listened to the voices and laughter coming from the floor above. She tried to distinguish between Jeremy's voice and those of his cousins, but they were all blended together like the sounds from a playground, a homogenized mixture of cheers and grunts and screams.

She was happy her son had his cousins close by so he could see them and play with them, even if it meant she had to listen to Eve fifteen minutes a day. Which really wouldn't be so bad if she wasn't so tired after a day's work. But Eve's willingness to pick Jeremy up every day after school was saving Angela a decent amount of money that she would otherwise be paying for childcare, and Angela appreciated it, even if she didn't always say so.

"Did you hear about Kimberly's latest squeeze?" Eve asked as she popped back into the kitchen and immediately took to setting the table.

"No, I haven't," Angela replied. She really didn't want to hear about another full-of-shit, conceited jerk her younger sister was sleeping with. It was always the same thing. She meets the perfect guy, gorgeous, rich and intelligent, and he always ends up being a loser of one sort or another. Like the one she made the mistake of marrying, twice. She didn't learn her lesson the first time around when he was arrested for picking up a prostitute. She had to marry him a second time when he somehow managed to convince her he was reformed. What he really meant was that he got so good at chasing women that he no longer had to pay to get laid.

"He's the vice president of…" Eve continued. But Angela just blocked it out. She didn't want to hear about Kimberly's prince, or Eve's asshole husband, or any man for that matter. She was tired and frustrated, and she had her own problems to deal with. She hadn't talked to Evan in well over a month, and as much as she thought he was different than most, she was growing ever more afraid that the marriage was over for good. But what scared her more than anything was how much she still loved him.

Eve finished setting the table and extended an invitation to dinner. But Angela wanted to get home and soak in a hot bath, and she hoped to be on her way before Wade came through the door sporting his smug smile and arrogant attitude. Just the sight of his face made her sick to her stomach, and she felt truly sorry for her sister having to live with him, clean up after him, and, worst of all, sleep with him.

"I better get going. I've got a busy day tomorrow and I have to give Jeremy a bath and help him with his homework. But maybe we'll stay Friday," Angela said.

Friday was the day Wade went out with his buddies after work, and usually he didn't make it home until Saturday afternoon. Eve would always say he was smart for not driving after drinking, and that he had such good friends to allow him to stay overnight. It was her way of ignoring the obvious signs, like phone numbers in his pants pockets, and empty condom wrappers in his car.

Angela gathered up Jeremy's things and retrieved him from underneath a beanbag that his older cousin was sitting on. He was sweaty and tired, but he was smiling and that made her happy. He'd been through a lot for a kid his age, and Angela was truly grateful for the close relationship he had with his cousins. They were good boys and she hoped they learned their morals from Eve and not their pig father, and she prayed for them every night as she prayed for Jeremy, and Evan and Emily.

Before they left Angela asked about Crystal, Eve's eleven-year-old daughter, who she hadn't seen around the house. Eve explained she was at swim practice at the Y, and that with any luck she would win her next meet and go on to compete in the city finals. Angela said to tell her she was asking about her, and then kissed her sister, who even at rest had the appearance of movement. Then she got out the door quickly, before being asked about Evan.

When they got home Angela bathed Jeremy. Then she made dinner while helping him write five homework sentences about his favorite activities. When they were finished eating she sat him down in front of the television for a while, then escaped to the bathroom where she filled the tub with hot water and bath oils. She undressed and stood in front of a mirror and inspected her body. She wasn't at all overweight but had a slight tummy that she vowed to get rid of by using her treadmill.

When the self-examination was complete she walked a few steps to a wicker shelf that held a radio. She hit a button or two and brought the box to life with the sounds of Mozart. She liked rock-and-roll while driving and country while working in the house or garden, but classical she reserved for relaxing in the tub, or making love to Evan, or occasionally while she cooking a fancy meal. It held a certain magic that could take her to places far away. Places she used to dream of one day going.

The music transformed the semi-outdated bathroom to an old world one found in a French chalet. When her mind was there the rest of her followed and she slowly eased herself into the centuries-old cast iron tub. The heat radiated throughout her body and loosened her muscles and joints, and her limbs turned to rubber. She closed her eyes and looked out a large picture window into a garden full of flowers. Then she slid under the surface, and the real world, with all its problems and opportunities and questions and answers, melted away.

CHAPTER TEN

The famous five, as Evan's mom called them in their high school days, was comprised of Evan and four of his buddies. Collectively they were quite a wild group of kids, at least by the standards of the day. They all owned motorcycles and were on the high school football team, and they all had one or two trips to the principal's office each year for pulling stunts that were oftentimes meant to impress the girls. Yet academically, they were excellent students who maintained good grades, and that, along with the pull their coach had, saved them from suspension on more than one occasion.

When they graduated they went their separate ways. One of them went on to play ball for Texas State, two went to college without scholarships, one went to work in the family business, and the last, Evan, went into the United States Navy's Nuclear Power program. He spent six years serving Uncle Sam, and much of that time was spent under the surface of the ocean in a state-of-the-art submarine. It was during the last year of his enlistment, when he was home on leave, that he met Angela.

Chuck, the one who went into the family business, had a serious girlfriend when Evan came to town, and his girlfriend had a friend who had heard all about Evan and wanted to meet him. So Chuck made arrangements for them all to go to a local club, which was more of a meat market than anything else, where they could dance and drink and raise a little hell like in the high school days.

The girl Evan was set up with was a complete knockout. She had long brown hair and hazel eyes, and breasts so large it was impossible for a man, married or otherwise, not to notice. Yet inside her head was little more than a person could gain from years of watching soap operas and talk shows, but

Evan didn't care about her intellect. He was home on leave and had been under the ocean for eighty-six straight days with a bunch of sailors, no women and no beer, so he wouldn't have cared if she didn't speak English and had warts on her nose. He was happy just to be around a woman again.

As the night progressed they danced and drank and danced and drank, and, before Evan knew what was happening, he was on the dance floor with one hand up his date's shirt and the other on her ass, and she didn't seem to have any problem with that at all. As a matter of fact she was doing just fine with her own hands, squeezing them down his pants and pulling him as close as she could get him. By the time they left the club there was little doubt that Evan would be returning to the submarine with one hell of a story to tell.

The club was in downtown Syracuse, about a block from Clinton Square, where Angela was working the night shift as a data entry clerk for a company that handled the ATM transactions for most of the larger banks in the northeast. She worked the eight P.M. to two A.M. shift, which allowed her to take daytime classes at Syracuse University and still make her bills. Plus, by working diligently and steadily, she would complete everything she was assigned by eleven o'clock and use the rest of the time for homework and study.

At quitting time she packed all of her books into a backpack and left the building, making sure to lock the door behind her. She hurried across a dimly lit courtyard towards the parking garage where her car was parked. Crossing the empty courtyard at such a late hour always made her nervous, despite the can of pepper spray she held firmly in the palm of her hand. She always sort of jogged or power walked, until she was in sight of the parking attendant who she knew by name and waved to every night.

The courtyard ended at the sidewalk where Evan's group happened to be walking towards a vacant lot where their transportation awaited. With perfect, or imperfect timing, depending upon how you look at it, Angela emerged from behind a block wall and slammed directly into Evan's date, knocking her to the ground. Evan made an attempt to catch her but failed, and instead caught Angela who was on her way to the ground with fifty pounds of books strapped to her back.

Angela, startled and afraid, pulled the trigger on the can of pepper spray and released a stream of burning liquid that hit Evan directly between the eyes, causing him to relax his grip on her and fall to the ground next to the big-breasted empty-headed girl. Blinded and in extreme pain, Evan rolled around and screamed and Angela took off for the safety of the parking garage, where she jumped inside the booth with her attendant friend and watched the action across the street.

It didn't take Angela long to realize she hadn't been assaulted and she had squirted an innocent person. She went back over and offered her assistance, which was met with bitterness by everyone except Evan, whose eyes were still on fire and swollen shut. Evan's date, the maddest of all for having been knocked to the ground, began spewing out a series of expletives more crude than most Evan ever heard, and he was a sailor. Angela paid little attention as she tried to rinse out Evan's eyes using a bottle of water she had in her backpack.

After about fifteen minutes Evan was able to open his eyes, and, when he did, his first sight was the girl he was going to marry. Angela was kneeling in front of him, wiping his eyes with a wet napkin, and apologizing profusely. He reached out and took her hand in his, and, in front of his date, asked her to have dinner with him the next day. As you can imagine, all hell broke loose.

Evan's date lit into him, calling him a no-good this and that and saying he didn't know what he just missed out on. She took off towards the parking lot, followed by her friend. Evan's buddy went after the girls, leaving Evan and Angela alone on the sidewalk. Angela, still in shock from the entire incident including a proposition from the guy she nearly killed, just stood there quietly until Evan asked her again. Even after hearing him twice she couldn't believe what was happening. She just knocked down this guy's girlfriend, or fiancée for all she knew, and sprayed him in the eyes with pepper spray, and the first thing he says to her is that he wants to take her to dinner. Wow.

"I can't go to dinner with you!" she said to Evan, whose eyes were still watering and hardly open.

"Why can't you? Are you married?" he asked, struggling to see her ring finger.

"No, I'm not married! But you have a girlfriend! Or at least you had one until you asked me out, or until I knocked her down," Angela said, gesturing in the direction of where his friends ran off.

"She's not my girlfriend. This was our first date, and, to be honest, it really wasn't much of a date at all. We just went dancing," Evan said, smiling.

"Well, I still can't go out with you. I don't even know you," she said as she poured some more water on the napkin and wiped his eyes again.

"I'm Evan Hayden," he said, offering his hand.

Angela stopped and looked at his smile and his bloodshot swollen eyes and then put her hand in his and introduced herself as Angela Cook.

"Well, now you know me. So how about dinner tomorrow?" he asked again.

The next day they met in front of the parking garage two hours before Angela was due at work. She purposely planned it that way so that no matter what happened the date was assured to last no more than two hours. That way, she figured, if he was a total bore, or some kind of maniac, she would just eat and run and never see him again. That thought vanished the instant she pulled up and saw him standing there in his Navy dress blues. The sight of him took her breath away. He was tall and muscularly slender, and had the most hypnotizing blue eyes she'd ever seen.

He was the same guy she'd sprayed in the face the night before, and at the same time he wasn't. Maybe it was the uniform, or maybe it was the fact that his eyes were no longer red and swollen, or maybe it was the lighting. Whatever it was, Angela fell hard, much harder than the bimbo she'd knocked to the ground the day before. Her stomach filled with butterflies and her heart raced, and when he smiled at her she became weak in the legs. It was the same feeling Evan had the night before when he opened his eyes and saw her for the first time.

Having grown up in Syracuse, Evan knew many people, and one of them was the owner of a small café only a few blocks from where Angela worked. The guy who owned it was a close friend of Evan's father, and a pallbearer at his funeral. Evan called him that morning and requested a special table, THE TABLE, for his date. Located on a private balcony overlooking a garden, it was reserved for special guests like the city's mayor or a close friend or relative, and it was set up with romance in mind.

At the cafe they were greeted by a jolly, gray-haired man who shook Evan's hand and made several comments about how much he looked like his father. He welcomed Angela in an old-fashioned way by kissing her on the back of the hand, which made her blush and made Evan smile. Then he led them to a spiral staircase that took them to the second-floor balcony where their secluded table waited. On it was a beautiful flower arrangement and two white candles, already lit.

The balcony's wall was covered with ivy and its floor terracotta tile, and it overlooked a garden full of so many colors a child would have to use the large box of Crayola crayons to even have a chance at coloring it. The fragrant aroma from below drifted upwards and filled the air with sweetness, and a fountain in the middle of the garden spewed water that created the sound of a waterfall.

Evan pulled out a chair for Angela and sat across from her at the intimate table so delicately set. In all the years he'd known the owner he'd never before asked for the special table because, quite frankly, he'd never had a need. There were other girls, and some that were quite serious, but none were as captivating and beautiful as Angela. Yet it was more than superficial beauty that sparked the flame inside of him. It was what he'd seen in her eyes when he'd opened his the night before. He saw kindness and tenderness, truthfulness and fate. It was like being hit by a bolt of lightning and living to tell about it.

The owner had a special treatment for his guests who occupied the balcony table. There was no menu or specials or descriptions of the cuisine. He conducted a short interview regarding the patron's likes and dislikes and prepared a dish he thought they would enjoy, and, in the twenty-plus years since opening the café, he'd never had a single complaint. There were, in fact, many couples who returned year after year to celebrate their anniversaries on the balcony.

Angela was overwhelmed, because she too had grown up in Syracuse and knew about the table, but she'd never known anyone who had the pleasure of dining at it, and she never expected to be on the balcony, overlooking the garden, listening to the gentle flow of water from the four-tier stone fountain, with a man who she had nearly blinded. Now, despite her efforts not to show her excitement, her face glowed with the thrill of the moment.

They sat across from one another and talked about their lives and what part of town they grew up in and what they hoped the future would hold. Angela's dreams were of family, friends and traditional holidays spent at home, while Evan's were of travel, adventure and discovering the world's mysteries. They couldn't have been more different when they sat down at the table, but by the time dinner ended, Evan saw himself sitting by a warm fire on Christmas Eve with Angela in his arms, and Angela pictured herself climbing Mount Everest alongside Evan. Their conversation flowed smoothly, without uncomfortable pauses or nervous stutters, and their smiles were genuine.

The food was served in classic fashion. First a rose was presented to the lady, and then wine was poured that Angela was at first hesitant to drink, but then decided, what the hell? How often is a girl treated to such a romantic dinner? And she was already thinking of calling in sick. Actually, the thought hit her the second she pulled up to park and saw him standing there.

The meal came in five courses, starting with a fresh garden salad and ending with the main course, a deliciously prepared baked salmon. Dessert was a big piece of the café's signature cuisine: chocolate mouse cake, so delicate it dissolved on contact with one's tongue. Sometime between the salad and the chocolate cake Angela excused herself, went to the phone and called work. She gave a brilliant performance of a woman with a headache and stomachache, and managed to free herself up for the entire night, which she hoped would be the first of many spent in Evan's company.

When dinner was over they walked around the city and periodically popped into a pub to have a drink and listen to some music, talk and dance. It was after the second stop, when Evan had consumed a few bottles of courage, that he reached out and took her hand. In the previous five years he'd been through boot camp, learned the ins and outs of nuclear power, and gone miles under the surface of the ocean in a submarine, but he had never been as nervous as when he made the decision to touch her. Their fingers locked and she squeezed with approval; his heart skipped a beat.

When the bars closed and the city began to empty, they made the walk back to the parking garage. The date that started almost eight hours before, seemed to last only ten minutes. He didn't want to let her go, and she didn't want to say goodbye. They had just met, and he respected her too much to even consider asking for more. She wanted a lifetime commitment and had no intention of ruining her chance by giving in to her desires. They exchanged numbers and said goodbye, but not before he leaned forward and kissed her.

Once in her car she pulled away slowly and waved, and he waved back. She threw on a blinker and turned a corner and left Evan in the road alone. He stood there and reflected on the past eight hours and hoped he had said nothing that would keep her away. When he had convinced himself there was no chance she would ever consider marrying him over all the men she could have, he walked to his car, started it up, and drove away.

CHAPTER ELEVEN

Derek found a renewed interest in his job, spawned partly by guilt at being bailed out of jail by his boss and partly by a desire, if only temporary, to pull his life together. He'd gone through similar spells of revelation before, but always took on more change than he could sustain, and would eventually crash hard before returning to the same old Derek. This latest reform kept him sober for several days and even brought him to work early to open the shop. He even designed a new layout for the place that he explained would speed the time it took customers to locate things, and make reordering and stocking more efficient. Evan didn't necessarily agree but chose to give the kid some autonomy to help the cause.

They were moving a large bait freezer from one side of the shop to another when the phone rang. Derek grabbed a grimy looking cordless from his back pocket and took the call. It was the same woman who had called for Evan before, and he informed her, in a rather anxious voice, that Evan was available to take the call if she wouldn't mind holding. His bulging curiosity to learn the connection between them eclipsed the part of him that said to lie and take a message; the agonizingly surprised expression on Evan's face served to heighten that curiosity. Derek held the phone at arm's length toward Evan, who said nothing, took it, and headed to the back office.

The room was dark; the result of a blinking fluorescent tube that was ignored too long and finally blew out. Evan closed the door and navigated clumsily to a wooden swivel chair located behind an ancient metal desk. He sat, and, for a very long moment, simply held the phone to his ear without saying a word. He heard faint breaths and running water and the clang of dishes in a sink. He heard Jeremy ask his mother for another glass of apple juice, and Angela's promise to get it as soon as her call ended. He pictured her standing in front of the kitchen sink, still in her robe, with her hair pulled back in a ponytail and staring out the window into the backyard where they used to barbecue and plant flowers and play with the kids. He pictured Jeremy, innocent and genuine, sitting in the family room, wrapped in his blanky, watching cartoons. Emily was there sitting next to him sharing a bowl of Froot Loops and laughing at *The Rug Rats* or *Sponge Bob* or *Hey Arnold*, and he was sitting at the kitchen table reading the newspaper and sipping a cup of Angela's coffee. It could have been any day at any time before the accident.

"Hello," he said, escaping the beauty of what was for the uncertainty of what will be.

"Evan, it's Angela," she said, her speech slow and weary and somewhat foreign to him after many weeks without hearing it. He sensed her despair and immediately felt ashamed for not returning her first call, but he knew damn well that he wouldn't have returned the second one either had Derek taken another message.

"I called twice before, didn't anybody tell you?" she asked.

"No, nobody told me. Is everything alright?" He felt stupid the instant the words left his mouth. Of course everything wasn't all right. He was twelve hundred miles away from his wife and son who he hadn't seen in a year, and she wasn't calling just to shoot the bull. She was calling to ask for a divorce and he knew it.

"Evan, it's Jeremy," she said as she started to cry.

The kitchen overlooked the family room where Jeremy sat on the carpet playing with building blocks. Angela turned away to hide her tears then headed upstairs to the bedroom with the cordless phone, where she closed the door behind her. She had become very protective of Jeremy since losing Emily, and didn't want him to know she was upset. Once out of earshot of her son she continued.

"Mrs. Miller, the school principal, called. She asked me to come in for a meeting, and…" She paused to hold back tears. "They think something's wrong with him, Evan. They want me to take him to a doctor." She started to cry again.

"A doctor? What the hell for, Angela? What do they think is wrong with him?" Evan asked, his voice loud enough to be heard outside the office door where Derek was listening.

Angela went on to explain that Jeremy had, in the last few months, been having nightmares, accompanied by bed wetting and at times even vomiting.

The dreams started shortly after Evan left a year earlier and were on and off since then. But a few months back they had become more frequent. Now they were happening every night. The bedwetting went along with the dreams and then he started losing control of his bladder in school. Other children began teasing him and eventually he withdrew and wouldn't speak to anybody except Angela. In the past six weeks he hadn't wanted to eat and he'd lost ten pounds. The principal called Angela and suggested a doctor, a psychiatrist that specialized in the treatment of children.

"I don't know what to do, Evan. He misses you, but what worries me is that he stopped asking when you're coming home. He even asked me one night if you went to heaven to be with Emily. I don't know what to say anymore. You haven't spoken to him in over a month. A month, Evan. For a kid his age a month is a very long time. What am I supposed to tell him, that you're confused and need some time to work things out? I can't lie to him anymore." She started to cry again. Evan held the phone, frozen. Tears rolled down his face, dripped off his chin and landed on the cold steel desk below.

"I can't take this anymore. It's been a year. A whole damn year and you're still gone. Can't you see what this has done to us? What it's done to him? People used to ask where you were and when you were coming home. Now they don't even ask about you anymore. Your own mother doesn't even mention your name when she stops by. The neighbors look at us like we have some weird disease or something. You just left without a word to anybody. Not a word!" Her crying was replaced by anger and her voice was louder and stronger.

"Angela, you told me to leave. You threw me out. Don't you remember?" Evan said meekly.

"For Christ's sake, Evan, I didn't mean for you to leave us like this. I just wanted you to pull yourself together. Emily's death hurt all of us, Evan, not just you. But we still have a son to raise, and now," she paused, "now we're losing him." She started crying again.

"I'm sorry, Angie," Evan said, crying.

There was a long silence.

"Evan, I have to know if you're coming home, and I have to know today. I can't live like this anymore. It's not fair to me and Jeremy, and it's not fair to the other people that love you, either. You have to tell me, Evan, are you coming back or not?" She had pulled herself together and said the words she had prayed to have the strength to say.

"I always planned to come home, Angela. I just can't tell you that it will be tomorrow or next week. I need a little more time and then I promise, when I get things…"

She cut him off. "No! No more time. I can't do that to him any longer. He loves you and he needs you here. I need you here. It sounds like you've made a life for yourself down there and we're just a part of your past."

"Angie, I…"

"No, Evan! No more. No more phone calls or letters. If you want to forget us then we'll forget you, too. I've already lost a daughter and a husband and I'll be damned if I'm losing a son. As far as I'm concerned, you're dead, Evan. Dead." She slammed down the phone and fell to the bed sobbing.

Evan's eyes, now adjusted to the darkness, focused on the puddle of tears below him on the desk. He looked at the phone, and after a moment's thought, put his finger on the first number and pushed. One by one he punched the numbers and listened to the tones. After seven numbers he stopped. Angela was four digits away, and all he had to do was tell her she was right and he was coming home, but he couldn't do it. She'd hit it right on the head. He didn't realize it until that very moment, but he *was* dead. He had died eighteen months before when Emily lost her footing and tumbled into the canyon. Only he kept breathing and eating and sleeping, and feeling the pain.

The final tear was enough to make the puddle run off the desk onto the floor below. He sat in the dark for nearly an hour before emerging into the noon rush. Derek and Candy were filling bait buckets and giving fishing tips when Evan left the office and quietly slipped out the front door. The bright sun hit his eyes and immediately shrunk his pupils. He squinted to see *The Secret*. The glare that shone from her white shell made her almost transparent, almost heavenly. He thought about his friends and what they would think if he vanished one day and never returned. He wondered if they'd miss him or even remember him after a year, or if they'd write him off for dead like Angela had.

CHAPTER TWELVE

The psychiatrist chosen by Angela for Jeremy was Dr. Sandborn, a woman very close to her own age who specialized in the treatment of children. When she met Jeremy she smiled widely and reached out to shake his hand. She was tall, slender and very pretty, which made it a little easier, even for a boy of seven, to smile back. She knelt down in front of him and spoke in a voice that was soft and smooth and exactly as one would expect, considering her appearance.

"Good morning, Jeremy, my name is Amanda. You can call me Miss Mandy if you'd like, or just Mandy. Would you and your mom like to come in and see the playroom?"

Jeremy looked back at Angela who was smiling and nodding her head yes.

"O.K.," he said, reaching out for his mother's hand.

Amanda led them to a very spacious and colorful room filled with toys, and he immediately started playing, unaware of where he was or why he was there.

"We can talk over here," the doctor said to Angela, pointing to a small alcove furnished with chairs and beanbags.

"You have a very nice-looking son, Mrs. Hayden," the doctor said, smiling.

"Thank you. He takes after his father," she said, feeling a bit anxious about her surroundings.

The two women sat across from each other in plush comfortable chairs.

"Can I offer you something to drink? We have soft drinks, or coffee or…"

"No, thank you," Angela said, sitting, stiff and rigid, like she was waiting to have a tooth drilled without Novocain.

The doctor opened a file she carried in with her and read for a moment, leaving it open on her lap.

"It says here that Jeremy's school recommended counseling. What type of problem is he having?"

Angela paused for a moment, unsure of just how to answer the question. Was he there because of the peeing in his pants, or the nightmares, or Emily's accident? Or is it possibly because his father left a year before and virtually severed all connections with her and Jeremy? She wasn't sure what to say, afraid that whatever she offered would give the wrong impression.

Angela was reluctant, and somewhat ashamed, to tell a stranger her son was peeing his pants and having such terrible nightmares that he could hardly sleep. She knew where it would lead, and she was tired and lonely and didn't feel like laying her life out on the table. But she was there for Jeremy, and that overruled everything else.

"His older sister died eighteen months ago," Angela said. It sounded so sterile the way it came out, like she was talking about Jeremy's pet goldfish. But the situation felt so terribly awkward and intimidating that she couldn't help how she sounded.

"Emily, her name was Emily. She was nine years old and they were very close," she said and turned to look at Jeremy who was curiously peeking inside a toy chest.

"She died in an accident at a park. He was there when it happened," Angela said.

"I'm so sorry," Dr. Sandborn said, reaching out and giving Angela's hand a squeeze. Angela looked at her and started to cry, then stopped herself, afraid Jeremy would see.

"How old was he when the accident happened?"

"He was only five," Angela replied.

"Has he talked to anyone about it? I mean besides you and your husband."

"A little bit with his grandmother. But we're... I'm always afraid it will upset him more to talk about what he saw. We always mention Emily in our prayers before bedtime, and he talks to her sometimes after that, when he's falling asleep. But I don't push him. Is that wrong? I mean, not to talk about the accident?"

"No, not at all. You've all been through a very traumatic event. People handle things in many different ways, and you're doing the things you feel are best for him." The doctor paused and smiled. "And bringing him here was a very good step. In many cases a child wants to talk, but just doesn't know what to say. They get easily confused, especially when it comes to the loss of a loved one, such as a parent or sibling, and that confusion can lead to feelings of fear of losing someone else they love." The doctor spoke with authority and compassion.

Angela felt a little more at ease and her muscles relaxed as she moved back in the chair. The doctor said what she needed to hear, that she had done the right thing. She needed to know she hadn't lost it like Evan. That despite what happened to Emily she could still hold things together for Jeremy's sake. There were times when she felt guilty for not completely falling apart. It made her feel as if continuing on with life meant she didn't love Emily as much as she should have. But she did love her, and she loved Jeremy and Evan, too, and it's that love that kept her going.

"Has anyone in the family had counseling since the accident?" the doctor asked once Angela regained her composure.

"No. Well, my husband did," she said, leaving out the part that he was ordered to by a judge.

"Is he still in counseling?"

The answer to the doctor's question would lead into what Angela wanted to avoid. But she knew it was inevitable, so she took a deep breath and told the story of what had occurred at the gorge.

"… and my husband, Evan, was with Jeremy when our daughter fell. We still aren't sure how it happened. But the police said she was probably climbing on the wall or walking along and lost her balance." Angela stopped briefly to wipe her eyes with a tissue. "Evan jumped over the wall when he saw her. He got hurt pretty bad when he landed. But then when he got to Emily and found that she was…" Angela stopped.

"You don't have to say it, Mrs. Hayden," the doctor said, again reaching out and squeezing Angela's hand.

"Well he just sat down there with her and wouldn't let her go. When the police showed up and tried to take her away he went crazy. He grabbed a police officer's gun and wouldn't let anyone near her. I don't know how much of it Jeremy saw. We never asked him about it."

"Where was he when all that was taking place?"

"A man and woman who were there picked him up and held him until I showed up. They said he was crying and screaming for Evan and Emily."

"You went there?" she asked, surprised.

"The police found me at work and told me what happened. They drove me there so that I could talk to Evan and convince him to put the gun down. But when I arrived he wasn't even holding it. He was sitting in the mud with Emily in his lap, just rocking back and forth and crying," Angela said, stopping when the doctor turned away to look at Jeremy who was playing with a plastic dump truck and some small cars. He was sitting on the ground, pushing them along the floor, paying no attention to the women who were fifteen feet away. When she turned back towards Angela she had a tear in her eye that she wiped with a tissue as it ran down her face. Then she leaned forward and gave Angela a hug and whispered, "I'm so sorry for your loss."

Angela cried for a while as the doctor held her hand and comforted her. Jeremy was lost in a world of cops and robbers, or something that required him to push little plastic cars at high speeds across the carpet, and therefore took little notice. He glanced over at his mother and the doctor once, but didn't seem to comprehend what was taking place. After a few minutes Angela regained her composure and the conversation continued.

"Have you talked to anybody since the accident?" Dr. Sandborn asked.

"I talked to the priest at my parish, and to a few close friends, and my family, of course, but not a doctor, not a psychiatrist."

"I'd like to recommend someone for you. He's a wonderful doctor. I've known him for several years and have sent many adults to him."

Doctor Sandborn pulled a pen from her pocket and began writing a name and telephone number on a piece of paper.

"Couldn't you work with me and Jeremy? I mean as a family?" Angela asked before the doctor could finish.

"I think you and your husband would do better seeing someone more experienced with adults," the doctor said compassionately.

"My husband isn't here anymore. He left a year ago and I don't think he's coming back," Angela said, dropping her head slightly before reaching for another tissue. "It's only me and Jeremy now."

The doctor stopped writing and after a brief pause tore up the paper she had written on.

"Well, in that case, we need to keep the two of you together," she said with a smile.

Angela returned the smile and thanked her. Then the doctor turned towards Jeremy and said, "Let's get that good-looking young man over there to come and join us."

CHAPTER THIRTEEN

Mary Sullivan had one notable weakness: she couldn't pass up a bingo game. It didn't matter if it was held at an Indian casino, a church social hall, or somebody's garage. She would be there. So, at the last minute, when she saw an ad in the local paper for a fundraising bingo game, she threw on an outfit and took off, leaving Art on his own for the evening.

Bingo was one of the few things Art and Mary didn't do together. She would tease him by suggesting that the reason he wouldn't go to bingo was because she wouldn't play chess. But in reality, it was because he couldn't stand being in a place where the second-hand smoke was so thick a person could swim in it. And Mary didn't play chess because she found it so boring she'd rather spend her time watching paint dry.

Since the evening was still young when Mary left, Art decided to knock on Evan's door and invite him to dinner. There was a new pub down the road touting baby back ribs so tender they melt in your mouth like cotton candy, and, being left with only frozen dinners and leftovers, he figured it was an opportune time to get a face full of barbecue sauce and enjoy an ice cold beer.

Evan was about to crack the seal on a new bottle of whiskey when Art's knock interrupted him. He knew at once it was Art by Art's signature: three taps followed by a brief pause followed by two taps. Besides, the only other person who ever came to his apartment was Charlie, and he didn't knock, he banged.

When he opened the door Art stepped inside and made an expression as if he had just entered the elephant house at the Bronx Zoo.

"Don't you ever air this place out? It's as stale as that old bread Sheila's always throwing to the gulls," he said without expecting a reply. He pulled back a curtain on a small window in the kitchen and opened it up.

"Mary found herself a bingo game and left me a bachelor for a few hours. Want to go chase some chicks?" he added jokingly after taking a deep breath of fresh air.

"Sure, why not? Anything beats sitting around here all night," Evan replied, and he meant it wholeheartedly. The last thing he wanted to do was sit in his apartment and let Angela's words torture him to death as they'd done since he'd hung up the phone earlier in the day. Hearing about Jeremy's problems ignited something inside of him he was having trouble controlling and understanding. It sparked feelings of guilt and anger and sorrow that were reacting like a strong base and a strong acid suddenly cast together. He was feeling downright explosive, and had Art not knocked on the door, he would have popped the seal on the bottle and drank himself into a stupor.

When they reached the pub Evan ordered two beers and then made a beeline for the pool table where Art had already dropped two quarters and racked them up. Unlike their chess games there was relatively little competition on the green felt; Evan was a much better pool player. But Art loved the game despite his questionable skills, and he tried at every opportunity to drop the eight ball before Evan, vowing after each loss to someday come out the victor.

There was a time shortly after they first met that Evan threw a game or two for Art's benefit, but it quickly became obvious and Art made him promise to play his best. One of Art's admirable qualities was his unyielding quest to be good at what he did, and another was his ability to gracefully and honorably lose. But he wouldn't put up with being patronized. As Evan learned more about his older friend, he realized that the best gesture he could extend him was to give him the very best competition he could.

Their first game went slowly with Evan missing shots he would normally make and Art making shots he would normally miss. The outcome was Art's first win since Evan agreed not to play down to him, but it was far from the victory Art would have liked. Evan's play was sloppy and by the way he guzzled his first two beers, Art could tell his mind was elsewhere. So, without a lot of fanfare, Art racked them up for another game.

They shot the second in much the same way as the first, with Evan drinking beer as if prohibition would be the law of the land again by morning, and missing shots he should have been able to make with his eyes shut.

"You feeling alright tonight?" Art asked, snapping Evan out of a daydream when it was his turn to shoot.

"Yea. Yea, I'm fine. I'm just a little tired," Evan replied, trying to clear his head long enough to finish the game. He didn't want to tell Art about the call from Angela and about the trouble Jeremy was having, at least not yet. His friend was having too much fun trying to conquer the geometry behind the game for Evan to bring it up, and the way Evan figured it, between the beer and the bottle back at the apartment, he could make it until the next day.

Art's style of shooting pool was unique and somewhat amusing. He would grip the pool stick in the very middle, and bend down into a stance similar to that of a sprinter waiting for the starting shot. Then he would balance on his toes and slide the tip of the stick in the palm of his hand. Watching him shoot pool would lead a person to believe he'd never seen the game before. But in reality he'd developed his style at a much younger age, and at the time, either due to better vision or a steadier hand or something that had since changed, he was quite good.

"Sugar!" Art yelled in a muffled voice when he scratched.

When the second game was over Art suggested they take a seat and order up some dinner. He'd lost count of how many beers Evan slammed back, and was concerned that he'd be carrying him home if he didn't get some food into him. But Evan talked him into playing another game. Not because he wanted to play, but because he wanted to drink, and he figured he could do more of it at the pool table than he could at the dinner table.

The brand new felt was smooth, and the table well balanced, and not yet christened with the customary beer and ketchup stains so often found in pubs. But as clean as it was it did little to help Evan's game, but almost magically improved Art's. After a fantastic break Art managed to clear the table of three stripes before turning it over to Evan, who barely made his first shot and didn't even come close on his second.

As Evan and Art shot pool the other patrons in the pub couldn't help but notice Art's unusual style. He drew the attention of several people at the bar and several more sitting at nearby tables. Most were only mildly amused, watching and commenting among themselves as people do when they see something out of the ordinary. But a couple of local boys, who had wandered in a few hours before and had been drinking steadily since, couldn't contain themselves and became quite vocal.

The larger of the two men was an overly tanned man in jeans and work boots, and, judging by the splatters of tar on his pants and tee shirt, he was a roofer. The other man was probably his partner since he was dressed similarly and carried almost identical black splatters on his clothing. But his skin wasn't tanned like the bigger guy. It was red and freckled and didn't contain the pigmentation needed for bronzing, and his hair, had it not been so closely cut to his head that it was almost impossible to see under his cap, would have no doubt been bright red.

It all started with some relatively mild chuckling from the strawberry-skinned fellow. He pointed and spoke low and caused himself to laugh at whatever drunken comment he made to his buddy. He took a swig of beer, some of which ran down his stubby chin, and wiped it with the back of his dirty hand. He had a look of satisfaction on his face and cast a grimy grin towards the pool table that Evan couldn't help but catch. Art, who may or may not have taken notice of them, continued to play as he always did, bending at the waist and sliding the stick in his palm. But Evan, who wasn't sure if they were making fun of him or Art, threw back a look that would have told anyone to back off, except two rednecks with several pints of draft in their bellies.

When it was Evan's turn to shoot again he took his time, chalking his stick between each shot and lining up each ball as if he were playing for the world championship. He bent down and slid the stick with purpose and power, causing the table to shake as the balls slammed into the pockets and dropped in the holes. The quality of his play was saturated with the evidence of a man who, as a teenager, spent countless hours with a pool cue in his hands. The rednecks, more stunned than impressed, didn't make a peep while he was at the table.

But despite being damn near tournament stature in his younger days, Evan was older and out of practice, and a little drunk, and eventually missed. When he did, Art approached the table and again crouched into that unique stance that separated him from every other pool player in the world. The littler guy gave the bigger one a nudge and then, in a voice louder than the last time, said something that made the bigger guy almost spit out his beer.

A feeling came over Evan that he hadn't felt in a very long time. He felt such intense anger that he wanted to smash his pool stick over their heads and drag them outside by their hair to beat the crap out of them. He felt a wave of heat climb from his stomach into his chest and up through his neck into his face, and it made his blood boil.

The last time such a feeling of anger towards another person overtook him was one afternoon four years before when Angela was forced off the road by a drunk driver, with Emily and Jeremy in the car. She was on her way home from the grocery store, and less than a mile from their house, a guy shot through a red light, brushed the front quarter panel of her car, and pushed her into a ditch. Her first reaction, after checking the kids, was to call Evan, who immediately jumped in his car and sped to the scene. When he arrived, the belligerent drunk was pounding on Angela's hood and calling her names. Both children were in tears, afraid the maniac was going to hurt their mother, and Angela was shaking so badly she couldn't even dial the police. Evan, seeing Angela shaking and his children crying, lost control and jumped on the guy. When he got him to the ground he gave him two or three punches before having the good sense to stop himself. Thanks to the statements of several cooperative witnesses there were no charges pressed against him when the police finally arrived. They considered Evan's actions appropriate considering the circumstances.

Outside of that incident he hadn't had a physical confrontation with another individual since his middle school days. It wasn't that he couldn't handle himself in a fight. He worked out regularly—at least he did before leaving Syracuse—and was big enough to give most men a run for their money. But his even temper and mild disposition kept him out of such situations, and, had it not been for the call from Angela and the beer, he would have just ignored the childish rhetoric from the two jerks at the bar. But in his state they could have merely looked at him wrong and it would have had the same effect.

As Art was doing his dance for the God of Billiards, Evan walked to the bar and stopped directly in front of the red-skinned guy, leaving less than two inches between them. In his left hand he held a pool stick and in his right an empty mug, both of which he gripped so tightly the veins in his forearms swelled. The bigger guy slid backwards and stood up, leaving his buddy somewhat trapped on his stool, and, when he did, he stumbled and fell to the ground. Evan didn't flinch; his gaze remained solidly locked on the bloodshot eyes of the smaller guy who was looking back in complete surprise.

"Do you find something funny?" Evan asked keeping his jaw locked and moving only his lips. The guy's red face turned white and his expression changed from surprise to terror as he looked around for his friend. Since he was sitting and Evan was standing, his view was all but completely blocked by Evan's torso, and he couldn't see his buddy who was on his feet again behind Evan and in total shock.

"I was, I mean we were just, uh," he mumbled as the place grew quiet and all eyes turned to see what the commotion was all about. But Evan didn't care if the audience consisted of one or one million. He was in a world of his own, and at the moment that world consisted of him and Angela and Jeremy, who was only six years old and was seeing a shrink, and Emily, whose smile he would never see again. The red-skinned guy was an incidental part of that world, a stranger who inadvertently wandered into a minefield and accidentally stepped on a bouncing Betty.

Evan was solid and stiff like a marble statue. His only movement was his chest, which rose and fell in concert with the deep fierce breaths he took. He didn't blink, or move his eyes, or even swallow. He was fixated on the source of the laughter and was like a loaded slingshot pulled all the way back and ready to fire.

The bartender, the son-in-law of the owner, grabbed the telephone and immediately dialed the police when he realized what was happening, while the owner, a beer-bellied balding man in his sixties, grabbed a baseball bat from below the bar and positioned himself within swinging distance of where Evan stood. The red-headed man's friend, having somewhat regained his composure, but who was still drunk, grabbed a pool stick from a rack on the wall and decided it would be in his, and his friend's, best interest if he were to get in the first swing. And that's exactly what he did. He swung at the back of Evan's head.

The pool stick traveled through the air, fat end first, towards Evan's skull, and just prior to making contact, came to a stop in Art's palm with a loud smack. Art closed his hand over the stick, pulled it away from the bigger man and tossed it to the ground. Before the owner could swing his bat, Art held up his hand in a gesture that said he was in control. He placed his arm around Evan's shoulder, and Evan released his grip on the stick and the mug simultaneously, allowing both to drop to the ground. The mug smashed into a million pieces and the sound startled Evan's prey so badly he almost soiled his pants.

Art threw two twenty-dollar bills on the counter and apologized. He guided Evan out of the pub and into his car, where Evan broke down and cried.

"What did I do in there?" Evan asked, his mind drawing a blank from the time Art interfered.

"It's alright, my friend. It's alright," Art replied as he drove towards the marina.

When they arrived Evan opened the bait shop and grabbed a cold six-pack. He and Art sat on the dock and he did what he should have done in the first place. He told Art about the phone call.

CHAPTER FOURTEEN

If the invitation had been given directly to Angela, without Jeremy's knowledge, she would have made up an excuse and avoided the party altogether. That's exactly why, Angela figured, Eve gave it to her in front of him. She pulled it out of a drawer as if she had forgotten to mail it and handed it to her with one of those innocent but manipulating smiles she spent years perfecting. It was the same smile that used to get her passing grades in high school from all of her male teachers, and the same smile that landed that prize of a husband who periodically beat the shit out of her. Having proved itself useful early on in life it became an integral part of her personality.

The party was held at one of Angela's most hated of places, Happy Hippo's, where teenagers run around dressed like blue hippopotamuses and the children run around like lunatics. The entire concept of the place, according to the annoying commercials, is to give parents a place to relax while their little angels partake of the many wonderful activities the establishment has to offer. The only problem is the little angels transform into animals once they hit the jungle, the play area of Happy Hippo's, which negates the whole relaxation ruse of the commercials.

The party started at noon with pizza being served for lunch, and cake and ice cream for dessert. The birthday boy, Kyle, sat at the head of a very long table filled with anxious children waiting to get sugared up and released into the jungle. Eve bounced from kid to kid, filling cups and wiping up spills while her husband, Wade, spoke on his cell phone to one of his buddies about football, or golf, or whatever bimbo he last screwed.

He was good at making appearances and playing the part of the involved father, and he perfected the art of slipping away undetected at precisely the right moment, which was usually when the situation was so hectic he wouldn't be missed. If, by chance, Eve took a break from whatever chaotic state of mind she happened to be in and noticed him gone, he would merely fall back on the defense that he was busy chasing this kid or that kid and she would buy it, or act like she did anyway. It made for peaceful relations and prevented black and blue marks.

When Angela arrived she brought Jeremy to his assigned seat and took a place at one of the booths surrounding the birthday table where many of the other parents were huddled. She immediately felt the thick blanket of whispers that circulated among Eve's friends, all of whom were kept well informed of Angela and Evan's separation via the gossip hotline run out of Eve's kitchen. The last they heard from Eve, who heard it from her mother in the strictest of confidence, was that Angela had contacted an attorney and was finally filing for divorce. All the members of the hotline had since waited anxiously for the next chapter of the living soap opera they so loyally followed.

Angela recognized several faces among the group, having seen them from time to time at Eve's house when she picked up Jeremy. They all seemed to be part of a common club with their similar hairstyles and outfits, manicures and gestures. They were like middle-aged dolls manufactured on the same assembly line with plastic smiles, plastic hair and plastic tits, and they spoke as if they were programmed by Martha Stewart software, about their homes and their children, their minivans and their health clubs. While underneath they worried about their aging bodies, their overdrawn credit cards, and their cheating husbands.

There was a time, when Angela was a stay-at-home mom, that she was briefly part of the group. She did coffee with them in the mornings and treadmills in the afternoons and Le leche in the evenings, and she shared recipes and joined the carpool. But they became clingy and overbearing, like those car salesmen that start off so nice and eventually prevent you from leaving the lot without first signing your life away. They would call at all hours of the day and night and want to talk about what so and so did, and what this one's husband said, and how that one's children misbehaved in school. Angela just got fed up with the entire scene and dropped it all.

For a while after that, the relationship with her sister suffered. Because they were Eve's friends before they even knew Angela, they were insulted when Angela stopped returning their calls and meeting for lunch. So being the honorable people they were, they took it out on Eve by locking her out of the group and treating her like Angela was treating them. But they ultimately came around and forgave her for being born of the same parents as her stuck-up sister. After all, Eve was their leader and every group needs a competent director.

Most of the looks Angela received were subtle, like eyes shot above the rims of glasses and heads turned as if to look for someone else. But Angela didn't care about them. Who she cared about was her sister, and for Eve's sake had decided long ago to hold her tongue if she was ever approached by one of her so-called friends. She didn't blame Eve for hanging around with them because she knew Eve was the type who had to have people around her. People who would help her hold things together so she wouldn't have a nervous breakdown. Since most of them knew the same misery she did they were aptly suited for the job.

At about the time the cake was being cut Wade noticed Angela and decided to pay his respects. He tucked in his shirt, ran his fingers through his heavily gelled hair, and swaggered on over to her and cracked a great big smile. For some reason, which Angela never understood, he thought she liked him, not in a sexual way but in a friendly way. Which confused her even more because he would have had to be a raging moron to believe she didn't know how lousily he treated Eve.

When he approached, Angela acknowledged him in much the same way a person pretends to like the taste of something they find quite repulsive. She smiled as if she was having a hard time swallowing a lizard sandwich and then shook his hand with as little skin contact as possible. His arrogance eclipsed her obvious disregard for him, and, without asking if the seat across from her was taken, he sat down.

There was a time, when both girls still lived at home and Eve had just started dating Wade, that Angela actually thought he was cute. He didn't have his beer belly then, and his hair was grown out. But, more importantly, he hadn't yet shown his true nature. It wasn't long before Angela started seeing the signs that something wasn't quite right. Eve would sometimes come home crying, and she and Wade would have the most awful fights over the phone. Fights that would have certainly ended up with Eve being thrown to the ground and smacked around a bit had they occurred in person. Before Eve had a chance to end the relationship for good she ended up pregnant, and, despite Wade's insistence, refused to get an abortion. The subsequent marriage to save face sealed her fate.

"How ya doin', Ange?" Wade asked after sitting down across from her in the booth. His smile was large, greasy and sincere, and Angela thought again how stupid he must be to believe she didn't hate his slimy guts.

"I'm fine, Wade," Angela replied without the slightest hint she was happy to see him.

"How's that boy of yours doin'?"

"He's doing well," she replied. It was short, to the point, and the rudeness went right over his head. His smile didn't subside a bit.

"Yea, he's a good kid. We're real glad he gets to spend the afternoons with us. A kid should be with other kids, and my boys just love him. They're all like brothers."

A pain suddenly developed behind Angela's right eye. It was very much like the beginnings of a migraine headache; only it responded to Wade's voice and pounded harder with every word out of his mouth. Being in his company, and worse yet smelling his breath, literally made her sick to her stomach.

It was never that bad before Evan left. But afterwards, when it was only Angela and Jeremy, Wade really started getting to her. Probably because she spent a whole lot more time around him than she ever had before, seeing him almost every day when she picked Jeremy up from her sister's house after work. He'd act like a big shot in front of Eve by insulting Evan and calling him a no-good bum who abandoned his family. In his own twisted way he actually believed the insults made Angela feel good, as if she felt the same way about the man she had spent a decade loving.

Angela knew where the insults originated. They were born inside of Wade long before Evan left Syracuse. They came to life the very minute Angela introduced Evan. She brought him home for dinner while he was on leave from the Navy, and, at her request, he showed up in his dress blues. Call it a family thing if you like, or chalk it up to the fact that Evan was well built and extremely handsome and would have attracted the attention of any woman, but Eve's reaction to him was very much the same as Angela's was the first time she saw him in his uniform. Wade picked up on it and had hated Evan ever since.

For that reason he would insult Evan every chance he got, and, after about a month of listening to his bullshit, Angela was ready to kick him in the balls. If she hadn't had her hours changed at work so she didn't have to see him anymore she would have probably ended up doing it. That's how angry and disgusted she'd become with him. But what angered her the most, more than his insults and advice, and even more than the abuse he gave Eve, was his complete incomprehension of how much of an asshole he was. He actually believed he was a great guy, and he thought everyone else thought so, too.

Angela reached up and gave her forehead a strong squeeze, then looked towards her sister who had her hands full of drinks, plates and cups.

"I'm gonna give Eve a hand," she said, knowing he would never follow her to where there was work to be done.

"All right, Ange. I'll catch you later," he said, as if Angela would be looking forward to another session with him.

Angela went to Eve, took a container of Kool-Aid from her and started filling cups. She worked her way from one end of the table to the other, topping off drinks and wiping up spills as Eve followed behind her scooping ice cream and shoveling pieces of cake onto small Styrofoam plates. Little hands reached in all directions as if they all belonged to some bizarre land octopus that was having a sugar fit.

When Angela reached Jeremy she bent over and gave him a kiss, which embarrassed him a little, but he smiled all the same. She filled his cup and rubbed him on the back as she took notice of his expression, which was a little bit distant and somewhat reserved, just enough for a mother to pick up on.

She knew him well enough to know what was running through his mind. He was thinking about his big sister, and how she was always right next to him no matter where they went, and he was noticing other children with sisters and brothers. He felt different, somewhat incomplete. He had a slight urge to run away and cry, but a bigger urge to stay and overcome, and for that she was proud of him. She prayed every night for God to give him the strength to fight his battles and not run from them as his father had done.

When the cups and plates were full Eve greeted Angela with a hug, as if she had just entered the place and hadn't already been there for half an hour. She gave her a quick rundown of everyone in attendance, and, with the exception of a few new faces, Angela knew each one from her short-lived affiliation with the group a few years before. She smiled politely as Eve discretely pointed to each one and then to their children. As she held up her thin arms her long sleeves crawled up and revealed blackened rings around one of her wrists, accompanied by the unmistakable indentations left by someone with lengthy fingernails and a strong grip.

They weren't the first marks of their kind Angela ever noticed on Eve. She'd been pushed around and hit and choked, on and off, for the entire length of her marriage. Through the years there had been cuts and bruises and bumps, and even hair pulled out by the handful. The worst was when he knocked her to the ground in a drunken rage one night and kicked her repeatedly until both her legs and buttocks were black and blue. It was a wonder he didn't break her back.

As bad as that beating was, she still refused to leave him or even call the police on the scumbag. She managed to convince herself, with more than a little help from Wade, that if she ever divorced him she would lose her house, her car and even her children. So she just put up with it and tried to persuade herself it wasn't really that bad, and that every time would be the last time.

When Eve finished the presentation of her many friends Angela pulled her aside and quietly asked what happened.

"Oh, that! It's nothing. I just banged it cleaning the oven," she said in her bubbly high-pitched voice. But Angela wasn't going to let her get away that easily. She took her by the hand, locked eyes with her and asked again. Eve smiled and made light of it and repeated the oven story. She said it convincingly and without turning her head or even her eyes, and that's the part that gave Angela a feeling as if her stomach was being squeezed in a vice.

When Angela let go Eve sped away to conquer spilled Kool-Aid, dropped cake and other issues pertaining to the multi-armed beast at the long decorated table. Angela stood for a very long time and watched the party and people. She wished so badly things hadn't gone the way they did with Emily and Evan, and she wished they weren't like they were for Eve, either.

As a little girl she had visions of a prince sweeping her off her feet and taking her to a giant castle where she could be a princess and live happily ever after. For a time, before Emily's death, the dream was as real as it could be in a grown woman's life. Evan was her prince and she his princess, and although their castle was a modest house at the end of a cul-de-sac in a middle-class neighborhood, it was still their castle. Had Emily not fallen on that awful day, they may have lived happily ever after just like in the fairy-tales. But for Eve that would never be the case. She would never know the happiness Angela once knew.

Angela's eyes eventually fell on Wade, who was bent over a table full of Eve's friends telling jokes. For the first time in her life she wished she were a man so she could drag him outside and give him back all the bruises he gave to her sister. It was a thought that had never before crossed her mind despite the long held knowledge he was an abusive self-centered son of a bitch. She had always hoped Eve would leave or, more miraculously, Wade would change. But Eve was comfortable, as odd as that sounded, being trapped in a life with a man who beat her periodically, and, on odd occasions, bought her flowers or candy or a piece of naughty nightwear. And Wade was comfortable being in control of another human being to the extent he could do and say anything he wanted.

The sudden anger and disgust Angela felt was not completely born from Wade's presence. Eve had bruises, but she did, too. Only hers were on the inside and easier to cover up. And her bruises weren't from sudden blows or strikes in anger. They were bruises similar to those found on the elderly when they are left alone in a bed for too long a period of time. They grew slowly and deeply, like bedsores, and they hurt from the inside out.

As she watched this man, who a year before was so very different from her own husband, she saw him change. Before her eyes his waist became slimmer and he grew several inches taller. His eyes went from those brown, calculating, distant ones to soft, blue, caring ones. His hands went from those that deliver pain to those that deliver pleasure. In an instant Evan was before her. Only he wasn't the Evan who once loved her and promised her a future of happiness. He was the Evan who fell apart and lay on the couch, drank beer and, eventually, left her alone. She saw him as one with Wade, delivering pain to her as it was delivered to Eve, and for that instant she hated him.

Before the tears could flow she stopped and turned away, remembering what she had told herself when she finally decided to talk to an attorney. She said the pain would eventually go away and she would someday be able to love again like she loved Evan. She convinced herself she was doing her best for her and Jeremy in the long run, and, most importantly, she convinced herself she had fulfilled the promises she made the day they were married.

She loved him for better or worse, in sickness and in health, until death do them part, and she had lived up to all of it. As far as she was concerned, Evan was now dead. She'd spent a year trying to convince herself otherwise, but he was gone. Just as gone as he would be if he had been hit by a bus or struck by lightning. He no longer shared meals with her, or took walks with her, or slept in her bed, or played with their son. Her heart was just as empty as that of a widow's.

When she was sure her eyes would remain dry she turned and looked with sadness on her sister who was serving more cake and filling more cups. She had jumped right back into that place where she spent most of her life. That place between soccer games and beatings where she could be anything she wanted to be. Where Wade was the man she knew before he threw the first punch and she was the woman who loved him. After standing and watching her for a moment, Angela approached her and gently took the spatula from her hand. She gave her sister a smile, and began helping her.

CHAPTER FIFTEEN

Emily's hair was perfectly combed in long straight strokes that lined both sides of her delicately prepared face. She had two small pink bows attached to her hair, with small pink butterfly earrings in her ears. Her tiny hands rested together across her stomach and held a rosary, her wrists were adorned with her favorite bracelets and a small gold watch. Surrounding her from head to toe were stuffed animals of every shape and color, and pictures of her from birth to shortly before the accident.

The dress she wore was picked out and purchased by Eve and her eleven-year-old daughter, Crystal. It was a soft pink, trimmed with white lace and held together with a tightly grouped line of brilliantly white buttons. A small pair of white gloves accompanied the outfit, but they were not put on her hands, at Angela's request. They were placed next to her and subsequently covered with a multicolored clown doll. Her legs were encased in white stockings with white shoes, and, as far as prettiness goes, she was almost as beautiful in death as she was in life.

She lay peacefully, like a sleeping angel, in a pearl colored casket trimmed in brass. Its small size, so incongruous, took the breath of each person who entered the viewing room. Young and old wiped tears away as they quietly sat and stared in sorrow at the small velvet-lined box. It sat center stage and screamed silently at every mother and father that entered the room. It brought out the fear that the natural order of things might get skewed and they may have to someday bury their children. Their frightened eyes couldn't look at it for more than a few seconds at a time, and yet the beauty of it, and innocence within, drew them to it.

Only the rustling of clothing and a mellow melody that seemed to seep from the walls and the ceiling broke the silence in the air. It was a tune of sorrow and hope played out on harps, violins and flutes. Like a sponge it sucked up sorrow—the sorrow that spilled and splashed around the room. Eyes met and relayed quietly the sadness that was shared. Small whispers passed from husbands to wives, mothers to daughters, and fathers to sons as each tried hard to understand the reason the little girl was taken.

In the front row Angela sat with her mother and father on her right side, and Evan's mother and sister on her left. In the row behind were Angela's two sisters; Eve, her older sister, who tightly clenched the hands of her husband and daughter, and Kimberly, her younger, divorced sister, who sat next to Eve's sons. Next to Kimberly sat Evan's younger brother Michael, his wife and two boys. Michael fought back tears as his better half whispered commands to their children who were already bored and totally creeped out at being at the wake of their cousin.

The room filled to capacity and then some, until people were standing against the walls and in the doorways. Family, friends, coworkers and people from their church were there to pay their respects and say their final goodbyes. Had it been ten years later the same people might have gathered at Emily's high school graduation party, and they would have been smiling and laughing and telling jokes. But there were no smiles and certainly no jokes as Father Anthony Terrentino entered the room and walked to the front.

The stocky man with a Brooklyn accent knelt down in front of Angela and took her hands in his. His eyes, eyes that could be as cold as steel or as warm as melted butter, met with hers as he squeezed her hands before bringing them to his lips and kissing them. She fell from the chair into his arms and he held her tightly as she cried. He asked the Lord above to be with her and him to get them through such trying times. The large man dressed in black, who, in another life, could have been a football player, or heavyweight boxer, was on his knees holding Angela and talking to Jesus.

A few minutes later he rose and walked to a small podium. Not everyone was Catholic. Some were Baptist, some Jewish, and some didn't believe at all. But they all knew when to listen. The father dried a tear in his eye then left the podium briefly to bend over the casket and kiss Emily's forehead. Another tear flowed and fell onto her in much the same way the holy water had nine years before when he baptized her. Except this time she was quiet and still; there would be no party afterwards.

Across town, at the same time Father Terrentino was kissing Emily, Evan was strapped to a bed on the fourth floor of Saint Mark's hospital. He was brought to Saint Mark's from the county jail and was ordered held without bail pending evaluation by a psychiatrist. He was sedated, as the doctor on duty explained, to prevent him from further harming himself. Which was the customary excuse used to allow the staff to drug new patients so they wouldn't have to deal with them until they were good and ready.

Evan was arrested and charged with a number of crimes including battery of a law enforcement officer, resisting arrest, assault with a deadly weapon, and interfering with a police investigation. Despite the fact that Angela immediately secured an attorney, there was no luck convincing a judge to free Evan for Emily's funeral, but he was in no shape to attend anyway. The lawyer did manage to convince his Honor to transfer Evan directly from the emergency room in Saint Mark's to the fourth floor of the hospital, therefore bypassing the jailhouse altogether and sparing him the humiliation of being booked alongside common criminals.

Father Terrentino's eulogy included memorable occasions such as Emily's baptism, first communion and confirmation. He spoke of her with sincere love and knowledge of her, having seen her several times each week in school and at religious services. He spoke of the family and the love they shared and the bond they had, and offered a prayer for Evan, who he rarely saw at church outside of special events for the children. Then he did something entirely unexpected. Unaccompanied by musical instruments he sang a song he had written especially for Emily.

From somewhere above, God sent us your love, God sent us your smile, He gave us your hugs.
From somewhere above, He lent us your touch, He loved us enough, to send us that much.
But somewhere above, He missed you too much; he called you back home, where you'll never be alone.
And somewhere above, is a place for us all, we will wait for his call, and then be together again.

When his voice fell silent Angela got to her feet, walked to the casket, and fell to her knees. Nobody moved for a long time as she knelt next to Emily and spoke to her and cried. She touched her face and her hair, straightened her dress and put her favorite stuffed animal in her arms. Then she kissed her. When she took her seat a procession past the coffin began. Some people stopped only briefly while others took enough time to kneel and say a prayer. Many left small notes or cards next to her, and her teacher left a small book with letters from her classmates.

When only the immediate family remained the doors were shut to allow for private time. That's when Angela pulled a piece of paper from her purse. The note was from Jeremy. He wrote it himself, and Angela neither corrected the spelling nor the content. She stood and looked down on Emily, unfolded the paper, and read the writing written in crayon:

by by emmi. i luv you. I will mis you veri much. Say hi to god.

Angela lifted her daughter's hand and placed the letter underneath, then bent forward and kissed her a final time. Her knees buckled on her way back to her seat and she was caught mid-air by her father, who placed her gently down into her mother's arms. The remaining family members took turns approaching the coffin to say their final goodbyes.

At very close to the same time, Evan was slipping in and out of a medicated state. His glassy eyes opened heavily and shut numerous times as he struggled to come back. His tongue, loose and numb, sloshed around inside his mouth as he tried to speak. Saliva ran over his lips and down both sides of his face as he formed eerie sounds that in no way mimicked speech. His eyes oozed fluid that wasn't tears but something thicker, and his hands and feet, excluding the foot with a cast on it, clenched and unclenched.

It all went unnoticed by the busy floor nurse who'd seen it all before and wasn't in the least bit sympathetic. Evan was surrounded by what she called nuts and maniacs of every imaginable flavor, and most were just that. They were society's crazies; the ones we hide out of sight and pretend don't exist. The ones we are afraid of on the street when they follow us begging for money or food or shelter, and the ones we incarcerate for stealing a loaf of bread or a bottle of wine or a warm coat. Lying there in formation was Evan, in the same white outfit on the same type of bed in the same ward. He blended in. He was perhaps a little different than the others, yet ignored all the same by a nurse who saw no difference.

As his eyes opened and closed he strained to focus, but the medicine was too strong. The cones and rods and tiny muscles in his eyes were useless. They were asleep and had no intention of waking up any time soon. What he saw was runny and shiny, with periods of darkness when his eyelids lost the battle with gravity. Open and closed, open and closed.

Then a hand touched his and its warmth and softness migrated up his arm and into his body. His muscles reacted and clenched down on it, and his eyes rolled to the left to see who was there. Another hand glided gently over his forehead once, twice, three times before brushing his face. His eyes locked onto the hazy image at his side, but he couldn't focus, couldn't see who owned the soft touch. The image came closer and closer until it was close enough to whisper in his ear, "I love you, Daddy. I love you." As it pulled away it became instantly clear. Her face, alive and happy, was there, right there in front of him. "I'll be alright, Daddy. Please don't worry about me. It's all right. I love you, Daddy." The image, instantly sharper than sharp and clearer than an Alaskan summer day, bent over and kissed him on the cheek. Then she smiled and drifted up and up and up.

The following day at eleven-thirty in the morning they laid Emily to rest. The same priest spoke again, but didn't sing. He kept it short and powerful, insuring all who were there that beyond this life was life again in the arms of the Lord. Angela took solace in his conviction and whispered softly to her daughter that she would see her again in heaven. She placed a flower on top of the coffin from the backyard garden Emily helped plant only months before. Then, very slowly and carefully, the beautiful little girl in the small box was given back to the earth from which she came.

CHAPTER SIXTEEN

Before the date of Evan's trial his lawyer managed to get most of the charges dropped. He explained the mitigating circumstances behind Evan's actions to the district attorney, who had children of his own. Once the man understood the situation he agreed to a rather accommodating plea bargain. But the presiding judge felt differently; he believed some form of punishment was in order for Evan's actions. After all, he explained, they could have resulted in the injury or death of a law enforcement officer or innocent bystander. So he exercised his judicial powers and ordered six months of psychological therapy coinciding with six months of probation.

The therapy took place twice weekly at Saint Mark's Hospital in a tiny stale office down the hall from where Evan was previously sedated and tied to a bed. On his first visit he hobbled in on crutches and sat in a tweed chair across from Dr. Bernard Shant of Long Island, New York. The doctor was a short arrogant little man who'd graduated last in his class and believed he deserved more than a hole in the wall in a state hospital. The truth was he wouldn't have even received the sheepskin had it not been for the academic connections his father had at the university.

The doctor blamed the world for his shortcomings and took his frustrations out on his patients, most of whom were ordered into his care by the courts as a compromise over going to jail. He could treat them in any way he desired without much worry of recourse, and he took full advantage of his position every chance he got by subjecting them to hours of condescending blather.

Each new patient was indoctrinated with the same haughty version of the doctor's life story including where he studied pre-med and at what fancy college he received his medical degree. The speech was always delivered the same way: The doctor would lean against the front of his desk and look down at his victim who would be sitting in the chair in front of him. He would cross his arms and speak as if he were addressing an elementary school child. Granted, many in the chair had the intellect of a third grader, but Evan was definitely an exception.

The doctor didn't know much about Evan and probably wouldn't have cared if he had. He just got into his customary position in front of the desk and began. He spoke with the angered arrogance often found in people in positions they felt were below them, and yet his words alone would lead a person to believe he was the most important individual in all of central New York.

Once the narrative describing the doctor's credentials ended, at a cost of thirty minutes at two hundred dollars an hour, he got down to business. He opened a folder and reviewed the facts of the case as he chewed on a cheap silver-plated pencil. He wrote down a bunch of medical mumbo jumbo to describe Evan's actions and made several references to another case that, in all likelihood, had no relevant ties to the current situation. Looking over the rim of his tiny square spectacles, he addressed Evan.

"I'm sorry about your daughter," the doctor said, his words lacking sincerity. Evan replied with a nod of his head and a forced gesture that somewhat resembled a smile.

"I see you were ordered here by Judge Montt. He seems to think that therapy is a better choice than prison in your case. He's sent me several people that would have otherwise been incarcerated, and I can honestly tell you that in every case, except one, he was right. I was able to send them all back into society without a repeat offense."

Evan sensed another "this is how good I am" session coming on and had to fight the urge to walk out the door. He already hated the pompous bastard, and was having second thoughts about agreeing to see him.

"This program was developed to give criminals…"

"I'm not a criminal," Even said, interrupting the doctor in mid-sentence and staring at him without blinking.

The doctor, clearly dismayed at being interrupted, folded his hands and looked down at Evan as if he were looking at a dog that just wet the carpet.

"Then why do you suppose you are here?"

The question was one Evan wasn't prepared for, so he didn't answer. It wasn't that he didn't have the wit to think on his feet and come up with a reply; normally he did. It was just that he wasn't operating on the same level as normal. His world had been so violently shaken in the previous weeks that his thought process was weighed down. So the doctor waited for a moment until he was confident he'd made his point and then continued.

"Like I was saying, this program was developed to give people a chance to avoid prison. People the courts feel would benefit more from counseling than incarceration. But you will only get from this what you are willing to put into it. You will come here twice a week, and, at the end of each week, I will send a report to your probation officer. It is my responsibility to notify him if you are late or absent. Your probation officer will…"

Evan sat staring out the window as the doctor spoke. He felt empty inside. He didn't want to cry, he didn't want to yell, he didn't want to talk. He wanted to know what happened. He made breakfast and took the kids to the park and ended up in some asshole's office. And Emily was gone. That fast. Just that fast.

The doctor left his podium and took a seat behind his desk, then fumbled with an ancient tape recorder until it emitted an annoying screech.

"I'd like to begin by asking you about your family, and how you are all coping with the loss of your daughter."

Evan's eyes didn't leave the window. He heard the question, the damn stupid question, but had no intention of answering it. His daughter was gone. Without warning and without reason she was taken away. He was walking in the gorge, like a million other people do each year, and she disappeared over the side, and the fucking moron wanted to know how they were coping. Evan had the urge to stand up and punch him right in the face.

"Mr. Hayden? Mr. Hayden!"

Evan turned his head slowly and locked his eyes on the one long eyebrow that ran across the doctor's forehead.

"Mr. Hayden, would you please tell me how you and your family…"

"I don't want to talk about it."

"Need I repeat what I just explained to you? You were ordered by the courts to…"

"I was ordered to come here twice a week. But I wasn't ordered to talk about things I don't want to talk about, and my family's affairs are none of your damn business."

"In order for me to help you I have to ask these questions."

"Help me? Are you gonna bring my daughter back? You can't help me! You think keeping me out of jail is helping me?" Evan said angrily.

The doctor slid his chair back and folded his hands on his lap, another of his patronizing postures. "Mr. Hayden, I can't help you if you won't let me help you."

"How are you going to help me? By tying me to another bed and drugging me until I pass out? Is that how you people help? I missed my daughter's funeral because of the help I got from this place!"

There was a lengthy pause before the doctor replied. "We will not hold you here, Mr. Hayden. You can leave whenever you like. But you know the consequences of doing so."

The doctor leaned further back in his chair and waited, and Evan thought for a moment before replying.

He didn't want to leave and he didn't want to stay. He had nowhere to go other than back home, and home had become torturous since Emily's death. There were colorings on the refrigerator door from when she was only two years old. Like the one she made of Mom and Dad and Baby. In it Evan had a huge head and one big eye and Angela was all hair except for one little round circle that Emmy said was Mommy's mouth. She drew herself between them with a big smile, and her little stick arms stuck out and held theirs. It was on the freezer door at eye level and caused him to cry every time he saw it.

Then there were the clothes. Things she wore that were never washed and still held her soft, powdery, fragrant scent. The nightgown she wore the last night she was alive still hung on her bedpost as if it was going to be picked up and put on again. Her bunny slippers her grandmother bought for her still sat by her bed waiting for her little feet to climb inside them, and her blanket, the one she used to wrap herself in to watch television, sat folded at the foot of her bed.

No place in the house was free of her presence. Not even the garage, where her bicycle waited for her little feet to propel it through the neighborhood. It hung on a hook next to Evan's and Angela's, and would never roll again to her friend Marsha's house where she would play Barbies or dress up in Marsha's mother's old clothes and pretend she was all grown up.

Outside in the neighborhood were the children she used to play with. They still ran through the yards playing hide and seek or chase, and their voices carried through the walls and into the house. Only they didn't sound the same anymore. They sounded queer, like an orchestra short a flute player, or a piano with a silent key, because Emily's laughs and shrieks no longer echoed off the walls of the surrounding homes and blended with them as they used to.

Evan couldn't take it, any of it. Everything in the house reminded him of the precious little girl that took her first steps in the living room and ate her first ice cream cone on the back porch. She was there, everywhere, but nowhere. He could smell her and hear her, but he couldn't touch her or kiss her. It was something he had tried to explain to Angela, but to no avail. The same things that tortured him comforted her and helped her deal with the loss.

So she hung pictures of Emily on the walls and placed her favorite toys and books out in the open because it made her feel closer to Emily. She didn't allow anything to be moved. Not even her lunch box that still sat on the counter in the very place Emily had left it. She needed it all to survive, and Evan knew that and allowed it, but it was killing him inside.

"I'm here because I was ordered to come here, that's not a choice. I fucked up when my daughter fell, and I did some things I shouldn't have, but I'm not a criminal. Until you lose someone you love you'll never understand. But I'll be damned if I'm gonna give you the opportunity to lock me up again. I'll come to your damn sessions and I'll sit here while you preach, and I'll pay you the money. But I'm not saying another damn word," Evan said.

The doctor rose and walked to the window. He opened it and a fresh breeze entered the room, displacing the stale air inside. He leaned against the windowsill and spoke with a more compassionate voice. "I'll tell you what. I won't ask any more questions as long as you'll talk when you're ready. Is that a deal?"

Evan looked straight at him and didn't respond. He didn't even nod his head. His eyes were dark and far removed from where they pointed; his mind was tumbling around in a vortex. The doctor could have yelled, "Fire!" and he wouldn't have even flinched.

For another hour the doctor talked to the walls. At some point Evan rose, walked to the window and just stood there looking out. When the session was over he picked up his crutches, and, without saying a word, made his way down the hall and out of the building.

The words he spoke that day were the last the doctor heard for quite some time. He attended the sessions as ordered. He didn't make eye contact, or talk, or acknowledge the doctor in any way until the very last minute of the very last session, when he rose to his feet, looked him in the eye, and said, "Goodbye."

CHAPTER SEVENTEEN

Evan's mother, Dorothy, called Angela on the evening after her and Jeremy's second visit with Dr. Sandborn. She had run into Angela's mother at a local grocery store and received the latest information about her grandson. Angela's mother purposely made Jeremy's situation sound more severe than it actually was, hoping word would get back to Evan and give him cause to come home or call, as if he didn't already have a reason to call his own wife and son. Dorothy hadn't spoken to him in almost a year, and his brother or sister hadn't spoken to him since before he left Syracuse, making the chance of anything reaching Evan via his family very unlikely.

Angela wasn't surprised when she picked up the phone and heard Dorothy's voice. Not because she received warning from her mother, who called the minute she got home to tell her about her encounter with Dorothy, but because Dorothy had been good about staying in touch with Angela. She usually called once or twice a week and would stop by on an occasional Saturday morning to spend some time with Angela and Jeremy. When Angela's mother heard that, she swore it was all a ploy to find out information Dorothy could relay to Evan. But Angela knew her mother-in-law well enough to know her concern was sincere. She too, in a way, also lost a child. In the year that had passed since Evan left, the two women became closer than they'd ever been.

When Evan pulled out of his driveway the night Angela told him to leave, nobody could have imagined he'd drive as far as Florida. He'd never been there before and didn't know a soul living in the Sunshine State, and he had plenty of places, assuming he didn't want to go to a hotel, to spend the night. His mother's house was a half hour's drive, and his sister's apartment was just a bit farther. His brother's house, which Angela considered his most likely destination, was only fifteen minutes away.

She figured he'd end up at his brother's place because his brother had, from time to time, spent a few nights at theirs when his wife reached her limit and sent him down the road. Each time Evan would counsel his brother and Angela would spend time on the phone with the wife, and, before long, they would get back together as if nothing had happened. So Angela hoped for, or actually expected, a little payback. She figured he'd stay there for a few nights, maybe even a week, and then return home and begin the task of rebuilding his life.

But he didn't go to his brother's house or his mother's house or his sister's apartment. He didn't even consider any of those places when he turned the key and stepped on the gas. He just drove. His destination was as arbitrary as a lottery number, and on that particular night the little ball popped into the tube and on it was written Interstate 81 South.

Finding out that Evan was fourteen hundred miles away, when she expected him to be only ten, almost caused Angela to faint. She couldn't believe her ears when she picked up the phone the following day and it was a collect call from Daytona Beach. It was the first time an argument between them ever resulted in either of them leaving the house, and she never expected him to run so far away, and neither did the rest of his family.

His mother was so upset she wanted to fly down to Florida and bring him home. When Evan called her, the one and only time after leaving Syracuse, she even resorted to cussing. But it did no good. Her son was immune to reason or coercion of any sort.

Before Emily's death and after his father's, Evan was the solid rock of the family. His mother came to count on him for all the things a good son does for his elderly, widowed mother. He called her daily to check on her, visited weekly, and made repairs around the house when needed. He treated her as if she were highly breakable and extremely fragile, despite the fact she was confident and very sharp for her age. After Emily's death, the phone calls, the visits, the concern all disappeared. It was as if everyone else died the day his little girl fell.

After the beating he took from his mother Evan refused to contact anyone except Angela, which put her in a very stressful position. She had to play the go-between with his mother and siblings, all of whom called frequently to inquire on his status. They wanted messages relayed to him he didn't want to hear, and they wanted to write letters he didn't want to receive. Angela was caught in the middle while trying to raise a son on her own and deal with the loss of a daughter and a husband.

The stress became so bad that she finally had to put a stop to it all. She called Dorothy and explained her position, and Dorothy's response, and subsequent actions, forged a stronger bond between the two women. Without hesitation the woman called her son and daughter and asked—insisted—they leave Angela alone. She told them she would pass on information when it came, and she told Angela she would never again ask about Evan as long as Angela agreed to call the minute she heard something. True to her word, she called only to check on Angela and Jeremy, to say hello and offer her help should there be something, anything, an old woman could do to help her abandoned daughter-in-law and grandson.

"Hello, dear, it's Mom," Dorothy said when Angela answered the phone. She called everyone dear, from the very young to the very old, and she did it in a way that made people feel close to her. It was a tactic, an unintentional one, which helped her in many situations since people tend to go out of their way for those they like.

"Hi, Mom. I had a feeling it was you. Mother called this afternoon and said she ran into you at the store."

"Oh yes, dear. We had a very nice conversation. Your mother's a lovely woman. Lovely," Dorothy said.

"I'm sorry I didn't call to tell you about Jeremy. I've just been so busy with work and everything," Angela said. She had meant to call Dorothy, but she knew she'd have to tell her about her conversation with Evan and her decision to contact an attorney, and that kept her from picking up the phone.

"Oh no, dear, not at all. You have your hands full with that sweet child of yours. How is he doing?"

"Well, like my mom probably told you, he's had a little problem at school."

"Yes dear, she mentioned it."

"We found a very nice doctor that he's seen twice now. She's really great with kids, and I can already see a difference in him. He saw her for the second time today, and he was actually looking forward to it," Angela said. What she meant by already seeing a difference was that Jeremy hadn't wet the bed in two nights. But, rather than the sign of some miraculous breakthrough, that change could have been because of the doctor's recommendation to halt fluids ninety minutes before bedtime, and make sure he went to the bathroom before hitting the sheets. Still, as the doctor explained, waking up dry will do wonders for his spirit, and for a six year old that can go a long way.

"Well, I'm glad to hear it. I'm just sorry he's gone through so much," Dorothy said. She was sorry for what happened to her precious little granddaughter, and sorry for what happened to her son. Now she was sorry for the damage it had all done to her grandson, a boy who reminded her so much of Evan.

After making her opinion known to Evan the last time she spoke with him she made the decision not to interfere further. She was raised to believe a marriage is the most personal and fragile of all human relationships, and when too many people are involved it can fall apart. On more than one occasion she was kept awake at night second-guessing her decision. She had even talked herself into calling him and telling him to get his ass home where he belonged, and she would have told him just like that had his phone number been handy when she got the urge. She came to her senses before she could call Angela to ask for it.

She felt her son's pain and sympathized with him, but she was from the old school where a man didn't run out on his family, regardless of the situation, and she was embarrassed by what he'd done, both for herself and her late husband, God rest his soul. She felt it was a reflection on how they raised him, and she spent many an hour trying to figure out where they went wrong. But they hadn't gone wrong. No more wrong than any other middle-class parents of the time. They gave him what they could and showered him with love. They had their problems, like every family did, but they were good parents. She found it harder and harder to believe that with each day her son stayed away.

"I'm sorry too, Mom. He's a good boy and he's been through so much for his age. I took him to see Emily the other day, at the doctor's recommendation, and you should have seen him. He sat down and talked to her, and I'll tell you, Mom, it just hurt so bad to listen to him. He was so sweet," Angela said, holding back tears.

"Did the doctor talk to him about his dad?"

"Not yet. She's been getting to know him. Or I should say getting to know us, because I stay with him during the sessions. She talks to him about school and his friends, his favorite television shows, and she tells him jokes and plays games with him. She even colors with him. It's amazing to hear the things she gets him to say. She asks him things that I never realized a child his age could comprehend. He understands so much more than I've ever given him credit for."

"So you think she'll be able to help him?"

"I think so, Mom. I think he just needs to talk about everything that happened, and have someone help him understand it all in a way that allows him to get some closure. To be honest, I felt a little threatened on our first visit. I thought, being his mother, I should be able to help him better than anyone. But the doctor told me that as a mother I was too close to him to do what she can do. She explained, as backwards as this sounds, that the bond between us contrasted with the degree of separation required for him to be able to open up. There are things he wouldn't want to say to me for fear of hurting me. So she spends some time each session one on one with him, and I believe it's good for him," Angela said.

After some more talk about Jeremy and the doctor and eventually the weather, Angela decided to let Dorothy know about the call to Evan. She reminded herself she was talking to his mother, and, being a mother herself, she knew that deep down inside blood was thicker than all else, especially maternal blood.

"Mom, I have to tell you something, and I hope you don't get upset."

"Certainly, dear, go right ahead," Dorothy replied, as if she expected Angela to say something trivial.

"Mom, I spoke with Evan the other day."

"Oh, your mother didn't mention that."

"It was after I saw her on Sunday. I never called to tell her."

"Oh," Dorothy said, sensing what was coming next.

"I called to tell him about Jeremy, Mom, and I did what I told myself I wasn't going to do. I asked him when he was coming home." Angela paused. She didn't want to continue because what she had to say next was going to hurt Dorothy and she didn't want to do that.

"Go ahead, dear," Dorothy said.

"He said he still wasn't ready. Mom, it's been a year since he left, and I still love him, but this thing is hurting Jeremy. It's hurting me, too. I honestly didn't call him with the intention of getting into an argument, but it happened anyway. I told him if he wasn't coming home that…" Angela stopped. There was silence on the line for several seconds. "Well, I said that it was over."

It took Dorothy a minute to digest what she heard. Angela held the phone and waited for her reply.

"Are you thinking about a divorce?" Dorothy asked.

"Mom, I don't want a divorce. But if he's not coming home, what choice do I have?"

"Do you want to see other people, Angie?"

"No. It's nothing like that. I just can't live in limbo like this anymore. I feel like my whole life is stalled. When Emily died it took the life out of me. I didn't think I'd be able to function anymore. God, Mom, you know that," Angela said. Dorothy did know it. She practically lived with Angela and Evan for a month after Emily's death. She cooked, cleaned and took care of Jeremy. She talked to Angela and helped her handle her grief. But Evan was a different story, he went in a shell and, when he started drinking, he was lost.

"I know that, dear, but divorce is a bad thing. It's not going to do anything to help Jeremy, and it may make matters worse. Please, dear, give it some more time. Give yourself a chance to think about it before you do anything rash."

But Angela had thought about it. What she didn't tell Dorothy was that she'd already made an appointment with an attorney to discuss her options, and she wasn't being driven strictly by emotions. There were financial aspects to what she decided to do. She wanted to sell the house and move into something she could better afford on her salary. Sure, Evan sent a monthly check, but it was a small portion of what he had earned at the nuclear plant, and if he stopped sending it she would be forced to sell. On top of that it didn't make sense to keep such a large house for only two people.

Angela assured Dorothy she wouldn't make any rash decisions, and then she changed the subject as quickly as possible. She didn't like upsetting Dorothy; she was a caring woman who was more alone than Angela was. Her husband, Evan's father, died a few years earlier, leaving her stranded in a house that was previously alive with activity. She once told Angela that the saddest days in her life were when her children moved out, and now she was alone with only photographs and phone calls.

Later that night, after Jeremy had fallen asleep, Angela sat on the back porch and drank a glass of wine. She listened to the rustle of the trees as a faint breeze moved through their branches and carried their loosened leaves to the ground. The sky above sparkled with a million stars that looked like diamonds scattered randomly out on a canvas of black felt. She looked up at them and tried to pick out her favorites from when she was a little girl. She remembered her father pointing to the heavens and telling her how far away they were, and she was amazed that she could see their light from such a distance.

As she lifted the glass to her mouth, a sparkle of a different kind drew her attention to her hand. It was the ring Evan gave her when he proposed, and, like the stars, it still shined as bright as the day she first laid eyes on it. She stopped and looked at it, thinking about her husband who was, for all practical purposes, as far from her as the Big Dipper. She remembered what he said, word for word, when he asked for her hand. He swore he would love her throughout this lifetime and the next, and he promised he would never do anything to hurt her.

She thought about those words as she finished her wine, and, after taking the last sip, she placed the glass on the table, removed the ring from her finger, and dropped it in. The gold band struck the bottom of the crystal glass and created a tone that carried through the trees and into the heavens.

CHAPTER EIGHTEEN

Jeremy and Angela's third session with Dr. Sandborn proved fruitful in some respects. The doctor managed to gain the little boy's trust much quicker than she expected, based on other boys his age she had counseled in the past. But she didn't attribute it to anything great on her part. She figured he was just following his mother's lead, as children his age tend to do. But what the doctor already sensed was his reluctance to talk about his father or his late sister. He was more than willing to tell her about school, his friends, and his cousins. But when given an open door to mention Evan or Emily he simply changed the subject, an involuntary defensive tactic the brain employs automatically in people of all ages when they feel threatened.

She didn't want to be the one to mention them. She felt it best to continue to provide the opportunities for him to bring them into their conversations when he was ready.

The doctor was generally regarded among her peers as a blazer of new trails. She'd been known to try things some professionals in her field regarded as unconventional; others called them ridiculous. Once, she was counseling two siblings who had lost their mother and were taking their grief out on each other in the form of fighting. Their father, a very decent, highly structured man, had lost control of them and had no idea how to relate to his own children. He was the corporate type who was used to a strict and rigid atmosphere, and he expected the same type of obedience from his boys that he received from his subordinates.

Dr. Sandborn went out on a limb and scheduled a special session with the boys and their father. The session was held at one of those paint ball places where they pass out air-powered pistols and rifles and people compete by shooting each other with small balls of paint. She teamed up with the father against the boys and they spent the afternoon just being kids. The father remembered what it felt like to cut loose and the boys remembered the bond they had before losing their mother. At the end of the day the three of them hugged each other and cried, and the doctor broke a barrier that might have taken her weeks or months in her usual counseling environment.

For Jeremy she decided to break away from the usual environment as well. The fourth session was held in a favorite place of his and Emily's, their backyard. She suggested removing, as much as possible, the therapeutic persona of her visit. So Angela bought some burgers and hot dogs and had a barbecue, and the three of them ate outside at the wooden picnic table where the family used to enjoy summer afternoons and evenings together.

Jeremy helped his mom by mixing a very strong batch of grape Kool-Aid and setting the table. He'd become so accustomed to meals for only two that he forgot to set a place for the doctor. He realized it soon enough and ran back inside, retrieved another knife, fork and plate, and, after a moment of intense thought, set them in his sister's old spot directly across from his. It was a gesture Angela took note of and pointed out to the doctor, because not even his best friend Tanner was extended the privilege of sitting in Emily's place.

As they ate, the doctor tried to imagine the scene that would have been played out if Emily had never fallen from that ledge. She saw a man at the barbecue, and, from pictures she'd seen in the house and Angela's description of Evan, the doctor pictured a man who was tall and muscularly slender with auburn hair and a devilish smile. He did the cooking while Angela set the table. At one point Angela went over to him, kissed him and ran her fingers over his scalp, and, ignoring the burning meat, he took her into his arms and squeezed her tightly.

In the yard a very cute little girl with a big smile played with her little brother. She pulled him in a plastic wagon that was now covered with leaves in the corner of the yard. She was his Clydesdale and he her master, and he sat on his knees and yelled "Mush!" as he pretended to crack a whip. When that game was over they became pirates or cops and robbers and ran around the yard, or climbed into the fort, or hid in the garden. Their laughs and shouts filled the air and mixed with the smoke from the grill, enveloping the home in love and innocence.

When lunch was ready they all took their places, Emily across from Jeremy, and Evan across from Angela. They filled their plates and maybe said grace, maybe not. They shared the meal as a million families do to celebrate the fact they are all together, safe and happy.

It was a very different scene from the one in front of her in real time, which was like a puzzle with missing pieces. Members who once formed a most perfect picture were missing, but the love was still there. Something else was there as well—pain so agonizingly real that it rumbled up from below like an earthquake and threatened to swallow them whole. It was the doctor's experience that such a rumble would never completely go away. But it could be tamed, as a wild horse can be broken, and lived with in peace. It was her job to saddle it and settle it for the benefit of the two people at the table with her.

After lunch Jeremy invited Dr. Sandborn to his fort, which was a nine-foot by six-foot tree house Evan built for Emily when Jeremy was only two years old. It sat up in an old tree in the far corner of the yard and fit so perfectly between the massive branches that it could have grown from the same seed.

She climbed the rope ladder behind him and managed to get through the small hatch in the floor. Once inside she fell into a corner to take in this world. The inside walls were almost completely covered with drawings in crayon and colored marker, and, despite being done by children they weren't done in haste. They were beautiful images of life through innocent eyes.

The doctor felt honored to be welcomed so openly into a place that was so obviously special to Jeremy. She knew immediately that it had become his and his alone since Emily's passing. A place he could go to escape the rumble of the ground outside and live in any time and any place he so desired. From what she saw on the walls, he had chosen a time when he had a sister and a father, as well as a mother.

"This is a very beautiful fort you have here," she offered as her eyes scanned the rainbow of colors so carefully placed on the walls.

"Yea. I don't let a lot of people up here, just my friend Tanner and my cousins. And my mom too, but she doesn't like climbing trees so she stays on the ground," he said in a bashful way.

"Thank you for letting me come up," she said, smiling.

"You're welcome. My mom says you like kid's stuff a lot."

"I do. Kid's stuff is my favorite stuff. That's why I have so much of it at my office," she replied, reminding him of the toys they both played with during their previous sessions together.

"Do you have any kids?"

"No, not yet, but I certainly hope to have some one day," she answered, and she did hope to have a child some day.

"Did you make all of these drawings?" she asked, well aware that some, or most, had to be the work of a child older than Jeremy.

"No, but I did this one," he said, pointing to a crayon coloring of motorcycle.

"That's really good. I like the colors you used," she said.

"And I did this one, too. But my marker stopped working and I had to finish it with crayon," he said pointing to a drawing of a person.

"Wow. That's really good. Is that a drawing of you?" she asked, hoping it was one of his father or his sister.

"Nope," he said simply before going on and pointing out several more he was proud to show.

The doctor saw a pattern emerge as Jeremy went from wall to wall showing his artwork. All of his pictures were on the lower third of the walls, and done with less skill than the ones higher up. She figured the others were the work of his sister. He was avoiding them, just as he avoided talking about her.

"This is a really great fort. It must have taken a lot of work to do all of this. Did you do it all by yourself?" she asked. The door was wide open and she was almost pushing him through it. That's why she was there, to get him through the door. She knew that if he was going to talk he would be more likely to do it in his special place.

"No," he said, glancing up at the other pictures.

"I did the bottom ones, and Tanner helped a little, too. Would you like to help, 'cause I have to finish this one," he said, pointing to an almost half complete drawing of a horse.

"Sure, I'd love to," she said.

Jeremy pulled two crayons out of a small bucket on the floor. He handed Dr. Sandborn a brown one and asked her to color in the head and neck, and said he was going to add a saddle. She carefully worked the rounded worn point inside the lines. Next to her hand, working with equal care, was Jeremy's small one holding a red crayon.

"How long have you been drawing in here?" she asked.

"Ever since..." He paused and his hand stopped. "For a long time," he finished and then his hand went back to work.

A long time in the life of a six-year-old can mean many things, but the doctor was quite sure she knew what it meant to Jeremy.

"There's not a lot of space left to color. What happens when it's all done?" she asked.

118

The little hand stopped again and he turned and looked at her curiously. He looked at the small area that was void of color and thought very hard about the question. It wasn't one he'd ever consciously considered before. Then he gently took the brown crayon from the doctor's hand and placed it, and his, back into the bucket.

"Wanna go see some of my toys?" he asked.

"Maybe in a few minutes. I kind of like it up here. Can we stay for a little longer?" she asked, thinking she was close to an opening.

"I guess," he replied uneasily.

"Which drawings did Tanner help you with?" she asked.

"Um, I think he did some of this one and maybe that one, too," he said, pointing from one to the other of several colorings.

"Did he do any of those?" she asked, pointing up top.

"No," he said.

"They're very pretty. Someone very special must have done them, that one's very good, too," she said, pointing at the wall in front of him.

The doctor waited silently as the boy's mind thought it over. He was gazing at a very pretty picture of two people holding hands. One was taller than the other and they could have been Emily and her father, or Emily and her mother, or Emily and Jeremy, or any number of other combinations. But she hoped it was a little boy and his older sister, and she was concerned about what was ricocheting around inside his hurt and lonely mind.

The doctor's work, although sometimes very satisfying, was at times sad and trying. She truly loved the young people and avoided what may have been a more lucrative career treating adults for the fulfillment of treating children. But to get to the end she must sometimes take them on a dreadful journey, one of painful memories that must be dealt with.

He turned and looked at her and his eyes were full of sadness. She reached out and took his hand and gave it a squeeze. That brought tears from his eyes.

"My sister did it. It's me and her," he said as a salty tear rolled down his face.

"She must have been a very special sister," the doctor said before taking him into her arms and giving him a hug.

"Yea," was all he could say as his bottom lip trembled and his eyes released a flood of pain they were fighting so hard to hold back. She held him tightly and let him. When his tears were spent she wiped his eyes and kissed him gently on the forehead and told him he was the very best little brother a girl could have.

After that breakthrough the two of them spent over an hour in the small box in the sky talking about Emily. Jeremy sat on the doctor's lap and told her stories about the drawings, each of which Emily had drawn to record a special event in her life. There was one of her last birthday party and one of her and her daddy swimming in the new pool. Another showed her baking cookies with her mommy and yet another depicted a scene where she and Jeremy rode a carousel together at a nearby mall.

When they climbed back down the ladder the doctor smiled at Angela, who had been waiting and hoping. The smile told her the doctor was pleased, that her little boy had taken a step forward. Angela took Jeremy into her arms and gave him a hug. His brown eyes were bloodshot and puffy, but he was smiling, and underneath the tiny red veins in the whites of his eyes, she saw a glimmer. A glimmer she hadn't seen in a very long time.

Chapter Nineteen

The fog surrounding them was so thick that Evan could only see Emily from the waist up as she dangled above complete nothingness. He had a firm grip on her hand and squeezed with every ounce of strength he could muster as she screamed, "Daddy, don't let go! Daddy, don't let go!" Her high-pitched voice cut through the dense cloud and echoed off the canyon walls as Evan held tightly to overcome the gravity that fought so hard to take her away. His arm tensed, and the veins protruded from under his skin as his muscles tore away from the bones. Sweat dripped from his nose and eyebrows, and his gut released a haunting grunt as the blood rushed to his head and threatened to pop his eyeballs out of their sockets.

Her face, its porcelain skin and blue eyes, looked back at his in a desperate plea for salvation. Her hair, fine like silk, blew in a violent breeze that surrounded her like the winds of a tornado. Her body, dainty and limp, hung attached to this world by only his grip. He stared into her eyes, her big round frightened eyes, and could see directly into her soul. It held the memories and experiences of a little girl's lifetime, and they played before him like an old, black-and-white, silent film.

After a minute his perspiration mixed with hers, lubricated the connection between their hands, and she started to slip away. She screamed, "Daddy, Daddy, Daddy…" in an unending string of panicked shouts. His brain sent the signals to his hand to squeeze even harder but his muscles had reached their limits. His fingernails popped from his fingers and blood shot from their tips and seeped between their hands, further lubricating the connection. Her screams grew louder as the surface area of their bond grew smaller, and, in an instant, she was gone. Her small body disappeared into the fog like a spoon dropped into a bowl of whipped cream, and her voice faded until it was gone.

He leapt from the bed, saturated with sweat and crying like a baby, and fell to the ground. Saliva and snot flowed from his face, covered the side of his head and formed a seal between his skin and the grimy surface of the faded linoleum floor. He cried out her name, over and over, and cussed at the ambiguous darkness that surrounded him. His anger grew and his fist pounded the floor until blood squeezed from beneath torn flesh on his knuckles. His body shook as an ice cold sweat covered his skin. The booze had failed.

He sat alone, very alone, until his body was milked of the venom that poisoned his sleep. When the final echo of her voice was gone he stood up and turned on a light. His hand was covered in coagulated blood that he wiped on his underwear before walking to the window and opening it.

Warm salty air rushed inside. He stood there and inhaled it deeply. He turned and looked at the bed and wanted to grab a knife and rip it to shreds. He hated it for taking him back to Emily's death. He hated it and everything around it. He hated himself for leaving her alone in the park, and he hated Angela for not blaming him and hating him back. But more than anything, he hated the power that controlled the world and decided when and how people died.

His arms tensed as the anger inside him grew. Swirling thoughts bounced around inside his head like bingo numbers being mixed in a hopper. Feelings came, and went, and came again, and pushed his emotions from one extreme to another. His heartbeat raced and sweat seeped from his pores. His blood got warmer and warmer until it boiled over and he lost control.

The first thing he grabbed was the nightstand. The lamp and clock crashed to the floor as it was ripped from below them. He launched it across the room into a wall, then picked up the lamp and did the same. Blood from his battered hand sprayed the walls. Adrenaline was released full strength into his blood and ignited like a roman candle. Whatever that element is that separates man from beast was long gone.

He picked up a one-hundred-pound reclining chair like it was made of Styrofoam and hurled it at the kitchen set in the adjoining room. The table splattered into pieces. Next he went after the bed, flipping it, frame and headboard attached, completely upside down.

The hurricane continued through the living room and kitchen until there was broken glass and shattered furniture everywhere. When there was nothing left to flip, smash or throw Evan stopped, took three or four deep breaths and sat down on the floor. He looked around as the anger drained from his body and was replaced, once again, with sorrow. The release was good, bad and necessary. It was a healing with no medical basis whatsoever, but a healing just the same.

CHAPTER TWENTY

The Secret sailed away at six a.m., just after Art left word with Derek that he and Mary would be gone for three or four days. She pulled away under her own power and was out of sight of the marina by the time her sails were raised, allowing the wind to pull her along. When Evan woke at ten o'clock and looked out his window, the first thing he noticed was the vacant slip where *The Secret* had been just hours earlier.

He skipped his customary morning shower and, after cleaning and bandaging his hand, raced down the stairs to the bait shop. The pounding in his head reminded him how much alcohol he drank the previous night, and his swollen knuckles reminded him of the boxing match he had with his apartment.

Derek was stocking shelves with a new line of artificial bait when Evan entered. He held up a sparkly faux shrimp that Evan all but ignored before asking about Art and Mary.

"He didn't say where they were headed," Derek explained, a little upset there was no interest shown in his little plastic friend.

"Didn't you ask?" Evan replied.

"What for? It's none of my business," Derek said bluntly, and he was right. It was neither his nor anyone else's business where customers go or how long they'll be gone. Many choose to leave such information in the event they run into trouble, but it's by no means required.

"Damn," Evan whispered under his breath. He needed to talk to Art about the conversation with Angela and about the dream. He was the only person familiar with Evan's situation, and the only one who's advice Evan could count on as being intelligent and pertinent.

"He did say they'd be back in three or four days, if that helps you any," Derek said. But it didn't help. Three or four days would be too long. Three or four days meant three or four nights, and three or four nights meant three or four more dreams.

"Maybe Dickhead knows where they went," Derek added. The remark caught Evan slightly off guard. But he knew instantly who Dickhead was, he had just never heard him called that openly before.

"Charlie?" Evan asked. The pounding in his head had gotten worse.

Derek just nodded.

"Thanks," Evan said before heading out the door.

Evan crossed the parking lot and found Charlie in the warehouse inhaling an Egg McMuffin and spilling a cup of coffee down his throat. It seemed like it would be painful for him to swallow the large un-chewed chunks of food, and the expression on his face as he did gave Evan the creeps. Charlie's eyes bulged out slightly, and he tilted his head back like a giraffe trying to swallow a tree trunk. Evan waited the ten seconds it took Charlie to gulp his breakfast before interrupting.

"Charlie, do you have any idea where the Sullivans went?" Evan asked.

A final slug of piping hot coffee chased the previously swallowed wads of food before he responded. "Didn't even know they was gone. Did you ask Shit-for-Brains?"

Before Evan could respond Charlie took the opportunity to complain about Derek. He didn't like the way the bait shop was changed around, and said the regulars wouldn't like it either. It had been the same way since old man Delcast owned the place and changing it was downright stupid. He went on and on about how the current owners were going to be upset, but Evan wasn't really paying attention. He was thinking about the Sullivans, and why they would leave without telling someone where they were headed. They must have told Derek and he forgot or just plain didn't listen. That had to be it, he reasoned. But Derek had heard Art say when he'd be back, so he should have heard him say where he was headed.

The throbbing in his head intensified; he needed his morning coffee. He thanked Charlie, cutting him off in mid-sentence, and headed to The Blind Minnow.

Sheila met him at the door as usual and directed him to the counter, then told him the daily joke about a midget and a dump truck. He laughed, despite the fact that it wasn't very funny, then asked if she, by chance, knew where the Sullivans had gone. She had heard them talking the other day, when they stopped in for lunch, about sailing to Sanibel Island or Key West. She only overheard a little bit, and wasn't by any means eavesdropping, but she thought they decided on Key West. The truth was, she did eavesdrop. She liked to know what was going on around the marina at all times, and she wasn't above a little harmless ear stretching now and then.

At about that time Dana came out from around the counter and placed a water and coffee down in front of Evan. Her long hair brushed across his shoulder and he couldn't help but notice her perfume, which she had refreshed only minutes before. She smiled, placed her hands on his shoulders and rubbed his muscles. Her flirtations were not at all subtle, although they had started out that way months before, when she had gotten the job.

Early on, when Evan became dock master, Sheila learned what she could through idle chit-chat and purposely leading questions. She prided herself on her ability to gather a wealth of knowledge about a person without having to actually come right out and ask. But with Evan it was a different story. He always steered the conversation away from himself and kept his answers vague, but that didn't stop her from forming her own blueprint of his past. She concluded that he recently lost his wife with whom he was deeply in love, and that he was the type of man who was very devoted to her, and, therefore, in an intense grieving process. It was the only reason she could come up to explain why he wore a wedding band and never spoke of a spouse.

When Dana started at The Minnow she had just gone through a nasty divorce. Her marriage of four years ended abruptly when her husband, a truck driver, called from New Mexico to inform her he wasn't coming home. He'd found, in his words, "a sweet little honey that knows how to treat a man." That left her alone to raise her six-year-old daughter from a previous relationship. So, after Sheila conducted her covert interrogation of Dana, she put two and two together and decided to play matchmaker by selling Dana on the whole dead wife thing. She told her story with such authority and conviction that the poor girl took it as fact rather than what it really was, a puzzle of speculation put together with mismatched pieces.

At first Dana's attentions to Evan made him uncomfortable. She had a friendly, outgoing personality that she relied upon to attract the attention of men she found attractive, and Evan was certainly the type of man who attracted her. He found her attractive as well, and what man wouldn't? She was tall and well proportioned with long brown hair and green eyes. But his heart belonged to Angela, regardless of how long it had been since he'd seen her last, and he was determined to honor the vows he took on that sunny day ten years before. But he didn't push Dana away because somewhere inside he liked, or needed, the closeness he felt when she rubbed his back or touched his arm. In a remote way it attached him to Angela, and reminded him he was human and still alive. In time he formed a relationship with her that, from his perspective at least, was slightly naughty but purely platonic. He had no intentions of crossing the line between flirtation and intimacy, and assumed Dana understood that.

It became part of his routine to have breakfast at The Minnow and sit at the counter and talk, or flirt, with Dana. He didn't need to be guided to the counter by Sheila, but allowed it because it too was part of the routine. The Minnow became his kitchen and Dana's counter his kitchen table. His seat was always available, something the girls made sure of, and his family always friendly. He'd sit at the counter and eat, laugh, joke and flirt, and never cross the line.

But that morning when he woke up something was different. He felt strange and out of place, as if he was seeing everything around him for the first time. He felt uncomfortable. He was in familiar surroundings with familiar people and yet it felt like the first time he'd been there.

He was lost in the woods and in need of a guide to find his way out, and in Evan's world Art had become that guide. He never realized before how important Art had become in his life. He had become family, and Evan needed him more than ever.

Art knew Evan better than anyone else, even himself. He'd spent a year listening to Evan spill his guts, and he knew what made him tick. Evan was a lot like he'd been at that age. He knew Evan's fears, weaknesses and desires. He knew every inch of Evan's soul as if it was his very own, and he knew what caused every scar on his heart. He would be able to help, if only Evan could find him and talk to him.

Art would be able to explain why Angela was no longer willing to wait for him to come home. And he would know exactly what she felt and would be able to describe it to him in a way he could understand. And if Evan asked his advice he would give it, without holding anything back. He would even be able to explain the dream, and why suddenly it lasted long enough for Evan's grip to give way. But most importantly he would listen, like he always did, and lend some order to the chaos of the situation.

But Art wasn't there. He was on *The Secret* on his way to Sanibel Island, or Key West or Mars for all Evan knew, which left Evan on his own.

Dana's hands worked slow as she rubbed Evan's shoulders. Her long fingers sank into the flesh of his neck, back and arms, and her fingernails periodically ran over the base of his skull and dug into his scalp. Evan's body, tense only moments before, melted under her touch. She sensed the anxiety in his body and continued on longer than usual.

As the seconds turned to minutes her previously benign touch became something more. The boundary widened from his shoulders and neck to include the upper portion of his chest as her fingers gently passed over his pectoral muscles and almost into the hair on his chest. He didn't stop her or make any gesture that would indicate his disapproval. He didn't want it to stop. She was a life raft of sorts, and he had nowhere else to turn.

It had been a long time since he'd felt the touch of a woman. Sure, Dana had rubbed his shoulders before, and Sheila had taken him by the arm many times to lead him to his place at the counter. But the skin that covered his body was numb, as if he had bathed in Novocain on a daily basis since leaving Syracuse. The numbness that prevented Dana's touch from reaching deep down inside of him disappeared when Angela hung up the telephone. He was suddenly stripped of whatever defense mechanism had been in place, and he found himself facing the world like a porcupine without its needles.

Her touch was gentle and stimulating and awoke feelings inside of him that had lain dormant since he'd last felt Angela's body against his. They were strong feelings created by chemistry somewhere inside his brain, and they drowned out their adversarial counterparts that told him to get out of there before it was too late. But, it already was too late.

When her hands slid free from his body he reached for them and took one of them in his own. The gesture caught her by surprise and caused her heart to skip a beat.

"You have no idea how great that felt," he said, keeping his grip on her hand and speaking with a solemnity she'd never heard from him before.

"I'm glad," she said smiling.

He returned the smile, and, for a long moment, they stared into each other's eyes without speaking before he let go and she walked away.

Sheila, having witnessed the entire episode, intercepted Dana and pulled her into the employee break room just off the kitchen area.

"My God, girl, what was that all about?" Sheila asked.

"I'm not sure," Dana answered, and she wasn't. All of Evan's flirtations up to then were innocent and unassertive, and she'd become comfortable with their temperate playfulness. But when he took her hand the innocence was gone. What she noticed in his eyes and felt in his touch was more than schoolyard flirtation.

"Well, you better get right back out there and talk to that man so you can find out," Sheila said in a demanding tone.

"What am I suppose to say to him?" she asked.

"Lord almighty, woman! You act like you're a virgin or something. You're off tomorrow, ain't ya? So ask him to come to your house for dinner. Hell, all the man ever eats is this diner food. Cook him something nice and let nature take its course," Sheila said with the giddiness of girl after her first kiss.

"Alright, just give me a minute," Dana said. She wanted to check her makeup and get a drink of water. She'd been busy all morning and hadn't had her break. But that was just an excuse—she was nervous. She hadn't wanted to attract a man's attention as much as she wanted Evan's in a long time, and now that she had, she didn't want to blow it by acting too eager.

Sheila, acting like a mother, pushed and pulled on small wisps of Dana's hair that were out of place. She unbuttoned the top button of her uniform and folded back the pleats, exposing Dana's cleavage.

"I'm not a damn hooker," Dana said, stopping Sheila from unbuttoning her shirt any further.

After a trip to the ladies' room, where she freshened her lipstick, Dana went back to the counter and refilled Evan's coffee cup.

She wasn't overly forward or bashfully shy. She was an experienced woman with several relationships behind her, as well as a single mother with the responsibilities of raising a daughter. She'd been involved with enough men to know they all seem great at first, and nine out of ten later turn out to be something quite a bit less. And, although she was ninety percent sure Evan was a decent man, she'd been burned enough times to remind herself to be careful. So she made a little small talk and then asked Evan to her place, and, as she expected, judging by what had passed between them earlier, he agreed.

Fifteen minutes after accepting an invitation for dinner and possibly dessert, Evan left The Blind Minnow. The double glass doors closed behind him and the sunlight hit his body and warmed his skin. A westerly breeze lifted his hair and tossed it around as he walked along the docks. His expression was as blank as a freshly cleaned chalkboard, and his memory was free of what it had held only an hour before. The call from Angela, and the dream, and even *The Secret* were no longer on his mind. They were stored away in that elusive spot where such things go when they become too much to handle.

CHAPTER TWENTY-ONE

The fourth session with Dr. Sandborn ended with a suggestion to Angela to take Jeremy to Emily's grave and allow him a few minutes of private time with his sister. Since her death he had only visited her on three occasions, and always in the company of his mother, who held his hand and stood with him the entire time. The doctor thought it would be a good idea to take along something he and his sister used to share, like a game, a stuffed animal or a coloring book.

The following day Angela left work early to pick him up from Eve's house. Eve was in one of her moods—or personalities, as Evan used to call her sudden shifts in character—when Angela arrived. There was no friendly greeting or offer of an iced tea. There wasn't even an inquiry about Angela's day before Eve buried her long thin fingers into Angela's arm and guided her to the kitchen. Such action on Eve's part was usually the result of some juicy information she had to share, like this friend's divorce or that friend's affair. So Angela was surprised when her sister cornered her and asked why Jeremy had been seeing a shrink, and why she wasn't told.

It wasn't a part of Angela's character to lose her cool, at least not on the outside. She was one of those people you sometimes meet who seem to be in complete control of their emotions, and, regardless of the circumstances managed to come up with an appropriate, and civilized, response to a situation. Only Angela had a weakness, one shared by most people, regardless of their character: her children. She had already lost her daughter and was trying to save her son, and at the time nothing was more important in her life than Jeremy.

Angela envisioned what had taken place in the hour before she arrived. Eve, picking up on an innocent comment of Jeremy's about his visits to a doctor, ascertained through subtle interrogation that he was seeing a psychiatrist. Then, annoyed that she hadn't been informed of this, probably pressed him for every detail until she heard Angela pull into the driveway, at which point she sent him upstairs and waited by the front door to give Angela a piece of her mind. The only decent thing she did was to drag Angela out of earshot of the children before demanding an explanation.

"I'm very hurt that you didn't tell me, Angie. I'm his aunt and I take care of him almost every day, and I should know about his medical condition in the event something happens to him. If he's having mental problems, then I…" Eve said while still holding on to Angela's arm.

Angela listened to the words until Eve reached the part about mental problems, then something snapped. Had it been said in another way Angela might have pacified her with a few minor details and politely requested that she refrain from talking to him about the sessions. But Eve hit the wrong button on Angela's keyboard and saw a side of Angela she had rarely seen before.

"What gives you the right to talk to me like this? Damn it, Eve, do you have any idea what I've been through in the past two years? Or what Jeremy has been through?" Angela said while pulling her sister's hand free from her arm.

Eve's eyes widened and her mouth sank in, and before she could think of a response Angela continued.

"If you must know, then I'll tell you. He's been having some problems dealing with everything that has happened in his life. So I took him to a psychiatrist, Eve, someone who talks to him and helps him deal with the issues. He's not having *mental problems*, as you put it. He's having emotional problems. Because he's a little boy who misses his father and his sister, and he doesn't understand why they're not here anymore. I hope that's something you never have to explain to one of your children, because it will tear you apart inside," Angela said, stopping momentarily to take a breath, and to hold back tears. She wasn't going to give Eve the satisfaction of seeing her cry.

"I appreciate everything you do for me, Eve, God knows I do. But you have no right asking a little boy about things like this, and you have no right telling your husband or your friends about it either, that is if you haven't already. The last thing he needs is other people making him feel different," Angela said.

She had already said more than her reasonable side told her she should. After all, Eve was helping her out by picking Jeremy up from school and watching him until she got off work. But Angela was paying an emotional price for Eve's generosity. She had spent a year listening to Eve's and Wade's comments regarding the situation with Evan. Hardly a day would go by without Eve saying that everything was Evan's fault and Angela should just divorce him and get on with her life. Then she would tell Angela she never really liked Evan, she only pretended to so she didn't hurt her feelings.

All along Angela held her tongue, confidently reminding herself of the jealous way Eve acted when she and Evan were first married. It was just about the time Eve suspected her husband was having an affair, the first of many, and she began making up stories about Evan flirting with her. She said he would comment on her clothes and how nice they fit her body, and that he would make little gestures when Angela wasn't looking, like winking and smiling in provocative ways.

Angela knew better than to believe her. They'd grown up together, so Angela was used to Eve's jealous ways. She knew her sister had some issues, and she felt more sorry for her than angry at her for the things she'd said. It just became a big joke between Angela and Evan.

It wasn't the first time Eve had made such accusations of a man Angela dated, but Evan made her especially jealous. He would send flowers for no particular reason, buy little love gifts, and make up awful poems that Angela just loved. He would call her two or three times a day just to hear her voice and tell her how much he missed her. Sometimes out of the blue he would surprise Angela with little weekend getaways to the Finger Lakes region where they would stay at a bed and breakfast and spend the weekend visiting vineyards during the day and making love at night.

"And I'll tell you another thing, Eve. I don't like the way you and Wade are always bad mouthing Evan. For all I know you talk like that in front of Jeremy, which would explain why he's been having such a hard time lately. He doesn't need to hear that kind of stuff about his father, regardless of how long he's been gone."

"I…" Eve started, but barely spit out the syllable before Angela cut her off.

"We have to get going. I'm taking my son to visit his sister," Angela said, ending it there.

Angela hadn't intended to come to Evan's defense. The words just rolled out along with the others. She felt odd defending a man who left his family a year ago and had not been home since. But whatever Evan's shortcomings were, they didn't warrant the constant bashing by Eve, and they certainly didn't warrant as much as one cross word from Wade, the asshole of all assholes.

Eve was speechless, and Angela took advantage of the silence to gather up Jeremy's things and get him loaded into the car. She shut the front door using a bit more muscle than usual, and left without saying goodbye. It took her a few minutes to calm down, and, when she finally did, a few blocks away from Eve's house, she talked to Jeremy about visiting Emily. She spoke softly and compassionately, and told him she wanted to give him some time alone with her, the way they used to have when they cuddled up and watched cartoons on Saturday mornings. She said Emily would like it, and that God would let her know he was there.

Jeremy sat in the back seat and listened, ignoring his toys and coloring books, and tried in his innocent way to understand what she was saying. He didn't want to be alone in a cemetery with a bunch of dead people he didn't know, and he told Angela that. He wanted her to be there with him and hold his hand like she always did. She said she would, and that she would only take a few steps away so he could talk to his sister in private if he asked her to. That made him feel better and then he colored a picture that he said was for Emily.

On the way they stopped at a flower shop near the cemetery and bought a beautiful arrangement of carnations and daisy poms in a brightly colored wicker basket. Jeremy picked it out, saying it matched the flowers on Emily's bedspread and that it would remind her of her bedroom at home. The young girl behind the counter almost cried when he told her it was for his big sister, who was in the cemetery down the road. Jeremy reminded her of her own little brother, so she gave him a kiss on the cheek and told him his sister would love the flowers. It brought a smile to his face.

When they arrived Jeremy carried the flowers, and Angela a bag that she had packed the night before. In the bag were several items Jeremy and Emily used to share—a set of plastic walkie-talkies, a Frisbee, a pack of Mother Goose playing cards and a Winnie the Pooh hat that Emily outgrew and gave to her little brother only days before her death. When they reached Emily's headstone Jeremy set the flowers on the ground and immediately took his mother's hand. Angela gave him a hug, knelt down beside him, and together they talked to Emily.

"Hi, sweetheart. We brought you some flowers. Jeremy chose them especially for you," she said, smiling at the headstone with a tiny porcelain angel in each upper corner. She removed a basket of dried up daisies she had brought on a previous visit so Jeremy could place his in the spot. "We miss you very much, my little girl. But we know God is taking good care of you in heaven," she said, fighting back tears for Jeremy's sake.

Emily rested in a peaceful and quiet spot in a corner of the cemetery away from the noise of the road. It was in sunlight most of the day, with oaks and elms providing shade in the early mornings and late afternoons. A slight breeze would sometimes come over a small hill and carry butterflies over her grave, and it wasn't uncommon to see a deer grazing in the early evenings along the tree line. It was a place Emily would have picked to place someone she loved, and a place she would have visited often to say hello.

Angela went from kneeling to sitting, and pulled Jeremy onto her lap. She wrapped her arms around him, kissed the top of his head and told him she loved him. Then she talked some more to Emily. She told her about her Nanny and Poppy, and about her friends in the neighborhood and about Jeremy's first grade class. Then she reached in the bag and pulled out a children's book and read her a story. After about thirty minutes she decided to give Jeremy some private time. She stroked his head and told him she thought Emily would like to be with her brother alone for a few minutes. His expression tightened as he looked around at the many different stones belonging to all the other people in heaven.

"I'll be right over there," she said, pointing to a small tree only fifteen feet away. "You'll be able to see me, honey, I promise," she said, waiting for his approval.

He looked at the tree and then at Angela. Then he smiled and said, "OK."

She stood up and his eyes followed her. She looked down at him and smiled, and told him to show Emily what was in the bag. He opened it, pulled out the hat and put it on. Then he grabbed the Frisbee and placed it next to his flowers. Angela stepped back and waited for him to grab the walkie-talkies and the deck of cards before slowly moving to the tree. Jeremy watched her until she reached the tree and sat down. Then, feeling comfortable with where his mother was, he turned his attention to Emily.

He sat for several minutes and fiddled with the cards and the Frisbee without saying a word. Angela watched him and her heart ached as she thought about what might have been, and she started to cry as she imagined what was going through his innocent mind. For a long time he didn't look up, he just stared at the toys and arbitrarily manipulated them as his brain thought about what little boys' brains think about. Then, when he was ready, he spoke, and Angela turned away to give him privacy.

"Hi, Emmy," he started, looking at Angela to make sure she couldn't hear. "I miss you a lot. I'm in first grade now, and I got Mrs. Baxter. She's not mean like some kids said. She brings us cookies on Friday if we're good. And she lets us have free time twice a day."

Despite being fifteen feet away Angela could hear, and tears ran down her face as his gentle voice broke the silence. He paused for a moment and looked at Angela, and when he was sure she wasn't going anywhere, he continued.

"Mom bought me a new bike for my birthday. It's the blue one from Wal-Mart with six gears and big boy brakes on the handlebars. And I got a cake with blue icing, too. I had a party, and Mom invited your best friend Marsha. She was the only girl there, and it was OK because she was your best friend." He stopped to think, and his head turned to look around the cemetery. Angela didn't move, she sat still and waited for him to come over to her. But he didn't. He continued talking.

"You have the bestest spot in here. And I like all the trees and stuff. It's like that place that Mom and Dad took us to ride our bikes." He stopped again and stared at the writing on the marble stone in front of him. He didn't know what most of it meant, but he recognized her name. He reached out and put his index finger on the first letter and pushed it around in the lines. Then he went to the next letter and did the same thing, until he'd traced her entire name. Then he reached down and picked up the Frisbee.

"Mom brought some things you liked. I 'member when we played with the Fizbee in the back yard. You showed me how to throw it so it would fly." He stopped again and looked at the ground, and the tears came. He pushed his little hand into the grass and spoke as he cried. "I miss you so much, Emmy. I wish God didn't take you away. Mommy says God takes the people he loves the most and misses the most. But I miss you, too. I asked him to send you back. But Mommy says he doesn't send people back when he takes them. He keeps them and loves them forever."

Angela heard him and decided it was time to go to him and help him understand. She rose and walked across the grass, but when he saw her he yelled, "Not yet, Mommy." She stopped and looked in his crying eyes. Her maternal instincts called to her to scoop him up and dry his tears, but something else told her to leave him alone. So she wiped her eyes, smiled at him and returned to the tree.

"I think about you all the time. And me and Mommy pray for you every night and ask God to say hi to you. And I ask him to tell ya I love ya. And sometimes Mommy cries, and I cry too sometimes." He stopped and traced her name again.

"Daddy's been gone a long time and Mommy don't talk about him a lot no more. I thought he was going to heaven with you, but Mommy says he's in Fourida. I think that's on the other side of the world near China. He used to call us sometimes, but not no more." He hung his head for a moment and some more tears rolled from his eyes. Then he picked up the walkie-talkies and turned them on. A hollow sounding screech came from them. Then he spoke into one and his crackling voice came from the other.

"I can leave one here, Emmy, and talk to you tonight from home so that you're not lonely. And I can talk to you every day when I get home from school. And maybe Mommy will let Marsha come over and talk to you, too. And if Daddy calls I will put the phone on it and he can say hi," he said, a little upbeat from a few minutes earlier. Then his eyes dropped to the ground again, before he spoke of the accident.

"I'm sorry about how you fell down. And I'm sorry I didn't help you, Emmy. I don't member a lot about it. But I heard Mommy and Daddy talk about it sometimes, before Daddy left. And I'm sorry Daddy was with me when you fell. Maybe if he was with you God would have left you here."

A flood of tears escaped Angela's eyes as she listened, and her mind raced back to some of the hurtful things she and Evan said to each other on those final days before he left. She couldn't remember where Jeremy was when they argued. But certainly, she thought, they wouldn't have spoken so he could hear. But maybe they did. Maybe he heard Evan describe the accident, how he lost sight of Emily because he was following Jeremy. Or maybe he heard Angela call Evan whatever name she called him when he was lying around like a bum. She couldn't recall everything that was said, so much of it was out of anger and sorrow.

She took deep breaths to calm herself down and wiped her eyes dry. She wasn't supposed to have heard what he said. It was his time alone with Emily and she was afraid she would undermine Dr. Sandborn's strategy by interfering. She sat as still as she could and struggled to contain her emotions.

After a long silence Jeremy spoke again. "Mommy says you're one of God's angels now, and that you're with us all the time. I like that, Emmy. I hope I can be an angel when I go to heaven, too. We can be angels together. And we can fly around the world like the Powder Puff Girls. But I would be a Powder Puff Boy, if they have that. And..." he continued for several minutes talking about angels and then toys and what he was going to be for Halloween.

Angela listened and smiled. She was proud of Jeremy for being so brave and caring, and she was glad she left him alone to be with his sister. In a way he reminded her of Evan. The Evan from a few years before, who was loving, compassionate and strong. The Evan that wasn't afraid to face the things that scared him. She sat for a few more minutes until he walked to her and put his hand on her head.

"I'm done, Mommy," he said.

"That's good, honey. I'm proud of you, and I know Emmy is happy you talked to her," she said.

Together they gathered up the toys, leaving one walkie-talkie next to the flowers. Angela took a piece of paper and placed it over Emily's name and rubbed a crayon over the paper. The letters transferred to it and Jeremy's eyes lit up like it was magic.

"Whenever you miss her you can look at this and she will be a little bit closer to you," she said smiling at her son.

He took the piece of paper and traced the letters with his finger, then smiled up at her. "Thanks, Mommy," he said.

Before bed that night Jeremy said his prayers as usual. When he was finished he turned on his walkie-talkie and pushed the button.

"Good night, Emmy. I love you."

CHAPTER TWENTY-TWO

Evan fired up Old Blue, a fourteen-year-old pickup truck that belonged to the marina, and headed towards Dana's place wearing new shorts and a new shirt he purchased an hour before when he couldn't find a clean outfit on the floor of his destroyed apartment. He hung the clothes in a steamy shower for fifteen minutes in a halfhearted attempt at loosening the profound creases that accompany new clothing. It did little to hide the fact that they were wrapped in plastic on a shelf in J.C. Penney only hours before.

He pulled the truck onto the road and switched from first to second gear then second to fourth, skipping third altogether. Third gave up the ghost a year before and was never repaired since the value of the thing was substantially less than the cost of the repair. Plus, with three of its four gears still operational, it could get around town just fine.

Evan glanced at Dana's directions written on a napkin before shoving it in the ashtray and turning onto Highway 41 to take what he was sure would be a short cut. After a few miles he made a right, then after a few more miles a left, and then a right, and a left, and just when he thought he might be lost he came to Highway 41 again. He retrieved the directions and decided to follow them despite his belief there was a better way.

He pulled back onto the highway, and, over the rumble of the leaking exhaust, heard the sirens for the first time. He glanced in the cracked rearview mirror and saw the lights, a few miles away but approaching fast, and kept his speed for another minute or two before pulling over and yielding to two fire trucks and an ambulance that sped past him heading for what looked like a black tornado rising in the east.

When they passed he continued on, keeping an eye on the street signs for his next turn. He made a right on Sand Dollar, which put the smoke to his left. Then he made a left on Conch to Ringling to Dover, which put the smoke directly in front of him. He drove down Dover and heard the sirens grow louder and saw the smoke get blacker until he was a block away and close enough to hear the screams.

The building was seven stories high and built during an era when fire sprinklers had about as much of a chance of being installed as satellite television. So when the building went up in flames it went up fast, leaving several families trapped above the fire with no way down except the fire escapes, which were only on the south side of the building. The northern end of the block-long apartment house was engulfed up to the fifth floor. Above the fire, on the sixth and seventh floors, were several people screaming for help in panicked harmony. Among those pleading to be saved was a mother holding her two young children in her arms.

Four fire trucks were directing massive streams of water at the upper floors in an attempt to clear a path for a ladder truck as several teams of firefighters entered the south end of the building.

Evan parked Old Blue on the sidewalk and ran towards the building. The scene was complete chaos as people flooded out of windows and doors, screaming and crying. A man on fire leapt from a window on the sixth floor and landed on a car and was immediately extinguished by a stream of water that knocked him to the ground so violently that it most certainly killed him if he wasn't already dead from the fall.

Once the ladder truck got into position the hydraulic pumps came to life and lifted the boom into the air. Its massive steel ladder floated gracefully over cars and trees and screaming people until it came to the spot where the four tubes of water were aimed. The fireman at the controls pulled a lever and the boom lifted, then another, and it telescoped out towards the sixth floor. Waiting anxiously for it to come to rest were two firemen dressed in full battle gear. It stretched closer and closer like a giant's life-saving arm. When it came within ten feet of the building a large pop rang from the truck and a thick red fluid ran like blood from a broken hose onto the ground. The ladder fell and crashed into the wall just below the fifth floor. The man at the controls pushed buttons and pulled levers in a frantic attempt to revive it, but nothing happened. The fluid was hydraulic, and without it the large steel structure was dead.

The two firemen climbed on the truck and raced up the ladder to the building. They smashed a fifth floor window with an axe, which released an explosion of smoke and flames that nearly knocked them to the ground. Shards of glass and broken bits of wood rained down on the people below. One of the pump trucks directed its stream into the window, and, within a minute, the flames disappeared. Then the two firemen climbed inside and vanished in a blanket of thick smoke.

Evan stood watching in horror as people continued to pour from the building coughing and wheezing. Several came out and collapsed on the ground while others were carried out in the arms of firemen or other escaping neighbors. One half-dressed woman walked calmly from the building under her own power. Most of her hair had been singed off and she had burns over a large portion of her body. She managed to stumble to a nearby ambulance and climb in the back before collapsing onto a stretcher inside.

The woman with the children continued to scream from a window on the sixth floor, seemingly unaware that fire was crawling up on her from behind. Two men on the ground below stretched a blanket between them and were yelling for her to drop the kids from the window as blasts of high pressure water ran back and forth across the front of the building periodically hitting her and knocking her off balance.

The two firemen who had climbed the ladder and entered through the fifth floor window had located the stairwell leading to the sixth floor. Fire rushed up both sides with the intensity of a blast furnace as one of them instinctively ran up the stairs in an attempt to reach the woman and her babies. But, halfway up, the stairway collapsed and fell five floors, carrying him with it to certain death. His partner, who witnessed the event, pulled away and ran for the window. When he reached it he literally jumped through it and landed face first on the ladder then stumbled down the long metal structure as quickly as he could. When he hit the ground he pulled off his respirator and yelled for the pumpers to aim their guns at the bottom floor where his buddy landed.

At that moment Evan jumped on the truck and took off up the ladder toward the building. He had no gear, no respirator, no coat, no boots and no chance, but he ran all the same toward the window. When he reached it he climbed inside and disappeared in the blackness. Another fireman, one who seconds before exited the front door of the building carrying an elderly man, saw Evan enter through the window and followed.

Richard Stocks was twenty-eight years old and in his fifth year as a fireman, and it was the first time he ever followed a man dressed in shorts and a polo shirt into the fires of hell. He was only through the window for an instant when a bell started ringing on his chest warning him that his tank had only minutes of breathable air remaining. He quickly got to his feet and started feeling his way in the darkness, yelling as loud as he could for the lunatic in the shorts.

The atmosphere was hot and dark. Wooden beams fell as the fire ripped them from the walls and ceilings. Rushing sheets of flames rolled out of nowhere with the ferocity of ocean waves in a hurricane and when they hit they bit strong and hot. The thick smoke made seeing virtually impossible and the lack of oxygen was certainly sudden death for anyone without an air tank.

The fireman took step after slow step, expecting to stumble upon the burned and dead remains of the man he had chased into the inferno. He went slowly and felt carefully with his feet, certain on each successive step he would run into the body. A minor explosion startled him, but only briefly. He remembered that canned goods and perfume bottles and cleaning supplies become small bombs when heated to several hundred degrees.

Another step and another and another. Nothing except heat and smoke and flames. His fire-resistant suit was simply that, resistant, and in the right environment it would most certainly burn. His mind told him that a few more steps would put him in such an environment and he might not be going home to his wife. But he kept going, slowly and carefully, curious to see just how far a suicidal guy dressed for a day at the beach could get in such conditions. He had no doubt the crazy bastard was dead, and if he wasn't he would surely wish he was. But he had to know for sure so he took another step.

Then, much like the opening at the end of a long dark tunnel on a bright day, the smoke cleared when he reached the missing stairwell. Standing at the bottom, a single step away from plummeting five floors to his death, was Evan, completely unharmed. It was as if he was standing inside an air-conditioned bubble. At the top of the missing stairwell was the woman who had been screaming out the sixth story window, in her arms were her babies. Between them was nothing except the massive hole that was created when the staircase collapsed.

Orange, red and yellow flames danced around them like burning rainbows as pieces of the ceilings and walls fell through the opening and disappeared. More loud popping sounds filled the air as Lysol cans, baked beans, or other previously benign products exploded like mortar rounds.

The fireman screamed. Unable to believe his eyes he took a step toward Evan with the intention of pulling him away and dragging him out of the building. As soon as he did the floor below him gave way and his right foot went through. He fell to the ground just as a ceiling joist broke free and crashed down upon his chest. It pinned him to the floor and lay on top of him, burning while the bell rang and reminded him of his dwindling air supply. He pushed on the six-by-eight wooden beam but it wouldn't budge. The bell rang and his breathing increased. He pushed and his breathing increased. He pushed harder and the bell slowed down. He pushed some more and the bell went quiet.

The only thing worse than hearing the bell come on when trapped in an oxygen-deficient environment is no longer hearing it at all. When it stops there's no air left in the tank. He took a final breath and pushed with his entire might and the beam still didn't budge. His head fell back to the floor and his eyes focused on Evan, who had his arms stretched out towards a little girl who was floating above the missing stairwell. She reached out, and when their hands met Evan lifted from the floor and floated over the opening to the woman and her two babies. At that instant Richard Stocks passed out.

When Evan reached the window with the woman and her two children a ground level cheer broke out. Another fireman rushed up the ladder to help her down as Evan went back into the building. A few minutes later he returned to the window carrying Richard Stocks, and placed him in the arms of two other firemen who had looks of complete and total shock on their faces.

They rushed the unconscious fireman down to the ground and started CPR while Evan stood silently by, looking up at the building as it burned. His eyes never moved as the flames consumed the sixth and seventh floors. The thick black smoke poured from every window and door as the building began to crumble to the ground.

When Richard Stocks started breathing on his own, they rushed him to the hospital. When he was able to speak the first words out of his mouth were, "I saw an angel."

CHAPTER TWENTY-THREE

Deloris Carlisle, the woman Evan rescued, was an illiterate black woman who learned from her mother, who learned from hers, not to trust white folks, and for the most part she didn't. She mainly kept to herself and didn't do much interacting with anyone, regardless of color. She spent her days cleaning rooms at a nearby Holiday Inn, and her nights raising her babies in the landlord-ignored, one-bedroom apartment she called home.

On the night of the terrible fire, everything she owned went up in smoke. She watched and cried from the street as dozens of firemen poured tons of water on the tower of flames. People gathered in small circles to comfort each other and describe their personal accounts of the horror before them. But, for all she lost, she still had her babies: they were safe. For that she had the Lord to thank, as well as a little white girl who floated without wings.

When the final wall of the building fell, and it was clear there would be absolutely nothing to salvage in the smoldering pile that lay before her, she gracefully carried her two young ones seven blocks to a shelter so they could sleep. She tucked them in amongst drunks and prostitutes and all of society's other undesirables, then knelt down on her knees and prayed. She thanked Jesus for saving her and her two young ones, and asked forgiveness for her sins. Before she climbed into the small bed with her children, she looked around the room and added a footnote to her talk with heaven. "And Lord, please help these poor people."

Richard Stocks was rushed to the hospital and admitted with three broken ribs, a punctured lung, a cracked collarbone, and a sprained ankle. He arrived unconscious, but breathing on his own, thanks to the quick and decisive actions of the paramedics who performed CPR at the scene, and Evan who carried him out alive.

Once stable, he was transferred from the emergency room to a semi-private room where his pregnant wife came to see him. She sat down next to the bed and laid her face against his hand, which woke him up. He turned a heavy head and spoke slowly against the pull of the painkillers that were given to him.

"I saw an angel," he whispered.

She smiled at him, then reached over and kissed his forehead. "Thank God you're alive. The Chief called me and told me you were hurt. And I..." She started to cry. "I'm just so happy you're OK."

He reached for her hand and gave it a weak squeeze, then managed a smile and an "I love you," which made her smile back. They had only been married a year and a half, and it had been her worst fear that she'd get a call saying he died in a fire trying to save someone. But she married him knowing the risks and the sleepless nights his profession would cause her. She knew it was his dream to be a part of the department and vowed not to stand in his way. But that was before he was hurt, and before her unborn baby was nearly fatherless.

"I spoke to the doctor. He said they had to revive you, that you stopped breathing. You were almost dead." She picked up his hand and held it between hers as if she was praying. She lowered her head and kissed his fingers. "I want you to quit. It's not worth this. We're going to have this baby and if something happens to you I'll be alone and it won't have a father. I don't know what I'd do without you," she said with tears flowing again.

"I saw an angel. In the building," he whispered, louder than before but still comparatively shallow. The words came hard as the medication continued to drip into his blood from a bedside I.V. unit.

His young wife barely heard him. She was holding his hand and thinking about the three-month-old life inside of her. She wanted so badly for him to quit the fire department and take any job that would have him home safely each night. But, like most firemen or policemen, he was drawn by the danger and excitement, and the ability to help others. Anything else, like selling cars or hammering nails, just wasn't for him. He had wanted to be a fireman since he was a kid, when his elementary class took a field trip to a station house and he first got to wear the oversized coat and gigantic boots, hear the siren and feel the adrenaline.

She looked in his eyes. They were droopy, tired eyes attached to a battered body that needed rest. The doctor gave her five minutes, and, as much as she wanted to hold his hand all night, she was afraid her presence would prevent him from getting the sleep he needed.

"I better get going and let you sleep," she said, wiping tears from her cheeks.

"No. I need to tell you what I saw." His voice was still faint.

"Shhh. The doctor said you need your rest. I'll be back first thing in the morning. I'm going to stop by your parents' house and let them know you're going to be alright before they hear about this on the news." She bent over and kissed him, leaving a smudge of mascara under his right eye that made him look like a beaten up boxer with a shiner. When she saw it she smiled and gently wiped it away with her fingers.

"I'm so happy you're alright. I really don't know what I'd do if anything ever happened to you," she said, stopping before the tears started rolling again.

"I love you," she said as she gently released his hand and left the room. Before she reached the elevator he was asleep.

Evan left the scene just minutes before Deloris Carlisle did. With all the commotion nobody noticed him leave. He simply fired up Old Blue and headed in a direction away from the smoke, away from the marina, and away from Dana's place. Eerily reminiscent of the night he left Syracuse, he drove without knowing where he was headed.

When he didn't show up at Dana's place she called the bait shop and the diner to find out if anyone had seen him. No one at the diner had any idea where he was, but Candy recalled seeing him leave in the truck before dark. She was outside having a smoke when he came down the stairs dressed like a million bucks and smelling of cologne. She said he just hopped in Old Blue and took off. Dana wasn't familiar with Old Blue, but after a brief description from Candy she assumed it had broken down somewhere along the way.

Dana quickly covered a tray of lasagna that she had prepared earlier, and put it in the fridge. She left a note on her door and went in search of Evan. As soon as she stepped out of her apartment she heard the distant sound of sirens and saw the smoke from the burning apartment building. There was a mildly sweet charcoal odor in the air that could have easily been mistaken for a neighbor's barbecue grill, had the darkened sky not told a different story.

It took her a minute to recall exactly what route she had scribbled down for Evan. There were several paths from the marina to her apartment, and which one she drove depended on the day of the week and the time of day she traveled. She remembered sending him down Sand Dollar, which would have put him near the tower of smoke she noticed in the sky. More than likely, she thought, traffic was detoured and he got lost. That is, if Old Blue hadn't croaked along the way.

She drove slowly and kept an eye peeled for the truck, which she expected to see on the side of the road with the hood up. She backtracked the directions she gave him and came to the fire only minutes after Evan pulled away. Traffic was being directed by a police officer, but it wasn't being rerouted, making the possibility of Old Blue being down for the count more credible with each mile she drove. She continued on, hopeful that at any minute she would find him bent over the engine compartment, tinkering.

But the miles unfolded and before she knew it she was sitting in the marina parking lot staring up at his apartment. For a minute or two she second-guessed what she wrote on the napkin. She had scribbled it down fast and could have sent him another route, or made a mistake and had him driving in circles. But her phone number was on there as well, and surely he would have called. No, she wrote it down correctly. She was sure of that. She turned around and drove back, hopeful that she missed him on a side street somewhere.

When she arrived back at the apartment the note was still hanging, untouched, on her door. She went inside and checked her answering machine. Nothing. Then she noticed the time. He was more than an hour late, far too long to be merely lost. He had obviously changed his mind, she thought, and she wondered if her forwardness over the previous few months was to blame. She reflected on the many playful exchanges the two of them had shared, and the things they had said to each other. Most were in fun. Well, not entirely, she had to admit. She liked him and some of the things she remembered saying brought a slight feeling of embarrassment.

She reminded herself that it wasn't her mother's era, when a woman merely sat back and waited for the man to make the first move. Times being what they were, there was nothing wrong with a woman being a bit forward. But maybe, she thought, he was old-fashioned, and she was a bit too forward for his liking. But then why didn't he just turn down her invitation to dinner rather than stand her up? She was both upset and angry, and she wanted an answer.

Old Blue went along rather smoothly although she sometimes only fired on six or seven cylinders and was missing third gear. Evan drove mechanically, pushing the clutch and working the shifter to maneuver the old girl through back roads and two-lane highways along Florida's west coast.

The sun went down in his rearview mirror as he drove a dirt road that cut through a housing complex under construction. He pulled a metal rod—the knob had fallen off years ago—and a single headlight illuminated the road in front of him. The moon's glow cut through the branches of oak trees, pines and palms as the truck rolled along.

Evan's eyes remained fixed ahead, seeing only what was necessary to avoid a collision. He stopped when he had to, and went when he could, sometimes after a honk or two from a car behind.

For two hours it went that way. Turn after turn for no particular reason other than to drive and think. But his mind wasn't really working in the sense that people's minds do when they contemplate or calculate. It was working on a level quite foreign to most people. A level where everything we hold true as human beings is not only questioned, but, for the most part, dismissed because it doesn't matter. In such a state of mind all of the ordinary parts of life are imperceptible, and the extraordinary parts, the unseen parts, become crystal clear.

The chunks of his brain that controlled, understood and remembered since he was born were numb, like an arm or leg that falls asleep. A previously unused spot, somewhere in the frontal lobes or cerebellum, awoke for the first time. It was learning to use its natural abilities just as a child does when he takes his first steps. It was the part of the brain that usually only awakes during the final moments of life, when a person has one foot on this side and one foot somewhere else.

He was in that place where people sometimes go and don't return. The ones that stay here are easy to spot. Some lie in doorways or under bridges, or, if they're lucky, in hospitals. They sit and seemingly stare at nothing for hours at a time, pissing and shitting in their pants and mumbling streams of sounds that make no sense to the rest of us. They point irreverently and scream or grunt, and we shake our heads and thank God we are sane while we assume they are not.

But what many of them see is what Evan saw. It cannot be explained with the words we know. It cannot be shared with a friend or portrayed with a painting. It is mortal in a deeper sense than most human beings will ever understand, and it is all around us our entire lives. We live it and breathe it every microsecond of our existence, and if we would only close our eyes and look within, it would become crystal clear.

Evan saw it. He saw it in the building as he stood at the edge of the missing staircase. At first it frightened him so badly his heart actually stopped. Then it melted like an ice sculpture in the sun, liquefied for lack of a better explanation. It became softer and brighter until it enveloped him. Then it blended. It's the only way it can be described. It blended into everything like chocolate does when mixed with milk, and, in much the same way, it gave everything a different color.

It was that power, or presence, or energy, or whatever you want to call it, that Evan was on the verge of understanding as he pushed the gas and hit the brake and turned the wheel and drove to nowhere. But don't mistake it for the vision of Emily that touched him and carried him and helped him save those people. No, her appearance is not what put him in the trance, or state of mind, that he was in. She was merely part of it, like the chocolate in the milk. What he saw was the glass and all.

What he was struggling to understand was whole and complete, and included everyone and everything. It is the dirt from which all things grow and the air that all living creatures breathe. It is life, death, sadness, joy, strawberries, and children and everything else you can think of and many things you cannot. It is what some people discount as chance or explain with science, and what others hope is real and fear is not, and eventually become part of when they leave this world. When Evan was in that building he saw it in a way most people never will.

He drove until it all aligned like a special arrangement of stars that occurs every thousand years. When it was clear, he pulled over into the sandy lot of an abandoned hardware store and stepped from the truck. He sat on the ground, leaned back against a tire, pulled his knees to his chest, and broke out into loud, choking sobs.

CHAPTER TWENTY-FOUR

WRTB out of Orlando carried the story of the fire on their eleven p.m. broadcast. They purchased an amateur recording of the dramatic footage from a tenant who filmed the entire event on his camcorder, including Evan's heroic rescue of Deloris Carlisle and her two children, and the rescue of the injured fireman.

The bouncy, and sometimes out of focus, recording would have had little value to them had it not captured Deloris Carlisle's desperate plea for salvation, and her and her children's subsequent rescue by an ordinary bystander after the fire department failed to get her out. To add a little more sugar to the frosting it also captured the rescue of the fireman who ran in after Evan and succumbed to the heat and smoke and had to be rescued himself.

One of the station's top reporters, the locally famous Tim Barnes, was assigned the task of finding the hero and the people he rescued, and getting the exclusive rights to their stories. Before the broadcast aired he was able to obtain the names of everyone involved except Evan, who nobody at the scene knew or ever saw before the fire. A few people vaguely remembered a truck that pulled away during the blaze, but they couldn't agree on the make or even the color, and none of them took notice of the license plate.

After exhausting his leads at the scene Mr. Barnes decided to locate Deloris Carlisle and get her story, which he hoped would shed some light on the whereabouts of her rescuer. He also wanted to talk to Richard Stocks, but was informed by a nurse, with little patience for reporters, that he was strictly off-limits to everyone except immediate family until further orders from his doctor. That, of course, was a lie, but one that had worked in the past to keep bloodthirsty lawyers away from auto accident patients, so the nurse figured it would work to keep a parasitic reporter away from an injured fireman. She gave it a shot with Tim Barnes, who snickered and whined but complied all the same.

His search for Deloris lasted a little over an hour. It wasn't the first time Mr. Barnes had to locate a person in her position, and there were only a handful of possible places she could have gone. Using a haphazard system of elimination he managed to find her at the third place he checked, Saint Michael's shelter in downtown Sarasota. A twenty-dollar bill slipped to the guy who answered the door got him inside, and since she was the only black woman in a bed with two children he located her in quick order.

"Mrs. Carlisle. Mrs. Carlisle," Mr. Barnes whispered as he gently shook her shoulder and aimed a small penlight at her face.

"Mrs. Carlisle," he repeated a little louder when she failed to respond.

"Shut the hell up!" a drunken voice screamed from somewhere amongst the sea of beds that faded into the darkness.

The tired woman slowly opened her eyes and focused them sharply on the man who pulled her from the only place where she knew complete peace.

"Mrs. Carlisle, I'm very sorry to wake you, but I need some information about the fire," the thin-faced Mr. Barnes whispered.

"Are you the police?" she asked impulsively, afraid the authorities might come for her children now that they had no home.

"No, ma'am, I'm a reporter for Channel Twelve News. Tim Barnes, WRTB."

Deloris didn't watch the news or read the papers, making her oblivious to his notoriety as a community icon of sorts.

"I don't know anything, Mr. Barnes. All I remember…"

"For crying out loud, can you shut up? People are trying to sleep!" It was the same faceless voice as before, only louder and angrier. Mr. Barnes bent over and whispered for her to follow him outside. Deloris carefully untangled her arms from around her children and stood. She looked down at them, then at the door, with obvious concern for leaving them behind.

"We won't be long. They'll be OK," Mr. Barnes said in a tone that could have convinced his own mother of his concern.

The small penlight led the way to the door, which opened with a rusty squeak. Deloris stepped out last and left a foot in the door so she could watch her babies.

"Mr…." she paused having forgotten his name.

"Barnes. Tim Barnes from Channel Twelve," he said, amazed she still didn't recognize him despite the increased lighting.

"Mr. Barnes, all's I know is that the place started burning and I had to get my babies out."

"Yes, ma'am. But the man who helped you get out, do you remember him?"

"Oh, yes, sir, I certainly do. I'll never forget him, he saved my babies," she said with a sparkle in her eye that could have been the beginnings of a tear.

"How did he save them? What I mean is, one fireman tried and fell to his death and the other gave up. How did this man manage to do what they couldn't?"

Deloris paused for a moment before answering, and when Tim saw the pause he knew what to do. He pulled a hundred dollar bill from his wallet and held it out, and Deloris took it. She took it because everything she owned was gone and she had two babies who would be hungry in the morning. But what she'd witnessed was a miracle, and, although she was poor and uneducated and all but forgotten about by the likes of Mr. Barnes and his upper-class society, she knew what had happened. It took her a moment to decide whether or not she wanted to share it with him.

Her life had been a constant struggle from the very moment she entered the world some thirty years before. She grew up poor, poorer than most white folks could ever imagine. The only parent she ever knew was her mother, who passed down to her what she had learned from her mother. In those lessons that were given over an ironing board or hot stove or mop bucket, she learned that most folks in the world would sell their souls to the devil for enough money. She learned there were things in life that a person had to hold onto at all costs, and Deloris remembered those lessons and decided her miracle was not for sale.

"I don't rightly remember the details. All I know is that we're alive and for that I have God to thank," she said, after deciding that Mr. Barnes, and others like him, would never believe the whole truth. It wasn't in their hearts. That she knew from what she'd witnessed over her lifetime, and from what she learned from her mother, God rest her soul.

"Did he tell you his name?"

"No, sir, he didn't. He just got us out of that building and then, well, he disappeared," she said, before pushing her face into the small opening to check on her little ones.

"Did you see him leave? Did you see where he went?"

"No, sir. I wasn't paying much attention to him. I was watching my building burn, Mr. Banes, just watching it burn to the ground with everything I owned," she said.

"Barnes," he said slowly to the back of her head as she turned to check the kids again.

"I need to get back to my babies," she said as she stuck out her hand to shake his. "I'm sorry I couldn't help ya more, Mr. Banes. And I thank you for the money."

"Yes, ma'am," he said, not bothering to correct his name.

At about the same time Deloris was pulled from her sleep, Evan was settling down behind the desk in the bait shop office. He obtained a list of marinas from a maritime book under the counter and began calling each one in search of *The Secret*. He turned the grimy dial of the fish phone hundreds of times via the flickering light of a battery-powered lantern. Between calls he sipped coffee and lined out those numbers to which he connected.

By early morning he had reached roughly half of the possible docking places between Nokomis and the Sullivans' two assumed destinations, Sanibel Island and Key West. The marinas he managed to contact were large, twenty-four-hour operations with around-the-clock staff, places Art would more than likely pull into for fuel or supplies, but no one Evan spoke with remembered seeing the sailboat or its captain.

Evan thought about the possibility that Sheila was wrong. She could have missed part of the conversation or simply misheard what was said. Or Art and Mary could have just as easily have changed plans at the last minute and headed elsewhere. But they did tell Derek they'd be back in three or four days, which in itself limited the possibilities of where they might have gone. If Derek were right *The Secret* would already be on her way back to Nokomis.

He sat for several minutes with his elbows on the table and his head rested in the palms of his hands. His mind tossed ideas back and forth as his body fought to stay awake. What he held as truth had been turned over in the previous hours, and he viewed everything around him in a different light. All the pieces of the puzzle were in front of him and they were coming together, but he needed Art, the one person in the world he was sure could fit the last of them into place.

If he just had the patience to wait they'd be back within a day, but there was a boiling inside that made it absolutely imperative he contact Art and tell him about the experience. Speaking about it, especially to Art, would somehow serve as a catalyst to making it real, the miracle it was. His friend was the only one who would believe him and understand what he was saying.

After running a line through the last number on the list Evan locked up the shop and boarded *The Shark Bite*. He had topped her off with fuel, fresh water, and a few edibles taken from the bait shop. He steered her out of the channel and into the Gulf. Ignoring the no-wake zones he opened the throttle and brought the two throaty engines to maximum power. Within seconds she was cutting through mild chops in the Gulf and heading south at forty knots. He was in such a deep state of concentration he passed within fifty feet of Bill Baxter, who was fumbling with his crab traps, and didn't even see him.

The sun was just breaking the horizon, which lit the tips of the waves like candles on a giant birthday cake. The water glistened as seagulls dove at the shallows for their morning meals. They crashed into the darkened water and came up with shiners, pinfish and scraps of seaweed. Several porpoise swam alongside the boat and played in its wake, and a school of rays floated in graceful contentment along the shore.

Evan wasn't paying attention to the action around him. Art had often mentioned he felt most comfortable sailing close to land, no more than twelve to fourteen miles out if he could help it. Evan figured he'd stack the odds of finding him by doing the same and scanning for white triangles in the distance.

A breeze blew cool and damp, not unlike many he'd felt in the air over the past twelve months. It chilled him a little and made him take notice of the weather. The sky held small groups of clouds that appeared unthreatening against the backdrop of the baby blue Florida coastline. For good measure he reached over and turned the knob of the ship-to-shore radio to hear a weather report. A forty percent chance of scattered thunderstorms with winds out of the east and waves three to four feet were expected in the late afternoon. It wasn't anything that worried him, considering how close he was to land and how long he expected to be gone. With a little luck he hoped to contact *The Secret* within the hour and be back at the marina by early afternoon at the latest.

Evan scanned the cluster of gauges on the instrument panel in front of him and noticed nothing out of the ordinary. Both fuel tanks showed full, all engine temperatures were good, and the bilge showed dry. The tachometer had the engines running well under their red line revolutions and they sounded solid and strong. Once he was comfortable with the state of the boat and its heading, he grabbed the radio's handset and began surfing the channels in an attempt to raise *The Secret*.

"This is *The Shark Bite* calling *The Secret*. Do you have a copy? Over," Evan said into the microphone hoping to hear Art's cheerfully surprised voice respond. He waited a minute, giving his old friend time to get to his radio and reply. After a long silence he repeated the call.

"This is *The Shark Bite* calling *The Secret*. Do you have a copy, over?"

Nothing. He changed channels and said the line again, and again until the knob stopped turning. There was no response of any sort on any channel. It was as if he were the only person alive in the world, and yet only an hour earlier he'd been at the desk dialing marinas up and down the coast. It is amazing, the feeling of isolation that comes with being even a few miles away from land.

He looked around and saw only water. The boat, so large at the marina, was now small and vulnerable. He knew a simple turn to the east could have him on shore in no time at all, and the sensation of being so alone and so far away made him think about Angela and Jeremy and the warmth and safety of their home in Syracuse. For the first time in a long time he wanted to go there, back to the place where he was a husband and father. Back to a life where he could tuck his son into bed and kiss him goodnight, and to where he could hold, comfort and make love to Angela.

But, as strong and refreshing as that urge was, there was another one equally as strong and calling out to him. It wasn't something he could define, but it was something he felt inside. He didn't question the instinct, he just followed it toward what he knew was a new beginning.

Two hours into the trip he tried the radio again, calling like the first time for *The Secret* to respond. The plastic knob snapped into place as he went from channel to channel, chanting his line of hope and waiting for a reply. There was still nothing except the roar of the engines and the whooshing of salty air as it flowed over the bow of the boat and onto his face.

He bent over and pulled a Coke from a paper bag that was being battered by the wind. He popped the top and swallowed a huge warm gulp. The fizzling tickled his throat on the way down and he coughed a bit before chugging the rest of it and tossing the empty bottle back in the sack. He looked again at his instruments. The only movement was in the fuel gauge, which came off the full mark enough to indicate it wasn't broken or stuck.

For another hour he stood behind the wheel and maintained his distance from land, all the while keeping the throttles full bore. The engines purred in unison, pushing the multi-ton vessel through the ocean almost effortlessly. Evan's knees automatically reacted to the rise and fall of the deck as he held the wheel and kept a sharp eye out for white sails. When he felt enough time and distance had elapsed since his last attempt to contact *The Secret*, he tried again.

"This is *The Shark Bite* calling *Sullivan's Secret*, over."

Channel one, then two, then three, then four. Just before he snapped the plastic knob to channel five he heard the reply.

"This is *Sullivan's Secret*. Is that you, Evan? Over."

Evan reached over and pulled back on the throttles, bringing the engines from an all out growl to a mere purr. The bow dropped instantly, bringing the large boat to an almost instantaneous halt. Evan responded excitedly to his friend's voice.

"Art, this is Evan. What's your location, over?" Evan said in a giddy voice.

Art replied with a set of GPS coordinates and an inquiry as to the reason for Evan's quest to find him. The concern in his voice was evident and Evan came back with an excited, "Don't worry, everything's fine. I just have to talk to you about something and couldn't wait for you to get back. I'll see you in a little bit."

He quickly punched *The Secret*'s position into his electronics. She was almost sixty miles due west, a little over ninety minutes at full speed. He hammered the throttles and the bow rose from the water, a massive wake rolled from her sides. Within seconds the vessel was at full bore heading due west into the Gulf of Mexico where Evan hoped to find *The Secret*.

CHAPTER TWENTY-FIVE

Derek opened the shop on time and quickly filled the buckets of some waiting fishermen. They were the weekend folks he didn't know by name, but had seen enough times to consider regulars. Unlike most of his weekly clientele, people who made a living from the ocean, these boys gave tips, and the tips got them a friendly joke or two and some questionable fishing advice that the smarter ones just ignored. But more importantly it got their buckets filled with big shrimp and lively pinfish. Derek reserved the floating pins and popcorn shrimp for those customers he remembered as being overly attached to their wallets.

It was sort of a special day for Derek, for several reasons. He'd been off the booze since Evan bailed him out of jail, and he had managed to be on time every single day since. But, more than that, it was a day of redemption. He managed, by saving his tips, to come up with the hundred bucks he owed Evan and he was anxious to give it to him to prove he wasn't lying when he promised to repay his debt. There hadn't been many people in the kid's life who would give him the time of day, much less bail him out of jail with their own money. When Evan did, it opened a door in the kid's life he didn't even know existed. For the first time he realized there were people in the world who were genuinely concerned about others, and not merely out for what they could get for themselves.

He watched the clock and waited for Evan to descend the staircase with all the anticipation of a child waiting for Santa. It was generally between eight o'clock and nine o'clock when Evan would wander in for his morning coffee, and that's when Derek planned on handing him the money. He thought about what to say, but everything sounded so stupid that he figured he'd just give him the cash and let him begin the conversation.

By nine o'clock Derek was pretty much camped out at the back window, where he could see the bottom half of the staircase leading to Evan's place. He kept his hand in his pocket wrapped tightly around the five twenty-dollar bills, anxious to pull them out when he saw his boss's shoes. Nine-thirty came and went, then nine-forty-five, then ten o'clock and still no sign of Evan. By ten-fifteen Derek had had enough and ran up the stairs to rattle his boss from what he assumed was another massive hangover.

He knocked on the door and waited, then knocked again and waited some more. When there was no answer he knocked a little louder, but stopped short of banging like Dickhead would have. He stood there confused for a few minutes, before remembering the date Evan had the night before. He heard about it from one of the mechanics, who in turn heard about it from someone Sheila had told. He assumed the date went well and that his boss was still in Dana's arms under the sheets in her bed.

When lunchtime rolled around Sheila sent Crystal, another of The Minnow's waitresses, with a box full of sandwiches and chips. Before she had a chance to hand them all out, Charlie had swallowed half of his along with some of the waxed paper it was wrapped in. Meanwhile Derek worked his moves on Crystal, a twenty-something birdbrain with giant tits and bright red lips. He told her a joke that went completely over her head, but she laughed all the same because she was as determined to get Derek in bed as he was to get her there.

As usual, Candy, who came in at eleven, stowed her sandwich in her cooler for later and worked while the others ate. She wouldn't have sat down among them even if she'd been there all day because she didn't like Charlie any more than anyone else did, and she had very little in common with Derek or the bimbo he was pursuing. She did find some entertainment value in watching her young male counterpart hunt his prey.

When the lunch hour was over, and before Crystal returned to the diner, Derek asked her if she'd heard from Dana. He hoped to find out when to expect Evan so he could get rid of the hundred bucks that was burning a hole in his pocket. Crystal looked a bit puzzled, not that she didn't normally, and said, "Of course I've heard from her, silly, she's at work."

Crystal went on to add that Dana was quite upset because Evan had stood her up and hadn't bothered to call to cancel the date. She said he was going to get an earful if he had the nerve to show up at The Minnow today. Candy, who was listening, added her two cents about seeing Evan leave and later getting the call from Dana who was trying to locate him. Charlie, who was still hungry and couldn't care less about any of it, immediately scooped up the extra sandwich when he heard Evan wouldn't be there to eat it.

When lunch was over Derek strolled outside to look for Old Blue. The truck wasn't in its usual spot, but it was there all the same, meaning Evan had returned at some point after Candy saw him leave. He ran into Bill Baxter who mentioned seeing *The Shark Bite* tear out into the Gulf at the wee hours of the morning. The old man said that whoever was behind the wheel should get an ass chewing for speeding in a no-wake zone. Then he took to complaining about some of his traps and his arthritis and something else that Derek simply ignored. He was too busy fitting the pieces together to pay any attention to the old man's bitching.

Within minutes he'd developed a few sketchy theories about why his boss would have passed up getting laid for going fishing, something Derek couldn't imagine any man doing for anything short of an all-expense paid trip to Hawaii, or Rio, or the Mexican Riviera. When he managed to convince himself that no normal red-blooded man would miss such an opportunity for the sake of a few slimy fish he headed back upstairs and knocked on Evan's door again.

He knew all too well the effect noise has on an alcohol-soaked brain and didn't want to impose undo torture on his boss, so he knocked softly and listened for any happenings on the other side of the door. The place was silent so he knocked a little louder, and a little louder, and was soon banging like Charlie would have done. But there was still no answer. That's when he tried the door and found it unlocked.

At first, in the dark, he couldn't see the smashed furniture or blood splatters on the walls, but when his pupils grew it all came into focus. The overturned bed, the broken furniture, the holes in the walls, and the blood. The blood was sprayed across the apartment as if it slid off the tip of a hunting knife, or machete. There really wasn't a whole lot of it, not nearly as much as it appeared at first. It was just spread around, fanned out from the G-forces that propelled it away from Evan's hand as he tossed the furniture. Derek froze as his brain crunched the numbers and when he hit the total button his cash register rang up a scenario straight out of a horror flick. He pictured Evan fighting for his life as some crazed lunatic chased him around the apartment in a murderous frenzy. Then he saw Evan get wrapped up in a sheet and carried to *The Shark Bite* and taken out into the Gulf and dumped overboard.

When he came running into The Blind Minnow, Sheila stopped him at the door and tried to make sense of what he was saying. He told her about the apartment and the blood and Old Blue being parked in the wrong spot, and how Bill Baxter saw *The Shark Bite* pull away. He said he knew something was wrong when Evan didn't come down for coffee and when he didn't answer his door. He wanted her to call the police and he kept mentioning the blood, Old Blue and *The Shark Bite* over and over like a broken record.

Sheila pulled him into the employee break room and shut the door, but not before Dana could get in there with them. He sat down on a chair and told them again about the blood and Old Blue, and when he started rambling, Sheila stopped him and told him to calm down. By that time Dana was spun up at hearing about blood and about the boat leaving so early in the morning. She was convinced, as Derek was, that something awful had happened to Evan. Before long Sheila was overwhelmed and decided to just call the police and let them handle it.

The officer that responded was careful not to jump to any conclusions. He checked the apartment and looked at Old Blue, and interviewed Derek, Dana, Candy, Charlie, and even Bill Baxter, who was more concerned with his traps than he was with Evan's disappearance. Finally, after two hours, he decided there was enough evidence to believe something out of the ordinary had taken place. He wasn't completely convinced Evan was the victim of foul play, but he didn't intend to take any chances.

An hour later there were investigators on the scene. Evan's apartment was roped off, as was Old Blue, and they carefully examined the evidence and re-interviewed all involved parties. Dana told them about the dinner date they had, and how he didn't show up and didn't call. She was so nervous her legs and arms shook as she spoke. The police asked her point blank if she was romantically involved with him, and if either of them might have had other jealous lovers. She swore they had never even kissed, and gave convincing testimony about how she wasn't the type of woman who dated more than one man at a time.

Derek told everything he knew. He said Evan had received a call the previous week from a woman with the same last name, and that he had spent an hour locked in his office talking to her. He added that when the call ended, Evan looked as if he'd been crying. He couldn't remember the woman's first name, but remembered she sounded angry, or at least a bit upset.

Charlie was of absolutely no use. Partly because he didn't give a damn and partly because, in the middle of everything that was happening, he was anticipating another chance at being dock master. He was as curious as the next person about what may have taken place, but it would suit him just fine if Evan were gone for good, and therefore he had no intention of being any help in finding him. He already had plans for firing Derek, but only after he made him put the bait shop back like it was.

Candy and Bill Baxter were the last ones spoken to. Candy told her account of seeing Evan drive away in Old Blue, and Bill his account of *The Shark Bite* tearing ass into the Gulf in the wee hours of the morning. The cops asked everyone about drugs and illegal aliens, both of which were often smuggled into the United States on small craft like *The Shark Bite*. The question brought accounts of Evan's weekly fishing trips, which added further suspicion to an already dubious set of circumstances.

When all the evidence was looked at and all parties interviewed, the cops figured it was a drug deal gone bad. A guy shows up a year earlier, doesn't say where he's from and never mentions family or friends. He takes all his calls in private, and makes weekly trips into the Gulf all alone. One morning his boat is seen speeding away and his apartment is ransacked and there's blood on the floor and walls. To them it all made sense, because they'd seen it a million times before. They figured by now Evan was dead, he and the boat at the bottom of the ocean. They also figured the guys who killed him were already back in Colombia, or Honduras, or wherever they came from, and would never be found. For good measure they took pictures of the apartment and of Old Blue, and pulled some fingerprints from the smashed-up furniture. They weren't going to put much more effort into it than that. It had been their experience that such cases were rarely solved, and people like Evan were rarely seen again.

They took the required step of notifying the Coast Guard, who, in turn, sent out a helicopter for good measure. But without an SOS or some other evidence that a vessel was in trouble they couldn't justify a large-scale search. *The Shark Bite* had only been gone half a day, and for all anyone knew Evan had just gone fishing again; at least that was their official position. Unofficially, they believed the same thing the cops believed because, like the cops, they'd seen exactly that a million times in the past, and they viewed any effort as futile.

By the time it was dark the excitement was over. The cops had packed up and left, and Evan's apartment and Old Blue were covered in fingerprinting dust. Derek stuck around and locked up the apartment while Charlie was on the telephone to the owners of the marina. Dana, Sheila and the other girls at the diner sat around and drank coffee as they mulled over the possibility that Evan wasn't who he appeared to be. All the cop's questions about drugs and illegal aliens had them wondering if he was a good guy or a bad guy. Dana swore there was no way he would have been wrapped up in something illegal. She said she had known a lot of guys, and she wasn't lying, and Evan wasn't the criminal type.

Meanwhile, some thirty miles out in the Gulf, a series of events took place that could only be explained as providence.

CHAPTER TWENTY-SIX

When Evan turned the boat and headed towards *The Secret*'s coordinates the weather was clear and he was in radio contact with Art. It should have been a simple matter of following the flashing dots on the console's liquid crystal display, and keeping the boat at the indicated heading. But like with many things in life, there would be some surprises.

The Shark Bite was cutting through the water and handling the swells just fine. But the three and four-foot seas that were expected in late afternoon came early. If that wasn't bad enough, there were occasional gusts of wind in the neighborhood of twenty miles an hour that made the ride somewhat exhilarating, to say the least. Evan remembered his training and kept the vessel heading directly into the waves, keeping the throttle to a minimum. She handled just fine for a while, and then something gave.

Down below deck, in a darkened engine compartment, a stainless steel reinforced flexible fuel line was swinging with every rise and fall of the boat. Each time *The Shark Bite* dropped, the fuel line rubbed against an exhaust manifold. It was a cycle that had been repeating itself since the day the boat was commissioned. Years before, when she was assembled, a mechanic forgot to install a one-inch retaining clip that would have prevented what happened next.

The years of rubbing against the extremely hot and somewhat coarse exhaust manifold finally took its toll. Coming off one particularly nasty wave the fuel line sprung a leak and shot gas onto the hot engine, which ignited immediately. The fuel line gave way moments later. A flame sensor, about the only thing that worked that day, sensed the fire and sent a signal to the fire suppression system to release the extinguishing agent, but the electrical solenoid valve that should have opened was frozen shut from years of sitting idle, leaving the fire to burn at will.

A loud buzzer and an indicator light warned Evan of the condition below. He instantly backed off the throttle and shortly thereafter saw the smoke. By the time he reached the fuel shutoff valve it was too late. Enough gasoline had been released to fill up half the engine compartment, and the vessel took to burning. Evan grabbed a fire extinguisher and went to town, fighting the waves to stay on his feet as he wrestled with the extinguisher. He emptied the first one in seconds and grabbed another one and did the same. It was no use; the entire aft end of *The Shark Bite* was on fire.

When the extinguishers were empty he snatched up an empty bucket and, scoop by scoop, doused the fire with water. He was in a panic, but a somewhat controlled one that allowed him to retain a little common sense. While his body was scooping and throwing, his brain was screaming for him to call for help before it was too late. But the flames were so fierce he didn't dare stop, not even for the twenty seconds it would have taken to make a mayday call. He continued to fight, and the fire fought back. At one point he stepped too close and his leg went through a weakened, burning portion of deck and he fell down. Flames from below ran up his leg and instantly cooked his skin.

He got back on his feet and kept right on tossing water, unaware of the second and third degree burns to his leg. The burning vessel swayed back and forth as waves slammed her from all sides. Evan lost his balance again and again but kept on getting up and scooping from the ocean, tossing the salty water into the flames.

Out of nowhere, a red projectile zipped by his face so close it almost took his head off. It was a flare ignited by the intense heat. Evan's eyes locked on to the source: an emergency kit too far inside the inferno to reach. The fire had melted through its thin aluminum shell and hit one of the many flares inside.

Without warning another flare let go, slammed into the forward part of the vessel and ricocheted off towards the ocean. Had it entered the cabin it would have been all over. Evan scooped another bucket of water and targeted the white metal box that held the rockets. He scooped again and threw, and again and again. He expected to feel a flaming fist hit him in the stomach and tear his guts out, and, when the third flare launched, it almost did just that. The burning missile ripped through the air and missed him by inches, literally charring his skin as it passed by.

He kept throwing bucket after bucket of water on the box. When the flames withdrew enough he reached in and grabbed it with one hand and dropped it overboard, hearing it sizzle when it hit the water. At that instant a fourth flare let go and illuminated the darkened water as it torpedoed toward the ocean bottom. The tips of Evan's fingers were seared, but he didn't feel the pain. He was too busy pushing back the grim reaper to even care.

The boat rocked violently as the waves pounded her sides and made it almost impossible for Evan to stay on his feet. The buzzer behind him screamed with an obnoxious howl, but Evan was making progress. The flames were dying with every bucket he threw, and despite the tremendous pain he continued to toss the water.

His body twisted and turned as he bent over the side and filled the bucket. The muscles in his arms and legs swelled as they worked to full capacity to keep him on his feet. He scooped and threw with an intensity that could only be found in a man fighting for his life, who truly wanted to live. When the last flame disappeared, Evan collapsed from total exhaustion.

The buzzer stopped when the fire died. It had nothing to do with the fire being out and everything to do with the fact that the boat's electrical systems were fried. The flames ate through every wire they touched, and the heat melted the casings of her batteries and liquefied their lead plates.

With the fire out Evan lay on deck and breathed deeply. He'd inhaled much of the black cloud that rose from the engine compartment while he fought the fire, and his throat and lungs stung, causing him to spit and cough for nearly half an hour. What made matters worse were the waves that continued to toss the boat around and Evan with it. He slid around the deck and occasionally slammed into the sides of the vessel as he tried to catch his breath. In time the pain in his neck and chest subsided, or at least it seemed to. It may have had more to do with the pain in his leg increasing, making all other feelings in his body pale by comparison. But, as bad as his leg was aching, his immediate reaction was to survey the damage to the boat.

The back end of *The Shark Bite* looked as if a bomb had hit it. There was a giant hole where the flames ate away the deck, and inside it were her two engines. Only minutes before they were cranking out six hundred horsepower at three thousand revolutions per minute, and now they sat silent and still. The hoses, fan belts and other plastic and rubber pieces that supported their operation were melted beyond recognition. Broken batteries oozed boiling acid into the bilge that mixed with oil, gasoline, and antifreeze creating a very nasty smelling brown gas that danced up and out of the hole and vanished into the air.

Once he had taken it all in, the pain in his leg overshadowed the severity of the destruction of the boat. The burned skin had broken loose on one or more of his falls and was pushed down around his ankle like a loose sock. There were shards of splintery fiberglass embedded in his flesh. There was gasoline, and oil, and battery acid on the red ripened tissue of his leg that could have been pure grain alcohol as badly as it stung.

He hobbled down into the cabin in search of a first aid kit or medicine cabinet. He gritted his teeth and moaned as he searched for anything that would help. In the hollows of a bench seat he discovered a watertight bag labeled medical supplies. He tore it open and its contents spilled onto the floor and rolled around as the boat continued to rise and fall. An array of products of varying colors and sizes lay before him like a spilled jar of candy. He grabbed them one by one and read their labels.

Antacids, clean wipes, hydrocortisone, antiseptic swabs, pain reliever. Yes, pain reliever. He tore into the bottle and poured a dozen into his mouth, chewing the dry tablets until he could swallow the thick paste that formed on his tongue and between his teeth. He reached again into the colorful pile. Hay fever tablets, sterile eyewash, iodine, spray-on blood clotter, compress dressing, gel-soaked burn dressing, and burn relief spray. He thought fast and tore the top off the eyewash and poured the cool liquid on his leg. It felt good for an instant, but the pain returned. He quickly shook the burn relief spray and doused his leg. It cooled and tingled, and, after a few minutes, the pain subsided enough for him to think more rationally.

He needed to remove the toothpick-sized fiberglass spears before he could apply a dressing. He grabbed the first one and slowly yanked. The boat took a roll that caused his hand to jerk, which drove the spear inward before he could pull it out. Pain shot up through his groin and into his spine. When it hit his brain he let out a thunderous scream. When he was able to breathe again he grabbed another one and pulled quickly, not allowing the ocean the pleasure of inflicting unnecessary agony. The pain was still horrific and he screamed again. The process repeated itself until the leg was free of debris and expelling blood from several deep wounds.

Now he used his fingertips to grab hold of the skin that was bunched up by his foot. He took a deep breath, bit down hard, and pulled. It unfolded like a cloth napkin as he stretched it taut and laid it back in place. He ripped into the burn dressing and applied it, wrapping it all up with a roll of elastic dressing.

For a long time he sat in the cabin and waited for the pain reliever to take effect. As he waited he moaned and groaned, taking short, quick breaths. But the small tablets were intended for headaches, muscle aches, minor bumps and bruises, not for the type of pain that accompanies severe burns and torn flesh. It took a long time for the pain reliever to have an effect, and, when it did, it only made the pain manageable. But that was enough for him to get to his feet and head back up on deck.

There was less than an hour of sunlight left and all around him there was only water. He wasn't far away from *The Secret*, and he knew it. He also knew he was dead in the water and had no way of letting Art know he was in trouble. He assumed his friend would figure it out and come looking for him, but he didn't even have a flare to show where he was, and the Gulf of Mexico was a huge place to be playing hide and seek. He'd heard the stories of men who'd gone to their deaths despite massive search efforts to find them, and he knew he'd better prepare for the worst case scenario: being at sea for a long time.

While he still had available light he took an inventory of the boat. There was an oar. A completely useless tool on a vessel the size of *The Shark Bite*, but a Coast Guard requirement all the same. There were several life jackets, two empty fire extinguishers, two Cokes, half a can of peanuts, three rolls of toilet paper, and a cigarette lighter. The galley had an array of cooking utensils and some spices, but nothing of any use, and the head had a half bottle of shampoo and a bar of soap.

He opened a Coke and took a few sips before recapping it to save the remainder for later. He wasn't sure if he'd be able to get any water from the potable tank without electricity, so he wasn't about to guzzle down half of what he currently had available to drink. He was hungry, but peanuts would only make him thirsty so he ignored them for the time being. His brain was up to full capacity and in survival mode, a state it hadn't been in for a very long time. He was listening to what it had to say.

When the sun went down he climbed into the cabin and lay down on the floor, wedging his body between a table leg and a stool. That position allowed him to stay in one place despite the rolls the boat was taking, but it did nothing to help him sleep. His blood and brain sloshed around for several more hours until the seas died down. During that time a slideshow took place inside his head. Pictures of places he, Angela and the children had gone flashed in and out. At one point he locked into a memory and it played several times over.

It was shortly after Jeremy was born. The air was cool but not cold, and there wasn't a cloud in the sky. It was apple season in central New York, and everyone in the area knew about Tanner's Apple Orchard. Family-owned for almost a century, it was the very best place to pick your own and take a hayride while sipping hot cinnamon-flavored cider. Emily was dressed in cute little red coveralls, decorated with strawberries, over a white long-sleeved shirt. She wore a matching hat and carried a wicker basket. The outfit was an original, designed and made by Evan's mother for, as she said, the prettiest little girl in the world.

When Emily first spotted the infinite rows of trees adorned with giant bright red apples she went crazy. She ran to the nearest tree, grabbed one, took a bite, then ran to the next and repeated the process. Evan trailed behind her with a camcorder stuck to his eye and recorded her every move. She managed to bite twenty-two apples before she was full, then she fell to the ground and stared up at the trees with the biggest, brightest smile Evan had ever seen. He and Angela just broke down laughing. Evan always considered it one of the very best days of his life.

Later, as they picked apples, he lifted her up so she could grab one from the top of a tree. Angela took a picture that was eventually hung in the den above their computer desk. Evan, frozen in time, arms stretched out, was holding Emily as she pulled on a giant red apple. Her strawberry coveralls and white shirt blended perfectly with the background of trees, and her smile told the world there was no better place to be than in the arms of her daddy. It was the type of picture that is often taken by professionals and on rare occasion by amateurs. The image, so outstanding, was permanently burned into the memory banks of Evan's brain.

When the memory was gone he managed to drift off, but not before he looked up towards heaven and whispered, "Please, get me back home."

CHAPTER TWENTY-SEVEN

Tim Barnes, with the help of WRTB's film editing department, analyzed the film footage of the fire, frame by frame. They searched for anything that would lead them to the mysterious hero who had saved Deloris Carlisle and her two children. But the film was shot using an antiquated VHS camcorder with a scratched lens. The images, although dramatic, were not very crisp.

For hours they sat looking at picture after grainy picture. They even analyzed the parts that were out of focus, hoping for even the remotest of clues. After three hours, and a half bottle of antacids, they got their wish. In the red polished reflection of a fire truck was an image of Old Blue. It didn't show the entire truck, only the front clip and half of the cab section. But on the driver's side door was what appeared to be the name of a business. They took the image and digitally enhanced and enlarged it. When it was the best it was going to get they began deciphering it.

The process was like trying to read a book through a piece of waxed paper. Some letters were loosely discernable while others could have been any of the twenty-six in the alphabet. The quest for the answer soon involved every available employee at the station. The station manager even offered a five-hundred-dollar bonus to each person who helped crack the code and locate the truck. There were people on the Internet searching the local business directory, some flipping through the yellow pages, others calling family and friends for help. They counted the letters and searched for every business with an equal number. Then they broke them down alphabetically and by geographic location throughout the county.

After several more hours they were down to less than one hundred businesses that could fit the bill. Tim made the call to concentrate on only those that began with a B, D, G, O, or Q. He was convinced, as were the others, that the first letter was one of those. That narrowed the list to less than twenty, at which point the station manager wanted to start making phone calls and asking about the truck. But Tim was convinced that the hero wanted to stay anonymous, and if called would deny ownership of any such vehicle. So he gathered up a team of people and hit the streets.

The marina was the fourteenth place they checked, and the minute they saw Old Blue they knew they had finally hit the jackpot. On the driver's door, in large black lettering, were the words "Delcast Marina." Tim high-fived his team of investigators and phoned the station to share the good news. The station manager was elated and wanted to show the world the bashful hero during the eleven o'clock broadcast. After a few rounds of backslapping and congratulatory handshakes Tim went in search of his big story.

Candy was the first person he could locate. She was hosing down an area of the floor in front of the shrimp stand when he entered the shop.

"Excuse me, can I ask you a question?" Tim asked with a great big fake smile. Candy figured him for a police investigator who was sent back for additional information.

"Sure," she said, releasing the handle of the spray nozzle.

"I'm trying to find a man who was driving that blue truck in the parking lot the other night. Would you know who I'm talking about?"

Candy realized then that he wasn't a cop, and with all the talk about drugs and illegal aliens she got a little scared.

"No. I have no idea," she said, obviously lying.

Tim showed her a grainy picture of Evan taken from the video. She knew right away who it was because she recognized the olive shirt and white shorts. She also knew enough not to mention seeing Evan leave in Old Blue on the night in question. She just shook her head as if she had no idea what he was talking about.

"I'm Tim Barnes, WRTB news," he said offering his hand. Candy cautiously shook it and tried to recall if she'd ever seen his face before. She wasn't much for the news, especially if there was a talk show or sitcom competing for her attention. "I'm trying to find him because he's sort of a hero. There was a fire and he saved the lives of four people, one of them a fireman," he continued.

Candy's mind raced. She wasn't sure what to think. It was only a day since the cops left, and they had Evan pegged as a bad guy. They hadn't mentioned anything about a fire or any hero business. Now all of a sudden he was a hero. It didn't make sense. Not to Candy.

"Look mister, I don't know who was driving that truck. There's a lot of folks who are allowed to use it," she said. But her lies were transparent, especially to a man who made his living interviewing people. He could moonlight as a human polygraph machine.

"He's not in any trouble, I just want to interview him. Like I said, he's sort of a hero to some people, and they would like to thank him. He saved the lives of a woman and her two babies. And a fireman, too."

It all sounded great, but Candy wasn't buying it. She just wanted him out of her shop so she could finish cleaning up and go home.

"You might want to try The Minnow," she said, pointing towards the door. Tim didn't know if that was a boat or a bar or a little person.

"The Minnow?" he asked.

"The diner. Out the door and to your right," she said, anxious to get him on his way. When he left she picked up the phone and called The Minnow to warn them about the suspicious-looking dude who claimed to be a reporter. Then after hanging up she ran to the back door and watched as he ambled across the lot.

Some of the girls in the diner recognized him instantly and were anxious to spill their guts in hopes of getting on television. They identified Evan as the man in the photograph and told Tim Barnes all about the strange circumstances surrounding Evan's disappearance. They left nothing out, describing, second-hand, the condition of his apartment and paraphrasing every statement made by every law enforcement officer who had responded.

In an instant a great story became a fantastic one. Tim already had visions of the broadcast. He would stand with the Gulf behind him and reveal to the world that the man who risked his life to save four others had disappeared under questionable circumstances, and may be, at that very moment, in need of help himself. He could interview Deloris Carlisle and Richard Stocks and get their reactions to the news their hero was missing. It would be great television and the ratings would soar.

Naturally he would leave out the part about drugs and illegal aliens. The man was a local hero and people wouldn't want to hear a bunch of unsubstantiated accusations. They would want to know what happened to him and what was being done to find him. Hell, the station could even sponsor an effort to rescue him, assuming he needed rescuing. They could use the story to show the community they cared about the people by sending out a search team. If, on the off chance they managed to find him, they would be heroes themselves.

The thoughts boiled inside him like bubbles in a shaken soda can. Something like that had never been done as far as he knew, and he wanted to get the ball rolling before the guy simply floated back and told everyone he was merely out fishing or gallivanting around the ocean with his girlfriend. He glanced at his watch and realized he had less than two hours to prepare a story that his boss would agree to allow on the air. He had to convince him that sponsoring the search would not only be within the confines of good reporting, which it wasn't, but would also come back ten-fold in increased ratings. But first he had to get out of the diner without making it appear as if he was overly excited. He didn't want anyone calling a rival station.

"Well, ladies, I thank you for your time. We might run a little piece on all of this at eleven, if we can squeeze it in somewhere," he said calmly.

"Aren't you gonna film us?" one of them asked.

"Not this time. But if he happens to show up we might bring the cameras out here and let you lovely ladies get on television," he said, throwing them a bone so they wouldn't spoil his feast.

When he was gone Candy ran over to find out what had happened. When she heard the details she became suspicious, and asked if anyone bothered calling Sheila.

"What for?" a forty-something bleached blonde asked.

"Because she's in charge now, that's what for," Candy said, annoyed at the blonde's tone.

"Well I don't think she would appreciate being bothered over such nonsense," the blonde shot back.

"Fine with me. Just make sure you explain to her why she wasn't called when she asks. See y'all tomorrow," Candy said with a grin. She left the diner and headed back to the bait shop to finish cleaning up. Her man was at home, and once she pulled out of the parking lot she wouldn't give a damn if the whole bunch of them dropped dead.

Later that night when WRTB went on the air they opened with Tim Barnes standing somewhere along the coast with the Gulf of Mexico behind him. He looked so concerned you would have thought Evan was his long lost brother. He spoke of him as a brave man who only days before risked everything for complete strangers. They cut to a live shot of Deloris, who was given another hundred bucks for her reaction to the news that the man who saved her life may be fighting for his own. With her two babies in her arms she broke down and cried. She cried real tears brought on by real emotion, and she would have done so with or without the hundred bucks. The cameraman zoomed in on her face, which made the tears rolling down her cheeks look like rivers.

After Deloris there was another live shot, this one of Richard Stocks. He was still in his hospital bed with tubes and monitors attached to him when he heard about Evan's situation. He made an attempt at standing up while vowing to help in the search effort. But his wife, who was at his side, pushed him back down and cried on his shoulder. Then it was back to Tim, who had to wipe the smile off his face before the red light on the camera illuminated. He had managed to beat that bitch, as he referred to the nurse that sent him away on his first attempt, and proved he was still the number one reporter in town. It didn't matter that the man was recovering from very serious injuries. All that mattered was that he got the story.

He turned and pointed at the black sea behind him and described it as an unforgiving vast wilderness of water where a local hero may himself be in trouble. But at this point Tim Barnes didn't believe for a minute that Evan was really in trouble. He figured the cops were probably right; he was somehow wrapped up in something illegal and was made an example by some pretty rough people. He figured Evan was most likely at the bottom of the Gulf wearing concrete shoes. But all of that was purely unsubstantiated speculation, and Tim wasn't about to mention anything that would interfere with the story and wreck his ratings. So Tim did what he did best. He stood and looked the camera square in the lens and pleaded for anyone with any information to contact WRTB or the local authorities. He said the community owed it to Evan Hayden to help him as he had helped others. He put the whipped cream on top of the milkshake by announcing that WRTB would be launching its own search-and-rescue effort to save the community's hero. He declared that people were preparing to take to the ocean to find Evan Hayden, and, in his defense, there actually were people getting ready to search. It was the only completely truthful thing he said all night.

What he didn't say on the air was that WRTB's investigative team had found out just about everything there was to know about Evan and even managed to contact his wife, who was on her way to Florida, at the station's expense, to be on the scene to greet her husband when he was found. They would meet her at the airport and get a private interview before transporting her to a secure hotel room, where she could be kept up to date on the rescue attempts and away from rival stations. When the rescue effort was called off, and Evan was pronounced dead, they could get her reaction on a live broadcast.

When the red light went out the smile returned, and Tim gave a high five to the cameraman who thought he was a jerk but would never say so. Tim hit a few numbers on his cell phone and inquired about Angela.

"Get her ass to the hotel and stay with her until she's checked in, then give me a call. And don't forget to register her with a bogus name. If she wants an explanation tell her it's for security reasons. If she's hungry, order room service. Remember, she talks to nobody about this. Got it?" he said.

When he hung up he looked out at the ocean and thought, "The only way this could get any better is if the son-of-a-bitch is found alive."

CHAPTER TWENTY-EIGHT

Evan spent most of the night lying in the cabin listening to the waves punch the sides of the hull. Once in a while he would hobble up on deck in the hope of seeing *The Secret*, but she never appeared. Her bright white sails failed to break the darkened sky as he had hoped they would. Throughout the night he dozed off numerous times. Sometimes for half an hour, and other times for only minutes. But the rough seas and throbbing pain in his leg, along with the expectation of hearing Art yell, "Ahoy!" kept his sleep shallow.

By morning the waves were down to mere ripples and the sky was clear. There was a warm gentle breeze that carried the sweet smell of fermenting seaweed, and the ocean's creatures were awake and frolicking in the water. None of it caught Evan's attention because *The Shark Bite* was still out of commission and his leg was still badly injured. It had become swollen, and the wound oozed a foul-smelling gelatinous substance similar to pus, only thicker and stickier.

When the sun was high enough in the sky to illuminate the blackened hole in the deck, he knelt down and got his best view yet of the damaged motors. There were bundles of charred wires and rubber hoses that looked like barbecued spaghetti and sun-dried snakes. A thick soup consisting of coolant, motor oil, battery acid, and salt water filled the bilge and covered the two massive steel blocks that used to be operational engines. It was worse than he remembered from the previous evening, and any hope he might have held of getting her underway was lost.

His stomach growled with hunger and the mucus membranes of his mouth ached with dryness as he thought about the can of peanuts and remaining Coke in the cabin. But, with ocean surrounding him for God knows how many miles, he was reluctant to squander anything. He knew he might be out there for days, possibly weeks, and decided his first order of business was to access the fresh water in the potable tank. He knew it was full because he'd topped it off before leaving the marina, but getting to it was going to be a trick since there was no available electricity to power the pump.

He opened an access panel underneath the sink in the galley and followed the cold water hose to where it penetrated the floor. He did the same to the sink in the head, hoping to get a better idea of just where the tank was located. But the hoses just disappeared through drilled holes in the flooring, leaving no clues to the whereabouts of their origins. Figuring the tank had to be accessible for maintenance purposes, he began pulling apart everything that could have concealed an opening. He removed pieces of carpet, moved shelves and tables, and pulled out the bench cushions, and finally found a hatch underneath the last cushion he removed.

The three-foot by two-foot panel lifted easily to reveal a darkened space much larger than he could have ever imagined existed below him. He remembered the cigarette lighter and grabbed it in haste and almost spun the flint wheel when he noticed a faint odor of gasoline. He had no other means of casting light into the hole, but knew what might lie ahead if he added flame.

He recalled his days in the power plant when he had explosive monitors that would tell him if there was enough vapor build-up in an area to cause an explosion, and he knew it only took a small amount of gasoline to reach the lower explosive limit. So he held the lighter for several moments as his brain ran the calculations. After reaching the conclusion it wasn't worth the risk, he tossed it behind him into the pile of medical supplies scattered on the floor.

The almost useless oar found a purpose when Evan lowered it into the hole and used it to survey the depth. He moved it from side to side and it came in contact with several items big enough to be a water tank. Then he examined it for signs of wetness, of which there were none, before deciding to lower himself down inside the darkened area.

Using his arms to support his weight, careful not to rub his injured leg against anything, he went feet first into the blackness. He went down almost four feet before his shoes made contact with the bottom. When they did, he carefully bent at the waist and lowered onto his hands and knees. His eyes adjusted rather quickly and he was able to see the outline of nearby objects, but couldn't make out what they were. He moved slowly and felt with his hands as he went. The first object he came across was tubular, standing vertically. It had an electrical cable attached to it but had no pipes or hoses so he ruled it out as anything to do with potable water.

The next item he reached was a square metal box that sounded hollow when he banged on it with his fist. He glided his hands over it and felt a large pipe, maybe three to four inches in diameter, entering it from above. He slowly circled it, hoping to find a pump attached near the bottom but there wasn't one. What he had found was the sanitary tank.

He moved again, crossing over a beam and a few smaller pipes, and, without warning, crawled head first into a blunt metal object that put a small knot on his forehead. He yelled a few choice expletives as he felt for blood, but he hadn't hit hard enough to break the skin. A touch of claustrophobia made him reluctant to go further, but his thirst overruled that feeling about as quickly as it came and he began to move again, this time with one hand protecting his face.

It wasn't a foot from where he hit his head that he banged his knee on something, and when he reached down and felt it, a smile crossed his face. It was a small electric motor attached to a centrifugal pump, no more than one horsepower, and just what he would have expected to find on a potable water system. He located the suction line and followed it back to a forty-gallon stainless steel tubular tank. He banged on it, and the sound was a solid thud, not the hollow ring one would expect if the tank were empty. His hands started moving around the vessel in search of a valve or petcock from which he could drain some water. In his excitement he moved too quickly and his injured leg was forced against the threaded end of a one-quarter inch bolt. The metal drove through the soaked bandage into the tender flesh below, sending a shrill of pain up his side.

When the pain sank to a manageable level he continued to search with his hands for some means of getting water. The tank was solid with no drain valve or discernable opening, and between the tank and the pump was rigid piping bolted firmly in place, the type that required tools for disassembly. The pump discharged into a stainless steel header which fed out in individual lines to the sinks and shower. There would be no water in the discharge lines without an operational pump, and there would be no operational pump without electricity.

After a few more fruitless minutes of searching for a way into the tank, Evan gave up and crawled out of the hull. He was sweaty and thirstier than before and reached for the previously opened bottle of soda, swallowing the few remaining ounces with total disregard for the situation. Despite being warm and flat, the sweet liquid felt good going down and left him with a stronger desire to pop open the peanuts and swallow a few handfuls. He reached for them, opened the lid and tilted the can to his mouth. The paste that developed as he chewed was smooth and salty, just as satisfying as a filet mignon would have been, considering how hungry he was. He stopped short of filling his mouth a second time and breaking into the last Coke. He had no intention of committing suicide by hastily consuming the little remaining food he had, not to mention the last sixteen ounces of drinkable liquid he could get his hands on. He covered the peanuts and set them aside, then lay back and closed his eyes to think about what he could do to get the water.

Meanwhile The Blind Minnow was buzzing with chatter and speculation surrounding Evan's whereabouts. Some theories had him in the Virgin Islands under an assumed name with a million tax-free dollars, some had him floating in the Gulf with a knife in his back. Others didn't even think he was on *The Shark Bite* when it pulled away from the marina. The most interesting guess came from Sheila, who figured him for an undercover Drug Enforcement Administration agent who had to stage his own death and disappear before some Colombian drug lord found him and killed him.

She said it all made perfect sense. He wore a wedding ring, but never spoke of a wife or children, and he never once mentioned where he was from or anything about his past. Charlie agreed with Sheila, saying there were many times when Evan would just wander away all by himself and not be seen for hours. He added that Evan didn't have any friends either, as if he had room to talk. He said all this while sliding a stack of hotcakes down his throat as if he were a ventriloquist doing an act.

Dana didn't believe any of it. She stuck with Sheila's original presumption that Evan was once married and had lost his wife. She saw the news broadcast and agreed with Tim Barnes that Evan was a hero. She saw the footage of how he had rushed into the flames and saved Deloris Carlisle and Richard Stocks. She didn't think a drug dealer would risk his own life to save some poor black woman and her children. Drug dealers, in her opinion, only thought about themselves and couldn't care less about what happened to other people. She viewed the whole undercover agent thing as the product of an old woman's imagination, but she didn't dare say so for fear of hurting Sheila's feelings.

Dana felt certain something else happened that sent him out into the ocean. She didn't know what, but she figured it was something nobody had thought of. He could have gotten hurt in the building and lost his memory or something strange like that. Whatever the case may be she was certain of one thing: Evan wasn't a drug-pushing bad guy like the cops believed. He was a gentleman, unlike most of the men she'd known. He never made crude remarks or unwanted advances to her like half of the single men who frequented the diner.

Candy piped up with an idea for the marina to get its own rescue team going. She said they should contact all their customers and tell them what happened. She figured many of them would be willing to take their own boats out to look for him. Charlie cut her off with a grotesquely arrogant laugh and asked who in the world would be willing to spend his time and money looking for some guy everyone thought was a criminal.

Derek jumped in and said he thought it was a good idea. Not that he really did, he just wanted Charlie to make some stupid comment so he could drag him outside and beat the stuffing out of him. He'd reached his limit with Charlie the day before when he overheard him talking about Evan as if he belonged on the FBI's Most Wanted list, and, had it not been for all the cops at the marina, he would have pounded his head in right then and there.

Sheila sensed what was coming and asked Derek if he'd like some more coffee, and handed him a few donuts along with it. She called to the back for another order of link sausage for Charlie in the hopes that getting food in their mouths would stop either of them from saying anything that would result in a fight. Having raised three sons she knew instinctively how to put out a fire, and, within minutes had succeeded.

A few minutes later the bell on the door rang and Sheila was on her feet to greet her customers. She grabbed a few menus, and, when she reached the lobby, came face to face with Tim Barnes. Outside the door she could see a van with a satellite dish on its top and the letters WRTB along its side. She smiled and then made eye contact with the woman to his right, who had obviously been crying.

"I'm Tim…"

"Barnes from the news. I know. I watch you all the time. I'm Sheila," she said, interrupting him. Her recognition of his face made him smile. Sheila shook his hand and then greeted the woman at his side in the same manner, and, before the woman could do it herself, Tim Barnes introduced her.

"Sheila, I'd like you to meet Evan's wife, Angela Hayden," he said.

It was the first time Sheila had ever been truly speechless.

CHAPTER TWENTY-NINE

Angela's existence was a shock to everyone at the diner who had assumed for the past year that Evan was widowed. But it was most shocking to Sheila, who had come up with the dead wife theory before changing her mind and making Evan a D.E.A. agent. Either way she was wrong. Granted, she was no Sherlock Holmes, but she had never been so far off base in the past and learning the truth embarrassed her.

Tim Barnes tried his darnedest to keep Angela away from the marina until Evan's fate was confirmed. He was afraid he would lose control over the situation if Angela's world met Evan's world, and he was concerned about how Angela would react if told the authorities had her husband pegged as a player in some sort of a sinister game like drug dealing or alien smuggling. Tim had been involved in situations in the past where people received too much information too soon. He'd lost control of some good stories and wound up having to share them with rival stations, which was exactly what he wanted to avoid.

But Angela wasn't Tim's typical subject. She couldn't be shamed into submission with a free airplane ride or complimentary hotel room, and she had no intention of sitting in a Holiday Inn watching soap operas while waiting for the phone to ring. She intended to find out as much information as she could to help locate Evan, and what better place to begin than where he'd lived and worked for the past year? When she insisted Tim Barnes take her to the marina to meet the people her husband associated with, she assumed they would have at least heard of her, but as she introduced herself their expressions made it evident rather quickly that they had no idea she had even existed.

Charlie, upon learning that Angela was Evan's wife, blurted out some off-the-wall comment about Evan having a screw loose for living apart from such a pretty little woman. The comment resulted in Sheila giving him an elbow in the gut that almost made him cough up the link sausages he swallowed only minutes before. Yet, as stupid as the remark may have been, it convinced Angela to sit down among them and give a brief synopsis of the past eighteen months. She didn't go into great detail, especially when it came to Emily's death, but offered enough for them to put to rest all their crazy speculations.

She painted a picture of a man very different from the one they thought they knew, and their feedback told Angela that the man she had lived with and loved for ten years was somehow different as well. It was as if they spoke of different sides of the same coin, and she wondered if maybe she had also flipped from heads to tails in the time since they had last held each other.

After giving the rundown on her and Evan's lives Angela sought some information of her own. She asked the expected who's, where's and why's and eventually inquired about the last time anyone saw Evan. Candy was the only person to speak up, saying she witnessed him leave in the company pickup truck the night of the fire, and she added there was nothing unusual about his demeanor. He just hopped in Old Blue and left. Sheila, sensing Angela's next question, made eye contact with Dana, who was so tense she would have shattered like glass had someone as much as tapped her on the shoulder.

Candy's answer, when Angela asked where Evan was going when he left the marina, was that she had no idea where he was headed, and she did so because she no longer believed Evan was involved romantically with Dana. She'd always sensed something good and pure about him, despite the fact his nights were spent with his head in a bottle and his days were filled with mysterious walks to God knows where. After hearing about the tragedy he'd suffered she understood his need to be alone, and she sympathized with his weakness for alcohol.

Charlie was a different case. He liked fireworks and saw an excellent opportunity to light some off. So when Candy denied having knowledge of where Evan was headed Charlie almost spit out, "Come on! You know where he was going—to Dana's place!" And he would have said just that had Sheila not grabbed his elbow and squeezed as tightly as she could, sending her brightly colored pink fingernails into his flesh. He wasn't the smartest fish in the tank but he certainly got the message to keep his mouth shut, and so did everyone else.

Angela picked up on the fact that the group was hiding something, or at least not telling her the entire truth. She took notice of Sheila's stronghold on Charlie's arm, of Dana's facial expressions, and of Tim Barnes's obvious discomfort. She knew there was more to the story than what she was being told, and that's when she asked to be shown Evan's apartment.

The request stumped the entire bunch of them: The marina folk because none of them had mentioned the disarray of the apartment or the blood splatters on the walls, and Tim Barnes because he had not told Angela the authorities had Evan pegged as a drug runner or alien smuggler. All of them knew damn good and well that the condition of the apartment would more than likely upset Angela, and, with the exception of Charlie, nobody wanted to be in the middle of what would likely unfold when she saw the place.

The silence was finally broken by Tim, who said the police had to check it out and they probably didn't want anything disturbed, for investigative purposes, of course. Derek shot to his feet and informed her they had already been through and he had locked the place up and could let her in using a spare key Evan kept hanging on a nail in the bait shop office. Unlike the rest of them, the situation had gone right over Derek's head. In his naivety he assumed she knew everything there was to know, and his offer caused everyone else to stiffen for fear of how Angela would react.

Angela and Derek left the diner with Tim two steps behind them, muttering something about disturbing evidence. When Angela heard all she could stand, she stopped and politely but firmly requested he stay behind. It had taken her less than fifteen minutes to figure him out and know what his angle was. She also knew he was responsible for WRTB's search effort and, for that reason, had agreed to put up with him. But she wanted privacy inside Evan's apartment, and, rescue effort or not, she was going to get just that.

On the way to the bait shop Derek told Angela he was the one she had spoken to on the phone, and that he had had no idea Evan was still married. He told her how everyone assumed his wife had died because of the ring he wore and because he never talked about himself or his past. He explained how Evan had bailed him out of jail and allowed him to keep his job even though he deserved to be fired. He said he hoped Evan was all right, because he was the only person who had ever given him a chance, and added that he was sorry to hear about what happened to their little girl. There was a shudder in his voice as if he wanted to cry.

Angela liked him immediately, and, when they reached the stairs to the apartment, she took his hand in hers and thanked him for being so helpful. She said she hoped Evan was all right too, and she was happy to see he worked with such a nice person. She smiled at the large young man with the teddy bear expression, and asked if he'd mind waiting for her and keeping Tim Barnes out of her hair while she looked around. Derek was happy to oblige

When she reached the door to Evan's apartment she paused and looked around. For the last year she'd had a picture in her mind of what the marina looked like, and it was far from what she was seeing. It wasn't better or worse than she expected, only different. It was odd for her to think Evan had been a part of something so foreign to her. Before the accident they knew everything there was to know about each other.

Standing in front of the door she realized, more than ever, that she no longer knew the man she married. She felt like she was outside of a stranger's door, or that of a relative she hadn't seen since she was a child. Before arriving in Florida she had a photo album of pictures in her head. They were pictures she developed during his time in Florida of where he worked and where he lived and what clothes he was wearing. Those images became familiar to her and gave her a comfortable feeling, as if she had been there and seen everything. Now she realized how inaccurate those images were, and she was suddenly nervous about turning the knob in front of her.

She slowly opened the door and took in what she saw in small pieces. A musty odor hit her immediately and she recognized the semi-sweet aroma of stale beer spilled onto dirty linoleum. The rooms were dark and drab, which made them seem dated, like a place that was left undisturbed for a few decades. She stepped inside and shut the door behind her.

It took her about the same amount of time it had taken Derek to notice the destruction and the blood, but the effect it had on her was quite different. She was shocked, of course, but not to the point where she ran out of the place in a panic. She had come a long way and had gone through a lot to get where she was, and, regardless of broken furniture or splattered blood, she had no intention of leaving until some curiosities were satisfied and some questions were answered.

Chalk it up to life experience, or a guiding grace, but whatever it was it allowed her to maintain the necessary composure to take in what she saw and honestly attempt to understand it all. There was the immediate gut feeling that something horrible had occurred in the apartment, but it lasted only seconds before she grabbed hold of it and stowed it away. She'd been through enough to know how to handle the unexpected.

After a slow careful walk through the bedroom, where most of the destruction and all of the blood was, she went to the kitchen. She stood on the worn linoleum floor and examined the cheap laminated cabinets. They had a baked-on layer of grease, dust and food splatter that was the culmination of years of pan-fried hamburgers and grease-soaked French fries. The former, and late, dock master was a fan of greasy foods, but didn't much favor the use of detergent when cleaning up after meals. He also fancied cheap cigars and low-priced beer, both of which had a major impact on the character of the eight-hundred-square-foot dwelling, and on the massive heart attack that took his life.

She pulled on the handle of a drawer next to the refrigerator and it opened to reveal a mottled collection of silverware that one would have to be famished to consider using. There were forks and knives stuck together from being stored in a less than clean condition, and there was a dusting of miscellaneous bits and pieces of insect parts and rodent feces. In a cabinet above was a scattered compilation of chipped coffee mugs and scratched plastic cups, and next to those a pile of unsightly plates and bowls that looked as if they were used more for ashtrays than for dinner service.

Next she inspected the fridge, which, surprisingly, was much cleaner than anything she'd seen so far. It was bare with the exception of a few jars of condiments, a six-pack of beer, a jar of pickles, and a half carton of spoiled milk. It brought back a memory of how Evan's refrigerator looked when he left the Navy and got his first apartment.

When she was done in the kitchen she went to the bedroom and looked again. She knew there was more going on than what that plastic, toupee-wearing son of a bitch Tim Barnes led her to believe. She realized why he wanted to keep her away from the marina, and she had a sudden urge to stomp downstairs and slap him across the face. She wanted to tell him to take his free plane ride and his cheap hotel and shove it. But, if she did that, WRTB might cancel their rescue efforts, and that possibility was all that prevented her from acting on her anger.

When he introduced himself earlier that day he told her Evan was a hero and he showed her the tape of the fire. He didn't mention anything that would have led her to believe that Evan was the victim of foul play. He simply said her husband had gone boating and never returned. She assumed he was fishing or sightseeing, or conducting marina business of some sort and had boat trouble. She assumed that because that's exactly what he led her to believe by telling her the Coast Guard was searching for him and there was an excellent chance he'd be found. But it didn't fit with what she was seeing. Despite her best effort to remain calm and focused she became upset. Her bottom lip started quivering and her hands started shaking. She knew that she'd seen enough.

Derek sensed her anguish when he saw her outside and rushed up the stairs, expecting to have to catch her in mid-faint. She managed to hold herself together when she saw that awful scene in the gorge, and again when she saw her baby lowered into the ground, so she wasn't going to collapse after everything she'd been through. No, she had no intention of lying in bed with her feet elevated and a cold compress on her head. She intended to find out what the hell was going on, and she knew who would tell her.

Derek started out unsure of what to say. When he realized she had no idea that the apartment was apparently ransacked, he was afraid to tell her what the police surmised. She assured him she could handle the truth as she once again took his hands in hers. His big gentle face filled with compassion as he told her about the drug deal theory and the illegal alien theory. When she asked where Evan was heading the night he disappeared, his head dropped. This business of being in the thick of other people's affairs wasn't turning out to be all he thought it would.

Hesitantly he told her about Dana, and how they had a date scheduled the night before Evan came up missing. He made a point of saying he never saw her in his apartment, and he'd never seen them kiss or anything. Even so, just hearing about the date was enough for Angela to believe that if something bad happened to Evan, it had to be connected to her. She knew her husband well enough to know he'd never knowingly get involved in something illegal, and she assumed his disappearance was in some way connected to Dana.

Her first instinct was to head back into the diner and find out everything Dana knew, but the likelihood of becoming outraged and losing her temper made her think twice. Instead she asked Derek if he would take her to the police station. When he agreed, she requested he not say a word to anyone, especially Tim Barnes, who was probably looking out the window of The Blind Minnow anxiously awaiting her return while rehearsing his explanation.

They walked together as if she was being given the grand tour, and when they reached Derek's dilapidated Mustang they jumped in and sped away.

CHAPTER THIRTY

When the second Coke was gone Evan made another attempt at getting fresh water. He went below and tried kicking the pipes in the hopes of breaking them or at least loosening them enough to cause even a small drip. But he twice banged his injured leg while maneuvering around in the dark, and the exertion made him thirstier, adding insult to injury when he failed again to break into the system.

Another idea he had was to snake a hose down the fill line and suck the water out. The only available hoses would have been in use on the engine, and they all burned up in the fire. So he tried stuffing his torn shirt down the fill pipe with the intention of wringing the water out of the material, but the line was too long and narrow for the material to reach. It merely bunched up as he pushed it in the opening. Finally, as a last ditch effort, he broke open the lighter and, using the plastic case as a small bucket, lowered it down the pipe on a piece of fishing line he had found. It seemed like it was going to work, but when he tried pulling it out it became hung up inside the tank and broke free of the line.

At one point he just laughed at the irony of being so thirsty and having available drinking water so close yet so unreachable. That was only a few hours after taking his last drink. When a day had passed without water touching his lips, there was no humor at all left in the situation. When two days passed he considered drinking seawater until his reasonable side posed a better argument than his primitive side. Anything with moisture was consumed, which wasn't much. He managed to get all of an ounce out of the sterile eye wash bottle, and maybe another ounce out of the bottom of the seemingly empty Coke bottles, but that was about the extent of it.

With the last bit of energy he had he built a catch basin out of material he tore free from seats inside the cabin. If it would rain his contraption would gather the water and route it into the live well where it would be stored. But the skies were clear when he retired to the cabin and collapsed on the galley floor.

His leg, that once ached so badly he couldn't sleep, was now numb to the touch. A day or so earlier he removed the first set of bandages because, among other things, the foul odor was making him sick. He also wanted to see if the torn skin was re-attaching itself. When he took them off he was shocked to find the skin had turned a grayish green color and had shrunk to the point where it no longer covered the tender flesh below. He considered cutting it away, but had no sterile knife aboard. He re-wrapped the leg using the three rolls of toilet paper he had left.

For a very long torturous time he lay on his back and looked skyward through the small windows in the cabin's ceiling, hoping to see a cloud. Eventually his eyes closed and he drifted off. In his condition a second was an hour and an hour a lifetime, and somewhere inside that twisted time zone he heard a horn. At first it didn't wake him, but when it got closer, and louder, it pulled him from near death. His eyes opened, but closed again under their own weight. Another long blast brought them open and they stayed open.

He crawled out of the cabin and used his remaining strength to lift his head over the side of the boat. His pupils painfully adjusted to the bright sun, and, when they did, he saw the sails. They glowed like God's robe atop *The Secret*'s glistening deck as she cut through the ocean like a surfing chariot. Standing topside like a warrior heading into battle was Art with his arm outstretched towards *The Shark Bite* directing Mary who was at the wheel behind him. Evan mustered the strength to lift an arm and wave, and then he fell backwards and passed out.

The news of Evan's rescue reached Angela via Tim Barnes, who was so worried he'd lost the story when Angela left the marina that his pleading gave new meaning to the term whining. When he finally located her he had her hotel room upgraded to a suite and provided her with a rental car, which he had followed without her knowledge. He also gave permission to room service to provide her with anything she asked for, which wasn't very much considering how upset her stomach had become.

She was on the phone in her hotel room, trying to reach the governor's office, when Tim knocked on the door. She had given up on the police department, who was convinced Evan was either dead or hiding out, and had concentrated on reaching someone at the state level who would be able to force the local authorities to do their jobs. She had been on hold for nearly an hour, and kept the receiver to her ear when she opened the door. She stretched the cord across the room and turned the knob with her fingertips.

Tim could hardly contain himself and shouted, "They found him, and he's alive!" Angela dropped the phone in her excitement. She asked a million questions, all of which Tim promised to answer on the way to the hospital where Evan would be arriving at any minute. As she gathered her purse and keys he warily asked her if she would mind a thirty-second on-camera interview when they reached the hospital. She agreed instantly. Little did she know the news van was already there and ready to go.

They cut across town in Tim's Lexus, rolling through stop signs and speeding up to make yellow lights. During the drive he told her the details of the rescue, taking advantage of poetic license by adding drama to the otherwise bland series of events. He said that had the people who found him not stumbled upon him when they did, he might have died out there. He told her that they would be at the hospital, and, with stealthy manipulation, tried to choreograph the scene he hoped would unfold when they arrived. He suggested she give Evan's rescuers a hug and refer to them as heroes, and he hoped she would cry so he could have the cameraman zoom in on her face for the full effect. She might have done all of that had she been listening to him, but she wasn't. Her excitement had quickly turned to anxiety and then reluctance at the thought of seeing Evan again after such a long time.

When she was in Syracuse it hadn't seemed like a year had passed. Relatively little changed in her environment while Evan was gone. Sure, she'd counted the days since he had left and she hoped every day that he'd return, but seeing the new life he had managed to create for himself, a life she found to be quite revolting, made the reality of the time span sink in. While she stayed true to her responsibilities and raised her son and paid her bills, he found a hole in the wall where he could live like a bachelor.

When she thought he might be dead, his supposed relationship with Dana didn't seem as important as it had suddenly become since hearing of his rescue. As Tim rambled on and on, Angela grew angrier and angrier. She thought about him prancing around the marina in shorts and flip flops, filling bait buckets, gassing boats and stopping in The Blind Minnow to see his girlfriend. She wondered how far the relationship had gone, and she felt stupid for not realizing sooner that there had to be someone else in his life.

By the time Tim pulled into the parking lot Angela had worked herself into such a frenzy that she got out of the car before it was completely stopped and ran for the hospital entrance. She intended to storm into his room and lay it on the line for him. "Come home, or stay and expect divorce papers." That's what she decided and that's what she intended to tell him. She was so adamant about her decision that she completely ignored the small crowd and camera crew waiting by the door.

Once inside she went directly to the administration desk, where she asked about Evan. The woman behind the desk informed her that he was in surgery, and directed her to a waiting room on the third floor. As she turned to leave, Tim took hold of her arm and started spewing out a line of crap about her obligation to WRTB and her promise to be interviewed. Angela, in no mood to deal with any man at the moment, requested he remove his grip before she had him arrested for assault, and she said it loud enough to make heads turn and cause the woman behind the desk to ask if there was any problem. Tim bowed out before he became the lead story of a rival station and stormed out the doors he had come through only seconds before.

Once on the third floor she inquired about Evan's condition. Not that she actually cared at the moment about his bumps and bruises, but because she wanted to know how long she would have to wait to get her hands on him. The nurse's unexpected analysis of the severity of Evan's injuries extinguished her anger in an instant. She was told he had a rather substantial injury to his left leg that might result in amputation, he was severely dehydrated and his kidneys may have shut down. She assured Angela that any updates would be immediately relayed, and the doctor would come out to talk to her as soon as the surgery was over.

Angela found the waiting room and dropped onto a couch. The previous several days of dealing with the authorities, Tim Barnes and the people at the marina had worn her out. The little energy she had left an hour before was spent on the emotional roller coaster ride she took on the way to the hospital. But she still had enough energy inside of her to worry. She worried that after all she'd been through to save whatever was left of her marriage she might still be going home alone. She said a prayer, asking God to watch over her husband and give him the strength to survive.

After being in the waiting room for about fifteen minutes, an elderly gentleman entered and asked if she was the wife of the man found in the Gulf of Mexico. Angela nodded and attempted to stand, but he placed a hand on her shoulder so she'd stay seated. He handed her a two-foot long roll of toilet paper with writing on it. He said it was in the boat when he found Evan. His voice was soft and his demeanor gentle. Angela accepted it, thanked him, and stood anyway to gave him a long hug, the kind that would have boosted WRTB's ratings through the roof had it been caught on film.

He sat with her for a while and told her the story of finding Evan, then excused himself so she could read the letter. She jotted down his name on a small pad and thanked him again before he left. She carefully held the fragile note as she read.

Angela. I love you so much and I am so sorry for leaving you like I did. I realize now that you had something inside of you that was missing in me, something that enabled you to go on with life when Emily died. I know there were many times in our life together when you tried to share that gift with me and I refused to accept it. But I want you to know that something happened to me that opened my eyes to what is real and true. Something terrific and wonderful that I wish I could explain but I don't have the energy to write down. You once told me, after Emily's death, that she was in a better place and that although we could no longer be with her, her love would always be with us. I didn't believe it then, but I believe it now. You also told me that she would be waiting for us when our times come, and I think that for me the time may be coming soon.

I wanted so badly to see you again, and to hold you and love you like I did on that magical weekend we spent in the Finger Lakes. I wanted to see our son and become the father to him he deserves. The father I haven't been for a long time. But fate has put me in this boat so far away from the both of you and so close to death that I fear I will never again touch you and hold you and tell you I love you.

But I need for you to know that I was never unfaithful to you and never stopped loving you for as much as a second. When Emily fell I stopped loving myself, and I had no idea where to turn. I just wanted the pain to end, but it wouldn't. It wouldn't end because I didn't know what you knew. But I know it now.

Please tell Jeremy I love him, and that I'm sorry I wasn't a better father. And please Angie, give him what you have inside of you. And if I die out here tell him I will see him again some day, and

that I'm with Emily and we are together in heaven.
I love you both with all my heart. Evan.

The tears ran down her face and whatever doubts she had about the love they shared were gone. Her reluctance to see him was replaced with nervousness, the kind she used to get when they first met and he was on the way over to take her on a date. Then a wave of fear hit her. Fear he may not come out of the operating room alive.

Her hands trembled as she folded the fragile piece of paper and placed it in her purse. They kept trembling as she picked up the telephone next to her and pushed the square plastic numbers. Doctor Sandborn gave Angela her personal cell phone number when she heard Evan was missing and Angela was headed to Florida. The doctor was concerned and would have gladly taken the call and spoke with Angela, and if need be she would have even hopped on a plane to be there with her. But Angela's fingers didn't dial the doctor's cell phone. They dialed her parents' phone.

The same tremble that affected her hands affected her voice, and her mother immediately knew her baby was upset. Angela needed to be close to someone as she waited in that sad little room where so many before her sat and waited for news about people they loved. The person she needed was her mom, because her mom was quirky and different and, more than anything loved, her in a special way.

They talked while the minutes ticked away about anything and everything. Her mom had a knack for knowing what to say and how to say it, and she used it perfectly to pull her daughter out of that hospital and bring her into the kitchen where she used to sit as a girl and drink lemonade in the summer and hot chocolate in the winter. Her words wrapped around Angela like a hand made sweater and her voice entered her heart and warmed it, despite the bitter coldness of the sterile hospital floors and overly bright hallways.

Angela was completely immersed in the sanctity of her mother's tenderness when a doctor touched her shoulder. She said goodbye to her mother and stood up to look the doctor in the eyes. She remembered the feeling that cut through her when she lost her daughter, and she wondered if she'd have to see another casket lowered into the ground. For the instant between the time she said hello and the time the man's lips started moving, she was awash in expectation.

"Your husband was severely dehydrated and had a very serious injury to his left leg. We gave him a lot of fluids and he's responding well. We managed to save his leg but he'll have some major scarring and possibly some nerve damage. We'll know more in a few days. For now what he needs is rest and nourishment," he said.

Angela's eyes lit up and a wave of relief passed through her when she realized Evan was alive, and, if she heard the doctor correctly, he was going to be all right. A smile crossed her face and some tears fell; She thanked him and asked if she could see her husband.

Once in his room she sat next to his bed and held his hand as he slept off the anesthetic. She studied his face, which had tanned since she last saw it, and ran her fingers through his hair, which had grown much longer and a bit grayer along the sides. She listened to him breath and kissed him gently on the forehead and cheek. She talked to him and told him she was there.

Hours later he opened his eyes, smiled and closed his weakened hand over hers. When he was able to speak he told her softly that he loved her and he was sorry. Angela touched her finger to his lips and told him she knew, and said he was never allowed to go for a drive by himself again, which brought tears to his eyes and a small smile to his lips.

That night, while Angela was asleep on a cot next to Evan's bed, a large figure appeared in the doorway. He stood silent for a moment before walking to Evan's side and laying a hand on his shoulder. The touch roused Evan from his sleep. The big man was in a hospital gown and supported himself with the use of one crutch. Tightly wrapped bandages surrounded his chest and gut, and his speech made evident his physical pain.

"I saw her," he whispered to Evan, who was trying to figure out who he was and if he might have wandered into the room by mistake.

"Who?" Evan replied quietly, not wanting to wake Angela.

"The angel in the fire. She's beautiful," he said.

Evan's eyes widened when he realized to whom he was talking.

"Do you know who she is?" Richard Stocks asked.

"Yes," Evan said, waiting for a moment in the dark before continuing. "She's my little girl," he said proudly with a smile on his face.

The beefy man smiled, reached out and gave Evan's hand a powerful squeeze. "She's absolutely beautiful," he said.

They stayed silent for a long moment and shared something only silence, darkness and truth can bring to light; an understanding that cannot be talked about because there are no worldly words to explain it. Then the big man returned to his room where he slept soundly and comfortably, and Evan returned to his dreams.

CHAPTER THIRTY-ONE

The following morning when Evan woke the sun was just breaking the horizon. A golden streak shone through an opening in the curtains and cut across his bed, and across Angela's cot. She was on her side, her hair covered most of her face, and her hands were together and tucked between her knees, which were pulled slightly upward. It was how she'd always slept, and seeing her filled him with inner warmth he hadn't felt in a long time.

He sat still and watched her for as long as it took the golden streak to move from her waist to her head. When the light finally reached her eyes she woke up and saw him there, smiling at her with tears in his eyes, but the tears she saw weren't from the same vintage as the ones he'd cried over the past eighteen months. They were tears that were bottled a long time ago when they visited the Blackberry Inn and spent the weekend tasting wine and farting on hayrides, and they were as contagious as the flu. They leaped from his eyes to hers, and, in an instant, she was as close to him as the tubes and wires coming from his body allowed.

He found her touch exciting and new like a schoolboy finds the touch of a girl whose hand he holds for the very first time, and yet it was familiar and comforting like a warm blanket retrieved from a closet on a chilly night. He touched her and took notice of all of her features as if he were an artist preparing to paint her from memory. He thanked God that she was there with him.

They spent the early part of the morning in bed together. Her head rested carefully on his chest, his arms wrapped gently around her body. They'd been apart so long they required time to become one again. They touched, caressed, and kissed until the morning nurse interrupted them with breakfast.

When the breakfast was gone Evan broke the silence and told Angela how much he loved her and Jeremy and Emily, and Angela told him the same. They both apologized for anything and everything either one had done to hurt the other. Then Evan told Angela about the fire. He described walking through the blazing building as a walk through the fires of hell surrounded by a blanket of ice, and said he wasn't really in control of his movements. He was pulled, in a sense, to the staircase where Emily appeared and took him by the hand and carried him to where the black woman stood holding her two babies.

He described reaching out and taking the woman by the arm and drifting through the flames with her, the two babies, and Emily to the safety of the window. He told her how Emily's tiny hand pulled him back inside to where the fireman was trapped, and how he was able to lift the massive burning beam off the man and carry him out. Finally he described how Emily's sweet soft lips touched his forehead before she waved goodbye and vanished.

When he began speaking about the visit from Richard Stocks she wiped her wet eyes and told him she was awake when he came in the room the night before. She said she heard what he said. She bent over and hugged Evan and they both cried. The tears were happy tears, for they shared the knowledge that Emily was indeed still with them. They could feel her love around them as they embraced.

Just before lunch Tim Barnes called and politely begged for an interview. Evan agreed;, not because Angela told him about the station's rescue effort, but because they were responsible for locating her and bringing her to Florida. Tim brought Deloris Carlisle to the hospital to meet the man who saved her life, and she provided him with exactly what he'd hoped she would. She stood next to Evan's bed and held her two babies, called him a hero and cried. Angela cried too, and it made great television.

Richard Stocks had been released that morning and declined any further interviews, saying over the phone that he spoke with Evan the night before and that something very special would always bond them together. He would not elaborate and politely asked the media to allow him and his wife their privacy.

Later, after Tim Barnes had left in search of his next big story, the man who had found Evan entered the room to see how he was feeling. He carried a small bouquet of flowers his wife insisted he bring, and he set them on the table next to the bed. He greeted Angela, who he had met the day before in the waiting room, before introducing himself to Evan.

Until that point, there was little mention of the details of the rescue. Evan assumed that Art and Mary were responsible since they were the last ones he remembered seeing, and Angela didn't think the who's and why's mattered. She was just happy someone had found him before it was too late. When Evan realized what had occurred he sprang up and asked about the Sullivans. The soft-spoken man just shook his head and said he'd never heard of them. He said he was fishing only a few hundred yards off shore and spotted the life raft. He described it as a small inflatable that was commonly found aboard larger vessels.

Evan's thoughts flew back to his last memory on board *The Shark Bite*. He heard *The Secret*'s horns and saw Art and Mary coming for him. He even waved and they waved back. He remembered that much. Unless it was a dream and they never found him, he thought. But it had seemed so real.

"Did they find the boat?" Evan asked.

"I don't know," the man replied, adding that he assumed they would have, considering how close to shore Evan was when he was rescued.

But Evan wasn't close to shore, and he knew it. He had gone at least thirty miles due west before the fire, and there was no way he could have drifted that distance in such a short time. Then again, he was malnourished and dehydrated, and had an infection in his leg that could have done strange things to the rest of his body. Maybe his mind played tricks on him and he never really saw *The Secret*, maybe he did drift all those miles. Or maybe he managed to get himself into a raft in his condition and paddle all that way. And maybe pigs really can fly.

When the man left the room he dialed the marina. He had to know if Art and Mary made it back or if they were out in the Gulf looking for him, as he would be looking for them had they failed to meet as planned. Derek answered the gooey cordless as he was cutting up some squid.

"How ya doing, boss?" he asked, before saying how sorry he was to hear about the fire and about Evan's leg. He said he would come to visit when Candy came in and he asked Evan if there was anything he could bring. Evan thanked him for his offer and said he was fine, and then he asked about the Sullivans.

"Who?" asked Derek.

"Art and Mary," Evan said. "They should be back by now."

Derek was silent for a moment and then again asked to whom Evan was referring.

"Art and Mary!" Evan said a little louder, looking at Angela as if Derek was out to lunch. But the kid said again that he had no idea who Evan meant.

"Come on, Derek. I'm talking about the Sullivans. You know, *The Secret*, in slip two-sixty-one," he said, rolling his eyes and thinking Derek had fallen off the wagon and was sipping the hooch while at work.

"Boss, there ain't no slip two-sixty-one," Derek said, "and there ain't no Sullivans as far as I know. Unless you checked 'em in when I was off."

"Derek, you're the one that told me when they left!"

"Man, I'm sorry, but I really don't know who ya mean," Derek said.

Evan disconnected and dialed The Minnow. He was sure Derek was hiding something from him. His mind ran the footage of the Sullivans waiting for him after he made radio contact and told them he was on the way. When he didn't show he pictured them getting worried. Then he saw them start to search for him and hit a storm, capsize and drown.

When Sheila answered he asked if she'd seen Derek and if he'd been drinking. She said he stopped by earlier for an egg sandwich and seemed perfectly fine to her. She asked if he had received the flowers from the girls and asked if they could visit after work. After a few more minutes of small talk, he asked her about the Sullivans and received the same run around he got from Derek.

"Sheila, if something happened to them you can tell me, but please don't act like you don't know who they are. You talk to them at least twice a week," he said. She swore that she had no idea who he was talking about and suggested he get some rest. Then she commented about hospital food and offered to sneak him in some home cooking, but Evan didn't plan on being there long enough to worry about the food.

It took some begging to convince Angela to find a wheelchair and get him out of the hospital and over to the marina. He told her about his friends and *The Secret*, how he was on his way to meet them when the seas got rough. His concern for the two elderly people touched her deeply, but she was far more concerned about his health than that of his friends. She finally agreed, reluctantly, to drive him there, but only if he promised to return to the hospital afterward, which he did.

She found a wheelchair, helped him get dressed, and then pushed him slowly down the hall towards the elevator. She felt a little bit like she was taking part in a prison break as they quietly slipped past the nurse's station where two young women in white were drinking coffee and gabbing about some doctor with a cute butt. When they reached the car she helped him inside, and hesitated in loading the chair into the trunk.

"We're only borrowing it, honey," Evan said, smiling.

On the way there he described Art and Mary in such detail that Angela felt she already knew them. He told her about Mary's cooking and Art's cigars and about their late night talks, chess games and fishing trips. He also spoke of *The Secret*, and how it felt warm and homey, and about the bell that Mary rang when dinner was ready. A bell almost identical to the one he'd seen at Angela's mother's house hanging outside the kitchen door. Angela sensed his deep concern for them in the intensity of his voice, and she hoped, like he did, that nothing bad happened to them.

When they arrived Angela unfolded the borrowed chair and loaded her escapee into it. Then she pushed him along the dock towards *The Secret*'s slip. The first person to spot them was Bill Baxter, who approached with the enthusiasm of a realtor about to close a deal on a million dollar property. He was delighted to see Evan was safe and, for the first time in a year, he smiled and shook Evan's hand. He didn't mention his traps, his hemorrhoids or anything else that bothered him. His delight in Evan's good health was driven mostly by the fact that Evan was one of very few people willing to listen to his whining and actually pacify him when possible. He feared having someone replace Evan who might actually make him pay for a new trap when one of his old ones fell apart

The second person to greet them was Candy, who happened to be outside hosing off a large rubber matt when they passed the bait shop. The last she had heard Evan would be laid up in the hospital for several days, so, upon seeing him, she rushed over.

"What in the world are you doing here?" she said after greeting him and Angela with a cheery howdy.

"Candy, have you seen the Sullivans lately?" Evan asked, looking down the dock in the direction of slip two-sixty-one.

"Who?" Candy asked.

"Never mind," Evan said. He didn't want to go through that again. Upon hearing her answer he gripped the rubber wheels of the chair and sped off down the dock with Angela close behind. Once they rounded a somewhat lengthy bend he expected to see *The Secret*'s bright white sails rolled up and her mast high in the sky, but there was nothing. As they grew closer he knew something was out of the ordinary, and when they could go no further, he realized just what it was. Derek hadn't lost his mind and Sheila had all her marbles, at least as many as she'd always had, and Candy wasn't pulling his chain.

Hammered into the wooden planks in front of each slip were brass numbers, the last set of which made the number two hundred sixty. Where two-sixty-one should have been was nothing but oyster flats leading into a dense growth of mangrove trees. Evan stared, in disbelief, at the place where he'd spent so many evenings in the company of his friends. He'd walked that dock past where it now ended and boarded *The Secret* on more occasions than he could recall. And now, if he moved the wheelchair any further, he would drop six feet onto the sharpened teeth of an oyster bed.

When something is there one minute and gone the next it defies all that is logical and of this world. Some people might call it magic, like when a man with a black hat and bow tie pulls a quarter out of a child's ear. Others might call it a hallucination, like a pool of water is to a man dying in the desert. Evan didn't know what to call what he was seeing, or, rather, not seeing. There were no words inside of him to explain it.

That night, as they slept side by side in the hospital room, Evan and Angela dreamed the same dream. A baby blue sky was painted all the way down to the aqua ocean below it, and, sailing across the glassy surface, was *The Secret* with her brilliantly white sails full of ocean air. She didn't seem to be touching the water, but gliding over the top of it like a seagull on the hunt.

Up on her deck stood Art and Mary, and, between them, was Emily. Her hair blew in the salty breeze and the ocean spray touched her lips as it had Evan's on many occasions. And, just like her daddy, she tasted it and liked it, and smiled. She seemed even more alive than she was before she left the earth.

There was something a little different about the elderly people who he had come to love so very much. It was something he couldn't quite pin down until Art bent over and scooped Emily up into his arms. It was then he saw them on Art's back. Wings. They were as bright as a Florida day and as soft as the sands of a Gulf beach.

THE END

AUTHOR'S NOTE

Thank you for taking the time to read my book. If you enjoyed it, please recommend it to the people you know.

Sincerely,
George Edward Zintel

Printed in the United States
39991LVS00007B/325-360